PAINTING THROUGH THE DARK

Painting Through the Dark

A novel
by

GEMMA WHELAN

Adelaide Books
New York / Lisbon
2022

PAINTING THROUGH THE DARK

A novel

By Gemma Whelan

Published by Adelaide Books, New York / Lisbon
adelaidebooks.org

Editor-in-Chief
Stevan V. Nikolic

For any information, please address Adelaide Books
at info@adelaidebooks.org

or write to:

Adelaide Books
244 Fifth Ave. Suite D27
New York, NY, 10001

ISBN: 978-1-956635-41-6

Printed in the United States of America

To Adam, always.

Contents

II: COUNTRY

PROLOGUE

June 20, 1982

A scraping of tires on stones woke her. Ashling peered out through the car window at the two-story house nestled in a clearing in a forest. Tall angular shapes jutted up, barely discernible in the still darkness. Bluish light from a television screen flickered through drawn curtains.

Charlie reached over and touched her shoulder. "Ready?"

She could see his face, dappled with moonlight, smiling. She nodded and shook herself to dispel her anxiety.

The gravel squeaked under Ashling's feet as she stepped out, and the sharp edges pricked her soles through the light sandals. Charlie led the way. She stayed close, following him through the darkness, towards the flickering light.

He took an oversize brass key from his pocket and inserted it in the keyhole. When it clicked, he eased open the thick wooden door as if signaling entrance to a fortress. They stepped inside. Charlie closed the door and locked it behind them. Ashling flinched. She was plunged into black.

Charlie's hand on her elbow guided her down the dim entrance hall towards the living room. Her body flooded with trepidation. She had imagined a light-filled space. They stood a moment in the frame of the doorway and looked in. It was like going back in time. Heavily fringed lamps cast narrow pools of light in the tightly shuttered room. Paneled walls blended with the floral pattern of the brown carpet and green brocade curtains. The TV light leapt across the furniture forming Rorschach inkblots.

Rose sat parked in her wheelchair in front of the television. Ashling was struck by her strong resemblance to Charlie—handsome, well-defined cheek bones, brownish eyes, and olive skin. Rose appeared to be much older and possessed none of Charlie's elegance. Her straggly greying hair was pulled back in a bun, and a grimy red velour bathrobe strained over her ample middle.

"You're late, Chas." Rose raised her arms in a ballet-like pose. He crossed quickly from the entryway, melting into the funnel of her embrace.

"Rosie." It seemed a familiar and oft-performed sequence, a refined *pas de deux*.

Ashling quickly banished the thought that there was something more than fraternal affection between them. Just because her brothers in Ireland would die of shame if she hugged them like that didn't mean there was anything amiss. Irish people like herself were the ones with the problem showing affection. Americans were open and free.

She couldn't as easily dispel the dread in the pit of her stomach that she'd made a massive mistake. Why had she left light-filled San Francisco for this?

I: CITY

SAN FRANCISCO

May 31, 1982

The surge of passengers propelled Ashling through the tunnel into the expanse of the San Francisco airport. She stopped and let the crowds swirl around her—people with skin colors from deepest black to her own palest white. Compared to sleepy Shannon Airport this was the far side of the moon.

She raked her fingers through her short blonde hair so hard she scratched her scalp. Mam had practically cried when she saw the new cut.

"Why did you have to chop off all your beautiful curls now that you're out of the convent?" she'd said. Her sixteen-year-old sister Brona said it gave her a *gamine* look. Ashling just wanted it gone. She wanted to start over.

"You'll be back before you know it, Ashly," Brona's twin said. "You don't have to go at all, pet," Mam said, desperate to keep her eldest child at home. Little Dermot puckered up his face and tried not to cry. Ashling pushed away her guilt that she was abandoning her family, refusing to continue to be a mother to them all. Her idea of home had reconfigured in the past few months. Her American visa was manna from heaven, though she didn't believe in heaven anymore.

Ashling looked around for the signs for Immigration. She joined a line snaking towards a series of glass booths with uniformed agents behind them. She tucked her artist's portfolio under her arm and pressed her spine against the backpack that dwarfed her frame. Her parents didn't understand why she burdened herself with the portfolio. In her secret mind it was her passport to freedom.

A cacophony of languages and dialects swirled around her as she inched along.

"Next." A voice boomed and Ashling jumped and stepped forward.

The woman opened her passport.

"How do you say it? A..sh-ling O'Leary?"

"Yes, Ash-ling."

"Do you have a sponsorship letter?"

Ashling handed the officer the letter from her friend Majella. The agent's ball-bearing eyes flitted back and forth across the page. "This a relative?"

"A friend. She was in my class in school, but she's married and living here now. She's meeting me."

"Says here you have eighty dollars?"

"That's right." Ashling was proud of her savings. It took hours of overtime in the art gallery to earn enough for the charter flight and manage to have a few pounds left over.

"How do you expect to get by on that?" the woman said.

Ashling's stomach dropped. Could this officer actually refuse to stamp her passport, and send her back? "Well...I'll be staying with Majella...until I find a job..."

"Show me your return ticket."

The drooping eyes scanned the ticket. "Three months," the officer said, "a temporary work visa. Expires August 31st." She brought the stamp down like a gavel strike, piled the documents one on top of the other, and shoved them across the counter towards Ashling.

"Do not overstay."

At the U.S. Customs station, the officer opened up her pack and asked Ashling to step to the side. He hooked the collar of her judo jacket with his finger and dangled it in the air like a fish.

"It's a judogi, for judo," she said. Getting through the airport was proving to be a feckin obstacle course.

She noticed his lovely blue-black skin and wondered how she would paint it. She'd only ever painted white skin.

"You some kind of black belt?" the officer said. He eyed her with suspicion.

She wanted to laugh. If only. "I'm a few belts away."

"And what's this?" He pulled a wooden contraption from her pack. Her precious easel.

"Be careful please…" She reached out without thinking and their hands collided. He gave her a sharp look.

He continued to rummage, and yanked out her clothes, her sketch pad, her Walkman, and her toiletries. She pushed back the rising anger and told herself he had to be careful. There'd been a recent spate of I.R.A. bombings, and airport officials were on alert for Irish terrorists.

The officer nodded his dismissal. Ashling stuffed everything back into her pack as well as she could. She slipped the straps across her aching shoulder grooves, gritted her teeth and hustled along with the rush of passengers towards the waiting area, Majella and freedom.

She scanned all the faces in the waiting area, searching out Majella's black curls. She watched as people called out names, rushed into each other's arms, hugged and kissed, and moved away. She had a sinking feeling as fewer and fewer people were left and there was no sign of Majella. Everyone from her flight was gone, but her.

Her chest constricted. Majella was the one and only person Ashling knew on this entire continent, and she wasn't here. She knew Ashling's family didn't have a phone, but if something changed she could have sent a telegram. She pulled out the letter. Majella's address was right there—Irving Street.

She hurried over to the Information Booth. A woman with frizzy orange hair glanced at the address and drew lines and Xs on a map with a yellow marker. It looked like gobbledygook to Ashling. At a currency exchange, she handed over her Irish punts and got miniature U.S. dollars and coins in exchange. She followed the passengers out into the exhaust fumes of taxis and buses and cars.

Collapsing onto the hard leather seat of the airport bus, Ashling dumped her backpack on the floor between her legs. A man sat down beside her and his leg brushed against hers. She snapped her leg away, then realized by his apologetic smile that it was accidental. She nodded back. The bus filled up, and the driver pulled away from the curb. She let her body relax. They were out of the airport zone. Whatever happened, she was safely on American soil.

She glanced around at the passengers of all different colors—Latino, Asian, Indian, Black. When she'd told her family she was going to San Francisco they asked, why not New York or Boston, they were closer and had plenty of Irish? But they didn't get the point: To move as far away from the country and its fake religiosity as possible. To have space and freedom to think.

Ashling looked out the window and saw a street sign for El Camino Real. She remembered reading about the Spanish origins of California—it made it even more exotic. The bus sped along through the drab grey outreaches, past rows of houses, all small and beige, piled up on a hillside. The sinking sun spattered pink blotches over parched yellow hills, the likes of which she had seen only in paintings.

It was Majella who sparked the idea of San Francisco when she'd come back to Timaleen the Christmas before. Ashling had just left the convent a few months before she was to be ordained and she was an emotional wreck. Majella was home for the funeral of the uncle who had raised her, and according to chatter in the village, had molested her. Nobody dared talk directly about this, let alone confront the bastard. Instead everyone remarked how generous Lanky Laverty was to have taken in his orphaned niece. It all made Ashling's blood boil.

Ashling was working long hours in the art gallery and squeezing in as many art lessons as she could from the owner, Brendan, who she'd studied with since she was a young teenager. Majella'd brought her husband Allen in to meet Ashling.

"How did you stick it out in that feckin convent for all that time?" Majella had blurted out.

"I thought I had a vocation," Ashling said. It sounded stupid now. She knew she'd been hiding behind those walls.

Majella turned to Allen. "We were far too young to know our minds." Her voice was razor sharp. "I suppose they'll hire you in the primary school the minute you qualify, Ashling."

"I'm only finishing up my teacher training to please my parents. Anyway, Sister Ignatius will never retire."

"They should get rid of that bloody witch." Majella's blue eyes blazed. "She knocked me to the floor once with a wallop to the side of the head because I sang a wrong note."

"I remember. And all the other poor kids she battered for no good reason."

"I don't get it. Why doesn't anyone complain?" Allen asked.

Ashling and Majella's eyes met. "Ireland," they said in unison.

"Priests and nuns—they're sacred cows," Ashling added.

"They get away with bloody murder," Majella said.

"I bet America's completely different." Ashling looked hopefully at her friend.

Majella flipped her head and her dark curls skimmed her cheeks. "It's lovely altogether. No one breathing down your neck. And you can be who you want to be."

"Even an artist?" Ashling said.

"Of course. San Francisco is teeming with artists."

The whisper of freedom and possibility rippled through Ashling. Within a week, she applied for a visa.

Ashling checked the instructions on the map and stepped down from the bus at 7th Avenue onto an actual San Francisco sidewalk. It was dark now. Streetlights illuminated the clusters of Victorians, and the flat-roofed houses with rambling fire escapes and businesses in front. She scanned the street and plodded across to the N Judah stop. Her legs were throbbing after the long plane journey.

At 46th Avenue, Ashling hoisted up her ever-heavier backpack and trudged over to Irving. There was the address. She approached the pink stucco house and climbed the red brick stairs to the arched entranceway. The glass door with the lace curtain looked comfortingly Irish. She could practically taste that cup of tea.

Ashling rang the bell and waited. Her whole body tingled with anticipation. With Majella, she could get the words out. Six thousand miles away from home, they could safely talk about all the topics that were taboo in Timaleen.

She rang the bell again. She heard a chair scraping and a rustling from inside. The front door opened, and she was face to face with a middle-aged Chinese couple who stood side by side.

"Jesus Christ!" What were they doing in Majella's house?

"Please. Please?" the man said.

"Hello. Sorry. I'm looking for my friend who lives here. Majella Laverty. Or Strang? Her husband's name?"

Two sets of eyelids flickered, and the pair moved even closer to each other until their matching tunics touched at the shoulders.

"Just a few months ago she wrote..." She heard the worry in her own voice. The woman gave a little jump, nudged her husband, and pointed to the house.

"For us. House. We buy." She tapped her hand on her heart.

"But...it has to be a mistake," Ashling said, and showed them the return address on the envelope. She double-checked the address on the letter against the one on the front of the house, aching for the alchemy that was going to change one or the other and lead her to safety.

"Do...you...know...who...lived...here...be...fore?" she said slowly. The woman's eyes lit up, she held out her finger to Ashling, darted into the house, and returned with an index card with Majella and Allen's names and a forwarding address in Stuttgart, Germany.

"Young people. They leave."

Ashling stared at the print in panic. "Oh, my God!" Why didn't Majella tell her? Maybe she wrote a letter and it got lost, or it was meandering towards Timaleen. The international post moved as slow as cold gravy.

"Thanks. Sorry." Ashling scribbled the address and hoisted her pack onto her exhausted body. The couple bowed. Ashling bowed back and walked away.

She stood on the sidewalk and stared through stinging eyes into the fog. Her heartbeat thrummed in her ears. The windows of houses were rectangular parcels of light, and old-fashioned streetlamps cast a yellow glow along the avenue. Majella was supposed to be her life raft.

A car shot by like a gust of wind. A streetcar chugged faintly several blocks away. Ashling was marooned in America.

ART TRIP

June 1

Ashling's eyes snapped open. They were scratchy, as if lined with grains of sand. She blinked, registered the cracking beige plaster on the ceiling, and remembered her trek on the streetcar through the late-night city to a bay front YMCA in an area known as Embarcadero. She had enough money for three nights in a tiny room.

She surveyed the clothes she had hung in the miniscule closet and focused on all she needed to accomplish. Immigration. Work. A place to stay. Every stitch of clothing—except for the ruffle wrap jacket from Goodwill—was made by her Mam. Six months ago, she owned nothing but the white uniform of the novice. She picked the short, black A-line skirt, matched it with a sea green top the color of her eyes, grabbed the vest, and hopped on a chair. She had to squirm around to see her whole body in the tiny, cracked mirror on the wall. *Would I give you a job in an art gallery or museum?* She pinched her cheeks to get some color, slipped on the burgundy vest, and her lips curled in a smile. She remembered the twins Brona and Breda saying in unison that the vest added a certain *je ne sais quoi*. At sixteen, they were already more savvy than she was about things like clothes and make-up. And, it went without saying, boys. She had a feeling that despite the death grip of the Catholic Church they wouldn't still be virgins at the age of twenty-one, like her.

In the months before she left Ireland, Ashling made a list for the family of everything she did to keep the household running. As soon as she started the list—planting a vegetable garden, raising hens, cooking, scouring pots and pans—pins of pain prickled her scalp, and as the list lengthened—creating and maintaining a family budget, stretching supplies to make the food last, sewing, repairing hems, darning socks—the pin pricks intensified and confirmed she needed to escape. Her parents had nudged her into taking over the running of the family when she was about eleven or twelve, and even after she joined the nuns at age seventeen, they still depended on her, and let things pile up for her visits home. When she abandoned her novitiate, she took over the household as before. She looked at her image now in the cracked wall mirror and felt that same angry pain again. She jumped down and pressed her palms against the sides of her head to squeeze out the ache. She had made it to San Francisco. Now she was bloody well going to puzzle out how to stay.

In the YMCA lobby, Ashling turned over each coin to read its value and dropped the quarters and dimes into a vending machine. She navigated the confusion of directions and knobs and stared at the murky liquid that dripped into a Styrofoam cup. She fed more coins into the metal belly, and a pastry wrapped in plastic plopped out of a slot. She tapped her fingers to avoid burning them on the hot cup and headed over to the front desk.

"I'd like a copy of the local newspaper, please."

The young man barely lifted his eyes from his comic book. He reached a skinny white arm to the pile behind him and handed her a paper—the *San Francisco Chronicle*.

"Thanks." Ashling counted out the coins. She spoke to a forehead of blonde curls. "Do you ever do barter? I'm in room 22, I could help in the gym."

"I'll check with the manager."

"I'm nearly a brown belt in judo."

His chin shot up, and he threw a glance over her body like a lazy x-ray. A patch of heat bloomed on the back of her neck. She stifled the urge to judo-kick him.

"Cool." He quick-scanned her again and scribbled a note on a pad. "I'm Joel. Check back later?"

She nodded.

Sipping her bitter coffee, Ashling entered the cost of everything she'd bought in her notebook. She scanned the Want Ads and circled temp agencies. She made a list of museums and galleries. She saw there was a Bergman film playing at a cinema called The Surf, on Irving Street, near where Majella was supposed to be. Ashling had seen her first Bergman films at a local festival in that mad frenzy of work and plans and savings in the months before she left Ireland. She was captivated by the light and shadow and mystery. Even when she didn't truly understand it all, she knew she was in the presence of true art.

Ashling stepped out into the cool San Francisco morning. She shivered, buttoned up her jacket, and stood back to take in the view. The glass mountains of downtown skyscrapers huddled together; the campanile of what must be the Ferry Building presided over the port; the Bay Bridge flickered in and out of the fingers of fog, and a ferry chugged towards shore trumpeting its horn. She was really here!

She hustled along towards Market Street as a cable car approached, jangling its bell. The operator jumped out, gripped a white metal bar and manually swung the car around on a turntable. It was an image from an art book that she and Mam had pored over years ago. The slatted wooden benches open to the elements, the passengers dangling over the rails, the conductor in his blue uniform and peaked cap. A patch of guilt landed on Ashling's heart. Her mother, and hordes of girls she knew from home would have loved to escape to an exotic place like San Francisco—but she herself was the one who had abandoned everybody and gotten away.

Pressing open the heavy wooden doors of the Immigration and Naturalization building, Ashling immediately faced a conveyer belt and a check stand with a line of uniformed officials. A burly woman with a halo of wiry hair shot out her hand and boomed: "I.D." Ashling fished out her passport.

"Place your purse on the conveyer belt, Miss. Remove any keys or metal objects."

She watched the royal blue purse with embroidered flowers that Mam had made from scraps disappear under the fabric fingers into the tunnel. Another official took her portfolio and carelessly flipped over the plastic sleeves. Her shoulders tensed. Those were her precious paintings.

"Please walk slowly through the metal detector," the official said. No alarm bells went off. They nodded her on. She crossed the expanse of white floor, her sandals clicking and echoing on the tiles, searched out the building directory and found the room number for Alien Visas. She headed down a dark, concrete stairway.

Pushing open the thick glass doors, Ashling saw a teeming mass of bodies crowded into a windowless basement. Bright blue and yellow saris and sarongs contrasted with the drab grey walls, and the air was thick with sweat, patchouli, and heightened expectation. Above a high wooden counter, the immigration workers were protected by iron grilles. Were they worried the "aliens" would storm them?

She found the machine that dispensed numbers, took one, and scanned the room for somewhere to sit. She spotted a place on a wooden bench between a young woman in a smart business suit, and an Indian woman, in a bright red sari, holding a young boy on her lap. Ashling wedged herself in, and inadvertently sat on the edge of the business skirt.

"Sorry." She inched over.

"It's no problem," the woman said in a precise accent, and gathered in a fold of fabric.

Ashling glanced at her. "English?"

She nodded. "Yeah, London." Her brown eyes were rimmed red and swollen.

"Are you applying for your visa?" Ashling asked.

"Renewing. I work for the New Zealand Consulate." There was a catch in her voice and her lip quivered.

"Is it really hard to renew?"

"No. Consulate jobs are great that way." Tears trickled down her coffee-colored cheeks and she quickly brushed them away.

"Are you all right?" Ashling asked.

The woman's lower lip quivered again. "I'm sorry," she sniffled. "I just…lost my boyfriend."

"Oh God! I'm so sorry."

She shot a teary glance at Ashling. "Not what you think." She narrowed her eyes and looked around. She lowered her voice to a whisper. "He got deported."

"Jesus! Where is he from?"

"Mexico. I was planning on visiting his family there this Christmas." A choking sound escaped from her throat.

"How did it happen?"

"It was like something in a film. Yesterday I was meeting him for lunch. I was walking down Market Street and Carlos was coming towards me when two INS officers appeared out of nowhere and grabbed him. I screamed and raced to him, but they pushed me back, though they let me come with them."

The woman scanned the room again and lowered her voice another few notches. "After hours at an interrogation center, I stood on the street, looking at the back of his disappearing head. He was on a bus, under escort, with a one-way ticket to the border…"

Her voice trailed off. She was dry-eyed now and stared at the floor. Ashling was barely breathing. She folded and unfolded her ticket. Would this be her fate if she overstayed her visa and tried to get lost in the shadows? She looked at the other faces. All had their own stories. All were requesting, petitioning—and they were the lucky ones who had some form of legal documentation. Yet they were "aliens." The little boy on her other side bawled, and his mother hushed him in her language. Hindi? Bengali? Her sari rustled, and she bounced him up and down on her knee. He cried in the same language as every other child in the world.

Ashling waited for over an hour before her number was called. From behind the counter a tight-lipped woman asked for her documents, slid her pink chipped nails under the bars and clawed the papers back to her side of the grille. Her eyes flitted over them, and she peered at Ashling above wire rimmed glasses.

"Date of birth?" she barked.

"March 16, 1961, I'm twenty-one."

"You were a student in Ireland?"

"Yes. Training to be a teacher."

The woman examined the visa stamp. Her lips moved silently as if she were deciphering code. "This was issued from… the American Embassy?"

"In Dublin, yes."

The nails slipped a form under the grille. "Here's an application for your Social Security card." Ashling filled in the address and phone number of the YMCA and passed the form back. The woman looked askance at the Y address, fixed her eyes on Ashling, and barked again:

"Where is your sponsorship letter?"

Ashling handed over the now useless letter from Majella. "My friends are away at the moment, so I'm temporarily staying at the Y." As soon as the words were out, she knew she shouldn't have mentioned the Y. But if she hadn't, her Social Security card would go to Majella's old address.

The thin lips tightened. "The purpose of a sponsor is that you are accounted for. So we can track you."

"Right…but between my application and arrival…it was several months..."

The laser eyes cut through the bridge of Ashling's nose. "You are required to inform us if there is any major change, and this is a major change."

"I'm sorry."

Ashling willed her legs to stop shaking but they wouldn't. The man at the next counter struggled in a faltering tongue through an interpreter. It was feckin hard enough in English.

The woman sighed, and with the smallest possible expenditure of energy she stamped the application. "Here." She dropped a card into the space below the bars. "This is your temporary

Social Security number—the actual card should arrive in about eight days."

"Thank you."

The woman gave a weary nod. She slipped Ashling's passport under the grille and the pink nails retreated. "Remember, you have three months. We can track you through your Social Security number. Penalty for overstaying is deportation, and denial of entry to the United States for life."

For life. She pictured herself in the same predicament as Carlos, seated on a bus, flanked by immigration officers, fading from sight, and returning to Ireland in shame. She squeezed out what she hoped was a confident smile and slipped away through the opaque glass doors.

Ashling blinked to adjust to the light. It was nearly noon. She flapped her elbows to get air circulating into her underarms, gripped her portfolio, inhaled a blast of biting air, and steamed towards the galleries on Geary Street.

She dipped into a fancy clothing store next to the first art gallery, so she could work up her courage. At home in Ireland, Ashling sketched patterns for her Mam from the displays in shops—that's how she started drawing, and how her family sported haute couture, at least by west of Ireland standards. When she entered the convent, she continued to draw and paint when she could squeeze out an iota of free time, but she abandoned all thoughts of a career as an artist. It seemed flimsy in comparison to devoting your life to God and service. The nuns did take advantage of her skills to design clothes for orphans, and shapeless shifts for the nameless girls who slaved away behind the high walls in the laundry. The clothes in this San Francisco shop looked like they were made for supermodels, and the cost of one dress could fund the O'Leary household for months.

Ashling walked tall towards the glass doors of the gallery. She glanced at the brightly colored paintings mounted on glaring white walls and was filled with a giddy melee of hope and excitement that she hadn't allowed herself to ever feel—the mad desire that one day her work might be shown in a gallery.

The gallery manager approached and smiled—a practiced professional smile that didn't light up her eyes.

"I was wondering if you had any summer work?" Ashling asked. Times like this, she wished she could still pray.

"I'm sorry. We're not hiring." Her manner matched her pinstriped suit.

"I have a good bit of curatorial experience," Ashling said, as fast as she could.

"We can't afford any extra help."

"I worked in a gallery very like this back home," she blurted. A wee white lie—the *Roisin Dubh* was in an old wooden building on a sheltered sea inlet and was attached to the studio of her art teacher, Brendan. He himself was an accomplished artist, and his oils and watercolors were for sale in the gallery, along with local arts and crafts.

The woman's burgundy lips parted. "I'm sorry."

Ashling took a breath. "Would you like to see a sample of my work?"

"I'm not sure why that's relevant," the woman said, shaking her head.

"Oh, I thought the fact that I was an artist might help." Ashling felt stupid. "May I leave my c.v. just in case?" she asked.

"If you wish."

Ashling slid her one-page vita from her portfolio, handed it to the manager, thanked her and said goodbye. She headed towards the door, swallowed the lump in her throat, and hoped her back looked dignified.

Hours later, weak from hunger and rejection, Ashling came upon an outdoor market. Her head spun with the sheer volume of goods—a cornucopia of pastas, baskets overflowing with pomegranates and persimmons, fruits she had never laid eyes on before and was glad were labeled, aromatic cheeses just as foreign to her—Stinson, Asiago, Parmesan—and jams like quince, and elderberry, that she'd heard mention of only in Shakespeare plays. She could afford one apple.

She plunked down on a metal bench in Union Square and sunk her teeth into the apple. She scratched off the eight galleries she had tried so far—there were nearly a hundred on the list. Two men sauntered past hand in hand. Ashling's heart warmed at the sight, a promise of the city's openness and inclusion. Gay men would never get away with showing open affection in the Ireland she knew. It was considered a sin, like almost everything.

Two women in sensible navy skirts and thick soled shoes, wearing silver crucifixes, strolled by arm in arm. Ashling choked on the apple. They looked like nuns. She coughed until the apple piece found the right way down. Through watery eyes she saw the women disappear, blocked out by a cable car that whished along Powell. Her mother had dropped strong hints about the Mercy convent where she could go if she needed help. Mam hoped she'd find her vocation again—as if she just lost it in the blooming street. She dug her teeth into the apple flesh and chewed until her jaw was sore.

Vaulting up the stairs from the employment agency, Ashling emerged at street level. She gulped in air. It was already after four. She had spent over two hours ticking off rote questions, had done typing and accounting tests, tried to solve pointless multiple-choice puzzles, and suffered through a stupid interview—all for the kind of mind-numbing office job she didn't want.

It was a long walk to the Museum of Modern Art, but she needed to save the bus fare. She set off down Market, portfolio strapped on her shoulder—she was going to get an art-related job if it killed her. She marched on. It'd be hard for Mam and Dad to argue if she said she was staying in the States for a worthwhile position. A wave of panic shot through her. This was her one chance and she had to get it right.

Ashling picked up her pace. Her throat turned dry. She coughed and pushed on. She had an image of herself years into the future, standing before a class of snot-nosed youngsters. She broke into a canter. A band constricted her chest. Her breath quickened, came in spurts, and scraped her rib cage. Timaleen primary school would be her prison, with the parish priest, Father Dempsey dropping in any time he felt like it. Her eyelids hardened, swelled, and pressed on her eyeballs causing the sidewalk to blur. She had to come up with an alternative and quick. She stopped. What was wrong with her? She eased herself onto a bench and scooped in an enormous breath. She exhaled and grabbed another breath. Three months was such a ridiculous amount of time to change your life.

When her breathing returned to normal, Ashling pushed on. She left the financial district behind, and the neighborhood changed. The smell of urine spiked her nostrils. Candy wrappers skimmed the street, then swept aloft on gusts of wind, soda cans and take-out containers tumbled out of garbage bins, a shape shifted in a doorway under a mound of blankets. Ashling drew in her portfolio and slid a protective palm over her purse.

She reached a wide, open plaza surrounded by classical brick buildings, and from her map recognized the Civic Center. A United Nations of people milled about the City Hall steps. On long stone benches, people in business suits drank coffee, ate, read newspapers. A woman in layers of filthy rags carried on a non-stop conversation with herself. It unsettled Ashling to see this person whose mind was rambling, and at the same time she was glad that everything was out in the open. At home she had schoolmates whose aunts or grandmothers had been shipped off to the mental hospital when they reached the change-of-life and went so-called crazy. Irish people kept their shame and secrets locked away. Her own secrets were piling up in her heart.

She approached the Veteran's Building where the museum was housed. Like City Hall it was classical in style, and the continuous series of arched entryways on the lower floor, mounted by a stately colonnade of pillars, made it feel sacred.

She clicked across the marble foyer towards a young woman at the front desk. "Excuse me, could you tell me how to get to the hiring department, please?" Her nametag read Madeleine Ng and Ashling wasn't going to chance pronouncing that.

Ms. Ng arched her pencil-thin eyebrows. "Do you have an appointment?"

"Oh...I'm an artist." She tapped her portfolio.

"You may go to Human Resources." She pointed a manicured finger in the direction of a grand staircase. "Ms. Rivera, third floor."

Ashling strode towards the marble steps. On the second story, she pattered along a corridor of golden tiles, up one more flight, and found the glass-paneled door with black lettering.

She caught her reflection in the glass—she looked a blooming fright.

She doubled back and found a bathroom. Her eyelids were swollen and partially veiled her eyes. Her lips were enlarged. Her skin was chalk. Did she have some kind of allergy attack back there on the street? She splashed cold water on her face, rummaged in her bag for a lipstick, dotted her cheeks pink and blended it in. This would have to do.

She pushed open the door and strode past an empty station towards the desk of a brown-eyed beauty with the name tag Ms. Dolores Rivera. Ms. Rivera's smooth black hair was swept up at the sides with silver clasps, and she had full lips and heavy brows like the painter Frida Kahlo that Ashling had come across in art books. This Irish girl was starting to feel white as alabaster in the darling city of San Francisco.

"May I help you?" Her voice was honey sweet.

"I'm Ashling O'Leary. I was hoping you might have some summer openings." She took a breath.

Ms. Rivera checked a calendar on her desk. "Did you have an appointment?"

"No, I..."

"We have a protocol," Ms. Rivera said in a stern voice.

"I have quite a bit of docent experience."

The brown eyes narrowed.

"I had excellent art training…" She slipped the portfolio strap from her shoulder.

"And most of our docents here are volunteer."

"I've done archival work, too…" Ashling's voice rose higher and faster.

Ms. Rivera placed her hands on the desk and her lips parted. Ashling gave it one final try. "And I took Dolores as my confirmation name."

A hint of a smile curled around the corners of the Kahlo lips. "What was your name again?"

"Ashling."

"Pretty name. Where in Ireland are you from?"

"The wilds of Mayo!"

Ms. Rivera's smile widened. "Ashling. We require a master's degree for full-time employment here."

"Oh."

"Sorry. Have you ever been to our museum?"

"No, I just arrived from Ireland yesterday."

"If you'd like to visit while you're here, it's our late opening tonight."

"Wow." She had never been inside a major art museum. "I can't really at the moment..."

"As my guest." Ms. Rivera opened her desk drawer. "If today doesn't work for you, you can come back another time." Her eyes softened, and she handed her a pass.

She slipped down a corridor with vaulted ceilings and sweeping open-air balconies and found the entrance to the museum. Ashling had intended to look for work in a few more galleries before they closed, but the artwork in the museum tugged at her with a silk hook, and she stayed.

Her immediate impression on entering the first gallery was wonderfully explosive colors, and figures shifting in dancelike motion. She stood before Matisse's *Femme au Chapeau* and her pulse raced. The hat was an elaborate confection of crazy greens and blues that bled over onto the woman's skin. In another Matisse, *La Conversation*, two women's bodies nestled together naturally as they conversed. She thought of her twin sisters Brona and Breda, opposites but inseparable, often perched on the same bench, reading from the same book, or chatting privately. One of Matisse's women wore a purple dress, the other a black one, and Ashling was in love with the bold colors and brushstrokes. She wanted to be this big and brave in her work.

She coasted through the rooms, and paused where the paintings lured her in. She had seen a reproduction in an art book of Magritte's *Les valeurs personelles*, but when she stood before the original painting—of a room with a normal-sized bed filled with huge, out-of-proportion, everyday objects like a giant comb—her mind spun with happiness. Inside and outside were reversed. The bright blue sky and white fluffy clouds formed the interior walls of the bedroom, and felt absurd, like life, when the things that are normal and familiar sometimes appear strange and incongruous.

She remembered the moment before she told her family she was going to San Francisco. Mam and Dad looked like a couple in a Renoir painting. They sat on the stone bench in their garden, all diffused yellows and blues and soft edges. Their shoulders touched, and they faced out, away from their children towards the sea beyond. Her youngest brother, Dermot, and oldest, Colm, were sprawled on the grass where they crafted a kite, and the twins were artfully arranged on the old wooden bench reading *Jane Eyre*. Then Ashling announced she was leaving. The family was so upset that her mentally constructed Renoir tableau dissolved.

Her head was already bursting when she got to Rauschenberg's *Collection*. A mixed-up mess of comic strips, newspaper headlines, paint drips, and crazy patches of color battled it out on the canvas. And then Pollock's *Guardians of the Secret*—another array of figures and symbols, some abstract, others vaguely distinguishable as mythological creatures—a hodgepodge of cryptic signs that set her heart racing.

"The museum will close in fifteen minutes." The announcement came over the air and snapped Ashling back to the present. It was a quarter to nine. She was filled with a wild excitement and a giddy hunger. Was this what a truly spiritual experience was for her—colors and shapes and textures and ideas spinning together and firing off into space—the heart rising from darkness?

She collided with two people before she even reached the stairs. She held onto the bannister and told her brain to walk her in a straight line. In the lobby she checked the map and adjusted her head to think straight about how to get back to the Y. It was already dark outside.

There were plenty of open seats on the light rail, but she couldn't bear to sit. She teetered down the aisle. She grabbed the leather strap every time the train chugged. She liked that it jolted her whole body, her bones, her nerves, her sinews. Everything and everyone looked sharp. Her vision was clearer now, her senses more attuned, her compass set. Her new life was just beginning. Here, in light-filled, art-filled San Francisco. She needed to hone her skills, expand her mind, find ways to express everything she had crammed inside. But she had no doubt that this was what she wanted to be. Had to be. An artist—not a nun or schoolteacher. She wanted this excitement and stimulation. This madness of invention. This terror of expression. This prayer that was art.

BRANDO

June 2

Ashling wove her way through the morning streets, shifting in and out of the skyscraper shadows. She clasped her portfolio to her chest for protection from the fog. Inching up the collar of her jacket, she crisscrossed a cavalcade of office workers armed with Styrofoam cups and briefcases. She carried a list of hostels in addition to her art galleries. If she could land an art job she needn't even go back to the temp agency.

After nine dead ends, Ashling was all set to slouch from yet another gallery run by two platinum-haired managers who were dressed in almost identical grey suits—she hadn't decided if they were male or female and was fine with that. She spotted the tea and coffee station and turned back.

"I make marvelous tea." She cringed inside. She was groveling.

The two looked at each other and burst out laughing in unison. "I don't think…" one began in a husky voice.

"Well… maybe we should have proper tea here," the other continued. She/he mimicked Ashling's accent, raised a hand and stuck out a pinkie finger as if holding a china teacup. Ashling felt a giant hand slap her forehead. Of course, coffee ruled in the U.S., the tea paraphernalia consisted of just bags—not much making there. She whipped out her resume to cover her embarrassment, added the YMCA phone number with a calligraphic flourish, and handed it over.

The bell jingled, and the door shut behind her.

The next gallery Ashling entered was on Geary, near Kearny, where huge vibrant works in a naïve style were set off against white panels. The slender silver-haired manager was polite, but he wasn't hiring either. Ashling sensed he was kind, so decided to risk it.

"Do you look at people's work?" she said, trying to keep her voice confident. "I don't know if it's the case here, but in Ireland gallery owners like their workers to know what it's like to produce art."

The man looked around at the two people who meandered through the gallery. "I'll take a quick look."

Ashling's heart leaped. The man lifted out her painting—of a woman in a flowing blue dress, opening a wooden gate under an arched trellis, gazing into the far distance.

"Brush strokes of the Impressionists, maybe Monet. But something darker, too," the manager said.

Ashling grinned. Her jaw relaxed. "I love Monet. Everything in his world looks like it's dancing."

The idea for the painting had come from one of Ashling's first experiences of creating a snapshot in her mind and storing it away. She was six years old, and her mother had asked her to mind the twin babies asleep in their basket in the sun. She didn't take her eyes off the gorgeous nut-brown girls for even a second. Pale pink petals fluttered down from the dog roses in the hedgerow, and she arranged them in patterns on the white cotton blanket. Then Ashling heard a rustling, raised her eyes, and saw her mother appear from the direction of the back garden with a bunch of rhubarb nestled in her arm. She was framed by an archway of hawthorn that cast a pink glow on her cheeks. Mam opened the wooden half-gate, paused as if she had just remembered something from long ago, and a faint smile shaped her lips into a tiny, pink boat. Her eyes shone. The sun set her hair ablaze. Ashling held her breath. She stiffened when baby Brona sighed and shifted, afraid it might disturb her mama's reverie. The seconds extended into an eternal moment as her mam stayed there, suspended. Then she blinked once, shivered, gently swayed the wooden gate over, clicked the latch into place, and sailed on into the house without even noticing the children.

Ashling's heart fluttered—like an angel had passed over. She glanced at the gate. She still saw her mother there, in her moment of private stillness. Later, when Mam asked her to see if she had left her wicker basket in the vegetable garden, the little girl couldn't bring herself to unlatch the gate. The closing of it in that way by her mother felt inviolable. She walked all the way around the back of the house and approached the garden from the gate near the edge of the cliff. She knew Mam wouldn't be happy with her going that way on her own, but the garden gate, for many hours afterwards, possessed a perfection she could not disturb.

"She has the reverence of a Madonna," the gallery manager murmured. The word "reverence" resonated with Ashling. In her six-year-old mind, she had already painted this picture, as if by trying to capture the mystery of a moment she might someday come to understand it. She remembered her own feelings of respect, even fear, a prohibition against undoing something fastened by her mother. That was the suggestion of darkness in the painting. Later on Ashling couldn't dare disturb her mam in her sewing retreat, her slip of a room at the end of their cottage with its squinty view of the ocean. Their mother sequestered herself there and hummed away, not in the least bit bothered by housekeeping, or even by childrearing. Her retreat was sanctified, and Ashling had always taken up the slack.

From the window of the Geary bus, Ashling watched the cityscape transform from the financial district through Chinatown—with its open-air markets, deep alleyways, red and yellow awnings, Chinese faces, and dress. In just two days of nonstop hustling, she had tallied twenty-three gallery rejections and eleven hostels with no empty beds. She was fit to explode with frustration.

A surge of people boarded the bus at the Chinatown stop. An ancient, stooped woman hobbled up the steps, pushed through a wall of passengers and propelled herself onto the seat opposite Ashling. The old woman pulled a newspaper from her canvas shopping bag and bent her wrinkled face over the Chinese characters. Ashling wondered how long she had been in the United States and if she felt at home here—if she missed living in a country where everyone looked like her and spoke her language. She wondered how she herself would feel if she stayed on. Would she be torn between the comfort of spending her life among her own people, and the wrench of leaving her native land for a place such as America? Would it come to feel like a splintering, or a grand expansion? Or both?

Ashling got off the bus in the Marina and flew through side-by-side galleries number twenty-four through thirty-one. Like a character in a French farce, she made an entrance, peddled her wares, got rejected, made a speedy exit, and then began the cycle all over again. She was determined not to pause until she collapsed with hunger.

Her spirits lifted as soon as she entered the sun-filled Rosen Gallery. The exterior walls were made of glass and when the swinging door closed and she looked out, she could see San Francisco Bay and Alcatraz. She glanced at the trickle of people who milled around the contemporary paintings and sculptures and aligned her internal compass towards the reception area. She remembered the voice of her judo instructor—walk with your hips, don't let your feet be too far apart or too close together so your head and shoulders don't bob. She moved smoothly across the floor, up to the woman behind the desk, and extended her hand. "Hello, I'm Ashling O'Leary and I wonder if you're hiring?"

"I'm Shelley." Shelley's lipstick was a perfect match for her magenta blouse. They shook hands. "That's an Irish accent, isn't it? Where are you from?"

"Mayo."

"I went to Ireland on my honeymoon."

"Is your family of Irish origin, then?" Shelley's dark blonde hair and periwinkle eyes made Ashling think she was more likely to be German.

"No, my husband is, but going back many generations."

Ashling whisked out her handcrafted calling card and handed it to Shelley.

"Unusual name. Is it Gaelic?" Shelley asked.

"Yes. An Ashling is a dream in which Ireland, personified as a woman, foretells the reversal of the country's bad fortune."

"So, you're the harbinger of good luck?" Shelley laughed. "What kind of work are you interested in?"

"I'm good at sales. I'm great with design, hanging shows, arranging spaces for exhibits."

"I don't want to get your hopes up. We really don't have an opening at..."

"And I'm a whizz with figures, accounting." Ashling squeezed her palms together like a supplicant. "Please, please save me from a deadly boring temp job."

Shelley's lips widened in a smile. "Okay. I'll talk to Charlie." She inclined her head towards the glass-walled office and Ashling followed with her eyes. A handsome older man, maybe late thirties, was in conversation with a fiftyish woman who wore a stiff buttoned-up navy dress. Ashling noticed his olive skin, dark-brown hair, and linen suit—probably Italian.

"He's the owner?" she asked. He looked a bit like Marlon Brando past his boyish stage. Maybe in the film *The Ugly American*. Charlie, like Brando, was drop-dead gorgeous.

"Yes, Charlie Rosen. He'll probably look over your portfolio another time if you like. He's very encouraging to students."

"Great. I'm not a student now, though. I'm a job seeker." Ashling slipped out her resume.

Shelley handed her a business card. "We do have an opening gala next Friday evening, so it's possible we'll need some help. Can you check back late Monday?"

It was a smidgeon of hope. She tucked the card in the special pouch with her passport. "Thanks a million."

Turning towards the door, Ashling was momentarily blinded by a shaft of light. She glanced over and saw that Charlie brandished what looked like a silver dagger. She swallowed her fear, but on second look saw it was a sleek sliver of a pen which he waved as if conducting an orchestra. His eyes met hers for the briefest of seconds—a flash of liquid brown—and he smiled. More generous than a Brando smile. She turned and kept herself from doing a jig through the doorway.

When the last gallery closed its doors, Ashling dragged herself over to the Marina Safeway. Her feet were sweaty, and blisters had sprouted on her toes. Her stomach was a hollowed-out cave.

The store was vast, the aisles like wide, straight roads. Smartly dressed people sauntered up and down pushing glinting carts. In Timaleen, all of the shops had their own specialty—the butcher, the baker, the greengrocer, the sweet shop, the haberdashery. In Iggy Grufferty's you could get a loaf of bread and a bottle of milk as well as sweets and the newspaper, but that was the extent of it. This store had everything. But how could you possibly find what you wanted?

Ashling roamed the aisles. At sample tables, handsome young singles dangled miniature paper cups, waved cubes of cheese on skewers, and conversed. It was a giant dating zone—men and women, men and men, women and women. This was a scene Ashling couldn't even imagine taking place where she came from. She was falling in love with this city where everything seemed possible. Except staying.

She toured the aisles, sampled the miniature offerings, and picked up a box of Band-Aids. She grabbed a hand basket. The produce section was misted like a tropical jungle and had a mindboggling selection of fruits and vegetables—she read the names: kale, okra, zucchini, mango, papaya. The mangos and papayas were hugely expensive. Ashling wondered if she'd ever fit in, or be able to afford such luxuries, and settled for a firm pear, a small package of white cheddar cheese, and a bread roll.

On the Marina waterfront, sailboats swayed in their slips. Ashling stretched her aching legs along an empty bench near the Golden Gate Bridge and bandaged her blisters. She nibbled on the cheese so as not to shock her contracting stomach—she was training herself to need less food. The bread lodged in her gut. She was lonely. She wished she had Majella to talk to, so she could start to sort out her tangled feelings. About Ireland, about men having all the power, about priests and nuns not being as holy as they were made out to be. And she wished she had that safe, haven in Majella's house. After tonight she could afford one more night at the Y and then she would be broke.

All around her people strolled, others lay on the grassy areas and read, or pic-nicked, like figures in a Renoir. Free. She herself was in a kind of Munch scenario—her scream pushed inside.

BREATH

June 3

After a hasty shower, Ashling dressed for her two-day, three-fifty an hour temp job at a downtown accounting firm. In the Y's lobby she stopped off at the front desk to speak to the manager with the moon-shaped face.

"Jorge could use help morning and evening, and we could give you half price on your room while you're here," the manager said.

"While I'm here?"

"You realize this is not a hotel." Her clipped voice reminded Ashling of Sister Ignatius. Her own hands smarting after being sliced by the skinny switch, and afterwards the broad smile as the nun pressed a sweet into her scalding palm, with a saccharine-voiced admonition not to tattle to mammy.

"The normal stay is three to four nights," the manager continued.

"Oh. I didn't know..."

"You can't treat this as a budget convenience. I can tentatively extend your stay to the beginning of next week." She pulled out a ledger and went back to her work.

That was just three more days.

The office supervisor, Mr. Pyle, sat at a large desk against the wall in the entry foyer. He looked like a Scrooge Ashling had seen once in "A Christmas Carol"—long and lanky with white curly hair and wire-brush eyebrows. He grabbed a box overflowing with papers. Ashling followed him into a huge room subdivided into a honeycomb of white plasterboard cubicles. There were no windows in the entire area—not a screed of natural light. She had a memory flash of her father's computer-chip factory—where he worked when his furniture business was slow. The tasks were monotonous, and after each shift her father came home drained and expressionless. Everyone in the family knew to keep their distance.

They arrived finally at an empty cubicle with a metal grey filing cabinet taller than she was, and a desk with a computer monitor. He gave her instructions and left. Ashling looked at his back disappearing into the labyrinth. She'd need a trail of crumbs to find her way out.

Ashling organized her documents. When a pile looked like it might topple over, she hauled it to the massive cabinet and her robot arms popped the documents into place. She repeated ad infinitum. By the first break, her brain had turned to cotton wool.

She opened her sketch pad. Ignoring perspective, she lumped the cubicles on top of each other to create a hillock of cells. She added more cells until the toppling hill became a mountain, sketched a footbridge in the foreground, and her own figure—head bulging, eyes round, mouth an elongated Munch scream. She smiled. It might be leeching her soul, but she would make $58 before taxes in two days at this job and had the chance of a higher wage if they kept her on for accounting work. Mayo might well be one of the cheapest places in Ireland, but it was dawning on her that San Francisco was probably the exact opposite.

Ashling's bare feet pressed into the ribbed gym mat. She pulled one knee, then the other up to her chest. Pushing away thoughts of the gallery rejections she'd notched up after the drudgery of the office, she leaned to the right, then the left, elongating her tired body. She reached her arms above her head, joined her fingers in a tepee and looked up. The high, ceilings and clerestory windows reminded her of a cathedral. She stretched towards the light. Next Sunday, for the first time in her life, she wouldn't have to go to Mass.

As a teenager she had started to wonder why everything had to be accepted on faith, but in the tiny village of Timaleen, not appearing at Mass on Sunday would bring a shame worse than death. There was no one to talk to about doubts or to ask for explanations. You weren't supposed to question why so many girls disappeared for months at a time to visit an "aunt" or "grandmother," and came back looking haunted—though you knew right well they had gotten pregnant. Or what exactly those girls behind the walls of the convent laundry had done that was so bad they were locked up, treated like outcasts by the nuns, and turned into zombies. Most especially, you didn't question why the males involved in these sex-related sins got off scot-free. She had pushed all those questions and suspicions inside, and now they were seeping out.

Ashling could picture herself, just six months earlier, and still in the novitiate, as she paused outside the convent parlor door. She breathed in the lemon scent from the polished mahogany and ground the soles of her feet into the doormat.

The Sacred Heart lamp above the door blinked red in the dim antechamber. She whispered a quick prayer. "Sacred heart of Jesus, guide me."

She'd mustered every speck of courage to request this meeting with the Parish Priest, who was as close to God as you got in Timaleen. The nuns worshipped Father Dempsey, and the villagers bowed down to his superior knowledge. He was a university-educated man from Dublin—God knows how he ended up in their remote corner of County Mayo.

The tiny antechamber linked the entrance hallway and parlor. Nuns waited there in the dark and prepared confessions or collected themselves for interviews with Reverend Mother. Ashling smoothed down the skirt of her robe and ran her finger under her veil to ease the pinching on her cheeks. After three and a half years it still felt strange to be covered from head to toe in the habit of the novice. In a few months, just after her twenty-first birthday, she would cut her hair, exchange her whites for all black robes, and take religious vows. But she had to be absolutely certain before taking that final step, and something was bothering her. She needed an answer.

Ashling stretched up to her full five feet, four inches, breathed in all the air she could, and knocked. She heard the priest say, come in, and she turned the brass knob and stepped inside. Father Dempsey stood over by the fireplace, framed by the portrait of the Blessed Virgin Mary and her baby Jesus. The flicker of flames from the fire were the only illumination in the room.

The priest was a tall, stately figure, even more so in his black soutane that shimmered down to the top of his shining shoes. His eyes were steely blue and his thick black hair greying at the temples, but he carried himself with the ease of a man who knows he is exceptionally handsome. Young girls went jelly-kneed in his presence.

"Good afternoon, Father." The room suddenly seemed huge, the fireplace miles away. Ashling turned and closed the door and tried to hide her own jelly knees.

"Hello, Sister."

Every morning since she entered the novitiate at age seventeen, she had kneeled in the pews of the convent chapel and listened to that silvery timbre as the priest intoned the Mass. "The grace of our Lord Jesus Christ and the love of God and the fellowship of the Holy Spirit be with you all." "*And also, with you.*" Ashling loved to ease into that pre-dawn ritual—candles illuminating the small private chapel, the mystery of the incense, the comforting assurance of the liturgy.

"Thanks for taking the time to see me, Father." She made her way across the expanse of the carpeted room, her footsteps muffled by the soft wool underfoot.

"Of course. Delighted." His words soaked into the lush draperies, which created a soundproofed privacy.

"The reason I came—"

"Was to have your confession heard before Christmas Mass, I assume. Take a seat." He pointed to a straight-backed chair next to the armchair. Many of the younger nuns preferred to come here rather than kneel in the forbidding confessional.

"No, Father. It's something else."

The turf sizzled and crackled in the grate and the flames glinted off the tinsel on the Christmas tree.

"You know that I'm doing my student teaching at the primary school at the moment," Ashling said.

Father Dempsey nodded, and smiled. "You must be nearly qualified by now?"

"Yes, I'll be finished in May." She glanced at the Virgin Mary with the sprig of holly dangling over the picture frame. "I came to talk about one of the girls in my class—Sheila Cullen."

"Who?"

"Sheila…Cullen. You know, she was in your Confirmation group."

All traces of a smile vanished from the priest's lips. "Yes. What about her?"

"It's just…well, I'm worried about her."

"And why would that be?"

Ashling pushed back against the force of his words. "She was a top student, Father. Now she's falling behind."

His eyes narrowed. "And why did you come to me instead of her teacher?"

"I did go to Sister Ignatius first. She said the girl probably just got lazy. But…"

Ashling wanted to say that Sister Ignatius was a sadist who beat children who were poor, or not doing well in school—but teachers and nuns were just one rung down from priests in the hierarchy. She couldn't tell Father Dempsey that Sheila's fall from star pupil to dunce gave the nun one more victim to torture.

"What do *you* think?" Father Dempsey said. His blue eyes were hard and focused. He was daring her to answer.

Ashling met his stare. "Sheila just has a few more months before she'll be going into secondary school, and I thought you could maybe speak to her in private, encourage her." She watched for his reaction.

The priest's eyes chiseled through the darkness of the room. Ashling's mind raced backwards, tracking, grasping at ideas unthinkable. She had a hunch that all was not above reproach in the convent, yet she had refused to allow herself to believe it. When the eleven and twelve-year-old's emerged from the parlor after private instruction from Father Dempsey, their eyes were downcast, and all color was drained from their cheeks. Everyone assumed they were steeped in devotion. Sheila got by far the most attention, and the nuns said she was likely being groomed for the religious life.

His eyes rooted her to the spot. "Do you think that I have special influence?" he said, his tone mocking.

Sheila's Botticelli face floated in Ashling's mind—the blonde curls that fell in tendrils, the pale skin, the lips a cherry heart. The vacant eyes. "My thought was, because you had singled her out..." Ashling heard her own words, repeating what all the nuns said. How lucky the girl was to be chosen. Wasn't Father great to give so generously of his time.

The priest's mouth curved into a set smile. "I made the same mistake as you, thinking she was clever."

Ashling recoiled from the coldness of his words. Father Dempsey was relegating Sheila to the dumping ground of lost causes.

"But Father...you kept on seeing her for...months. Why?"

The priest lunged his arm in her direction. Ashling jerked away, frightened by the sudden movement, thinking he was going to grab her. She had the sensation of spinning backwards in time to six years prior, her fourteen-year-old self, frozen, barely able to make out her own father's features in the dark of their kitchen, his arm reaching out, his hand groping towards her.

In the present in the convent parlor, Father Dempsey continued to reach past her and swept his prayer-book up from the mantle.

Ashling realized she was holding her breath. She exhaled.

"Sheila used to be among the top three in her class," she said, striking back. "She's clever."

Father Dempsey cradled his missal, the gold cross on black leather shielding his heart. "It's my God-given duty to seek out those who might be suitable for the religious life. But I eventually realized, as you must have, that there was no helping

Sheila." His words were cruel and measured. The fire sparked and turned his eyes a silvery red. Ashling suddenly remembered the day a few months before, when she had seen Sheila emerge from the parlor with a red stain on her yellow dress. Ashling was passing the door and asked the girl if she was alright. Sheila muttered that she cut herself and would wash off the blood in the bathroom before her mother came to pick her up. At the time, Ashling accepted this. She now recalled the girl's downcast eyes and eagerness to escape. Her aura of shame.

"You're a smart girl, Ashling." She saw the priest's lips moving, but his voice seemed to come from far away. "You'll make a fine nun."

In a matter of months, she was expected to prostrate herself before this man and accept his divine authority to ordain her. Her stomach heaved, and she swallowed to stop the bile rising. Father Dempsey's soutane billowed from a heat blast. His black figure loomed in front of the crackling fire, his vestments were fluttering wings. His entire demeanor was a study in hubris and in his smugness, he was assured of her silence.

The priest opened his prayer-book and lowered himself into the armchair. "Now, if you'll excuse me, I must pray, prepare for evening Mass. And remember your vows, blind obedience, Sister. Blind obedience."

Ashling turned towards the door. The rose and blue of the carpet swam before her eyes and the embossed wallpaper reduced to a blur. All the information in her brain was rearranging. Every concept, every belief. All she had not allowed herself to formulate let alone give credence to, because it had no place in the worldview of her faith. Not one person, nun, or novice, allowed themselves to even think anything could be amiss. She knew that her thoughts had trapped and confined her, had instilled the belief that fathers, both parental and religious were inviolable. She knew that the church had custody of their minds—the girls', the nuns'. And her own, until now.

She could deny it no longer. She knew at that moment, in her heart, the truth about what happened with Sheila. And countless other innocent girls.

She reached the door and stretched her hand towards the knob. Out of the chaos came the cool voice of the priest.

"Goodbye, Sister O'Leary. I'll see you at Mass."

As Jorge paired off the players in the San Francisco gym, the question crossed Ashling's mind now whether she had joined the convent at the age of seventeen in the hopes of recovering and solidifying the faith she had started to question years earlier. If so, then that final encounter with Father Dempsey had shattered any remaining remnants of those hopes.

Jorge teamed Ashling and a young woman with golden skin and almond eyes who was, like her, a blue belt. They bowed to each other. Ashling stepped in towards her partner with her right foot, turned on her left, and swept with her hip and leg to lift her off balance. Her partner countered by easing backwards, evading Ashling's advance, grabbing a shoulder fold of her judogi and pulling her towards the floor. Ashling reacted instantly, righted herself. They were evenly matched, quickly gained speed and momentum, and soon were whirling in a continuous series of attack, avoidance, counterattack.

The match accelerated. Ashling tried to keep her full attention in the present but it kept wandering. She had to make a success of San Francisco. She was already twenty-one and had wasted years stuck behind the bloody convent walls. After her encounter with Father Dempsey, she had requested a meeting with Reverend Mother where she confided her suspicions. The look of disgust and disbelief on the nun's face was seared into Ashling's brain. The supposedly holy nun had told her that her words were sacrilegious, that she should look to her vows, and bow to the greater authority of her superiors. That night Ashling packed her bags and left the convent forever.

She speeded up her moves and dived in for a throw. Suddenly she got that same scratchy throat and eyelids-hardening sensation she had felt on the way to the art museum. That same long-limbed monster inside trying to shut down her eyes, throat, heart. Her opponent's face blurred and morphed into that of Father Dempsey. Ashling's breath came in a rattle of panic and scraped her chest. She couldn't bear to face the smirking holier-than-thou fecking priest. She moved faster. And it pissed her off no end that he got away with damaging little girls and that it was endorsed by the so-called reverent mother. She flew her left foot back, shifted her hip into position over her opponent's leg. She dragged a wheezy breath up her windpipe. She slipped, wavered, and barely righted herself.

"Not so fast." Jorge tapped her lightly on the shoulder. "Maximum efficiency, minimum effort."

"Sorry." Ashling gulped in air.

"Start the movement with the hip, and the leg will follow."

She opened her mouth to speak but could only nod.

Jorge's palm brushed her shoulder blade. "You're speedy, but temper that with caution, mindfulness."

Ashling knew she had violated judo decorum. She had to keep that anger in its proper place. She drew in a deep breath and slowed down.

After class, Ashling helped Jorge clear off the tatami mats and stack them in the adjoining storage area. He glanced at her face. "Are you alright?"

Her throat was lined with nettles, and the edges of her lids still scraped against her eyeballs.

"I wonder if you're allergic to the mats?" he said.

There were no mats when she had similar breathing problems on the way to the museum, so she knew that wasn't the case. It felt related to anxiety—a very American notion. No one had time for anxiety back home in Mayo.

Jorge left. Ashling tidied up the rolled yoga mats on the shelves, and lined up the straps, cushions, and eye pillows in the prop box. She gathered the straying yoga balls. At the far end of the room, straightening the mats in the corner, she had a thought. Back here, on top of the mats would make a good place to sleep when she was kicked out of the Y. If they let her help in the gym first thing in the morning and last thing at night, she could sneak in. If she re-arranged the mats so that there was a taller pile closer to the door and a shorter one behind it against the wall, she could sleep on the short pile and be invisible from the doorway if someone came in.

She walked towards the double doors which closed the space off from the gym—they were almost as high as the ceiling. She closed one side and latched it in place, pulled the other towards her, staying on the inside, and closed it as quietly as she could. Her head spun. Her terror of the dark swallowed her up, and she thought she was toppling backwards into black. She saw her own fourteen-year-old self, frozen, barely able to make out her father's features in the dark of the kitchen. She tried to banish the image of his hand groping towards her, pushing himself at her. Tried to banish the stories told in whispers of girls like Majella, whose fathers/brothers/uncles/priests had done unspeakable things. Trying to reconcile that with Catholic Ireland and everything she'd been taught about the purity of the Church. Wanting to fight back. Gathering in all the force she could so she could say no. Could you really say no to your own father? The shock of his hand on her flesh, his body pressed into hers.

A filament of yellow light crept from the gym through the chink where the two doors met and Ashling's lungs filled with air. She opened the door and stepped out. Her palms were slippery as she pulled the door closed behind her. She crossed over to the women's bathroom. She guessed one of the lockers could house most everything she owned, and she could stash her portfolio behind the mats. She could pull it off.

Turning on the tap, she soaped and kneaded her sweating hands. She caught sight of herself in the mirror and understood why Jorge thought she had an allergic reaction to something. Her skin was chalk, her eyelids swollen, her lips puffed up, her eyes a watery green. Her face was a shell-shocked mask.

ROSEN GALLERY

June 7

Ashling swung open the door of the Rosen Gallery. She sauntered over to reception, where Shelley sat at her desk. Charlie stood by her, elegant in a tan-colored suit. A handful of people wandered around looking at the art.

"Hello there," Ashling said.

Shelley chuckled. "You sound happy. Did you avoid the really boring office job?"

"No. But, I'm rising above it." Ashling's smile crinkled her cheeks. She hugged her portfolio.

"Charlie, this is Ashling, the Irish girl I told you about."

Charlie grinned and reached out to shake Ashling's hand. His clasp was warm and firm. "Come on in and we'll have a look at your work. Just holler if you need me, Shelley."

Ashling swelled with pride that Charlie was willing to look at her paintings. He led her to his glass-walled office. When he closed the door all the gallery sounds disappeared.

"It's like a space capsule in here," Ashling said.

Charlie pushed aside several neat piles to clear a space on the desk. "Have to keep it tidy—being in the glass bubble." He smiled. "Okay, let's see what you've got. Want to sit?"

Ashling shook her head. "I'll meander if you don't mind." She handed over her paintings.

While he looked, she skimmed the edges of the room. She could see Charlie's linen suit out of the corner of her eye. He wore it like he was born to Armani. She and her family joked about Mam's haute couture creations, but this was the real thing. His arm rose and fell as he turned over the paintings, and he made murmuring noises she hoped were approval.

Ashling glanced at the framed posters on the walls—of painting exhibits with the gallery inscription. They were mostly abstract, with large splashes of color, and floating shapes. In her peripheral vision she could see people wandering through the gallery, drifting in to look at a painting, stepping back, making comments to the person bedside them. The paintings were contemporary—geometric shapes with bright colors, abstracted landscapes with tiny figures, objects that resembled tangles of threads.

He's going to feckin hate my work, she thought.

"Is this where you're from?" Charlie said, lifting up a canvas. Ashling crossed over—he was looking at a painting of a beach with several old bicycles strewn in the sand.

"It's where my brothers and sisters and I go to swim in the summer."

"I sense the excitement of rushing off, abandoning the bicycles."

Charlie turned over another canvas. "This is interesting, this young couple on the bench with their backs to us."

Ashling laughed. "They're my parents. They're in their early forties—I suppose that's not so old."

"Not really." Charlie laughed.

Heat seared Ashling's cheeks. Charlie might be close to forty.

"Is this Ireland, too?" he asked.

She nodded. "It's the Victorian promenade in a seaside town near us."

"They seem carefree, your parents. And you've created an aura of…romance...but something else too."

The whole family went on that outing. After a stroll on the beach Mam and Dad sat side by side on a high-backed stone bench looking out over the ocean, where they held hands and retreated into their own private world. Ashling had tried to capture their great love for each other, but also the exclusion of the children. Aisling was so capable that she had been made to parent her siblings. Looking at the painting now, she felt that entering the convent had been a cowardly attempt to escape all that.

"I can see you've been influenced by Degas." Charlie was still looking at the same painting.

He flipped back to some of the previous paintings. "You capture a lovely sense of spontaneity in many of these. Do you have Degas' favorites?"

"His dancers, of course. The way he can convey a sense of motion in his brushstrokes."

"Have you been to the *Galerie Nationale de Jeu de Paume* in Paris?" His pronunciation was perfect.

"Where they have the huge Impressionist collection? I wish."

"Paris isn't that far from Ireland."

"It is from Mayo!"

"But you made it over here. This is a lot farther."

"True…but sometimes it's easier to make a big break."

Charlie's brown eyes met hers—a flicker of sadness. He focused on another painting.

"This one reminds me of Richard Diebenkorn. Do you know him?" Charlie said.

Ashling shook her head.

"I'm thinking of his painting of a girl looking at a landscape —something in the attitude and the edges reminds me of your figure here."

Ashling had painted this a few months after leaving the convent. In her painting a girl sat indoors looking off into the distance. Her head was rimmed by a grey nimbus. The girl might be Majella, or herself, or Sheila, or any Irish girl. And the cloud— Majella's uncle, and men like him. The Catholic Church. The Father Dempseys, the Reverend Mothers, the Sister Ignatiuses, and all the reasons a twenty-one-year-old woman might want to get the hell out of Ireland. When she was working on the painting Ashling knew she was pushing past her limitations as an artist. She wanted to express through art what everyone around her in Ireland was blind to. What they wouldn't believe when using words to spell it out. The effort was a ring squeezing her heart.

Charlie's voice brought her back to the present. "Diebenkorn's grandmother was a painter, born in Dublin actually, and an important influence on him."

"Really? There's not a huge legacy of Irish painters. And not a lot of women."

Charley nodded.

"There's Mainie Jellett. She incorporated Cubism into her work," Ashling said. It was a rush to talk about art.

Charlie glanced back at the bicycle painting. "This one is also blurring the edges. Maybe a hint of Fauvism?"

"Because of the color? I think of Matisse, but I've only begun to experiment with that kind of color."

"You're pushing past the representational and playing with abstraction. Your work has an intensity, and you're painting what your life is about." He leveled his eyes on her. "You strike me as having the drive to keep at it."

She nodded, afraid to trust her mouth to work.

Charlie glanced out at the gallery. "You realize that even if something opens up workwise, the starting level's not very glamorous."

"I'm familiar with unglamorous!" she blurted out.

Charlie chuckled. "Would you be up for a few hours' work on Wednesday and Monday? Shelley could do with help prepping and winding up after the Friday event."

"That'd be brilliant."

Charlie closed the portfolio.

"Thanks for looking at my work," Ashling said.

He led her to the door. "My pleasure." He smiled the sweeter-than-Brando smile. He opened the door, and they left his space capsule.

"Shelley, I'm bringing Ashling in on Wednesday to help you with the prep for the gala," Charlie said.

"Fantastic. Want to come in at 10:30 in the morning?"

She knew Mr. Pyle possibly had work for her at the temp job through Wednesday, but she said yes.

"I'll walk you out, Ashling. Going to grab an espresso."

A few paces from the gallery, Charlie nodded to a man behind the counter of a tiny coffee shop. "*Buon giorno,* Gino." Gino nodded back. "*Doppio?*" and without waiting for an answer, revved up the espresso machine.

Walking away, Ashling heard Charlie speak to Gino in Italian. The sounds were delicious and muscular. He could be a European in Rome or Florence, having his daily espresso.

She hitched her portfolio at a jaunty angle. A surge of hope and power shot through her. Hope that she could somehow help Sheila and those left behind, by her art. It was a mad kind of responsibility. She tilted her face to catch the blood red glint of the sun, melting into a Dali clock over the Golden Gate Bridge.

Ashling followed her nose into a Mexican fast-food restaurant several blocks from the Y. It was packed with families—couples gay and straight and singles—all sitting on plastic chairs arranged around Formica tables attached to the floor. It looked like a playhouse with fake furniture. At home, furniture was made of wood.

She stood in line and inhaled the spicy smells. She picked at random something called a *carne asada* burrito and said yes to all the trimmings, even though she had no idea what some of them were. She couldn't waste money on a drink so asked for a cup for water. When the girl slipped the silver parcel into a brown paper bag and added a scoop of tortilla chips, she wanted to say thank you in Spanish, but it was the Irish *go raibh maith agat* that popped into her head.

Ashling sat on a bench by the pier. She itched to get working again. Art was now her prayer. She needed to find a place to paint so she could start to experiment. She had things to say—dark bits floating inside, weighing down her heart.

Seagulls spun overhead. She peeled back the silver foil. Even a few hours' work in the gallery was promising—it was an entrée into that world. She bit into the burrito and a fire lit on her tongue. Her eyes and nose watered. She used the napkins to catch the juices spilling out the corners of her mouth—the spiciest thing she had ever encountered at home was white pepper. She laughed out loud. She felt deliriously silly. The fire was in her head too—her conversation with Charlie crackling around. She took another deliciously punishing mouthful. It was thrilling to have someone she could talk to about art and who glimpsed what she was aspiring towards.

Ashling made herself stop when she had eaten half the burrito—she needed to keep training her stomach to expect less food. She re-wrapped the remainder for the next day's lunch and left behind a squawking flock of seagulls.

Ashling fervently wished there was a back door to the Y, so she could skirt around her nemesis. She tripped on something and careened towards the sidewalk, her burrito flying. She righted herself, rubbed her scraped elbow, and narrowed her eyes to look for the food. In the dusk she made out a pile of blankets in the threshold of a closed storefront. She gasped when she saw there was a person there—she had snagged her foot on his shoe. He blinked a few times, groaned, and pulled the blanket back over his head. She drew her jacket close to her chest and hurried away. Two doorways down, she came upon another man, already asleep, his belongings in plastic shopping bags at his feet. A shiver of sadness ran through her. She had never seen people sleeping on the streets before. She pressed on.

The lit-up sign for the Y was a beacon. She had a bed waiting for her—at least for one more night.

TATAMI

June 8-9

I have good news, Miss O'Leary," Mr. Pyle said, wiry eyebrows twitching and an almost-smile on his face. "I can offer you work tomorrow and Thursday, and likely on Friday."

Ashling froze.

"Mr. Pyle, I have another engagement tomorrow. Is there any chance I could skip, and continue…"?

"Are you signed with another agency?"

She shook her head. "No, not at all, I…"

"Well, then. You led me to believe you were available. Now you're saying you're not?"

Sweat rose on her palms. She was back in primary school with Sister Ignatius towering over her, arm raised, ready to pound the ruler down on her knuckles.

"I'm sorry."

"This will be your last day. I'll inform the agency I won't need you again."

Ashling slunk away. She should have been sensible—trading a few hours in an art gallery for steady work. She disappeared into her cubicle and buried herself in the mound of papers.

On her break, Ashling poured herself a cup of coffee in the lunchroom and sat down to read the letter from home that arrived that morning.

"Isn't it vile?" a voice piped up behind her.

A young woman, her face framed by a mass of blonde curls, was pouring herself a coffee. She took a sip and grimaced. "It could kill you as fast as the boredom in this shithole."

Ashling laughed. "I'm mostly a tea drinker. Haven't much of a basis for comparison."

"Tastes like piss. I'm Cynthia. Cyn." She gulped another punishing mouthful.

"Ashling."

"Never heard of it. No names like that in Phoenix."

"You're new to San Francisco?"

"Yep. Finished up high school last week and took to the road pronto." She waved her thumb in the gesture of hitching a ride.

"Your parents didn't mind you leaving?" Ashling said.

"Hell no. My old lady practically kicked me out. Couldn't stand me from the time I was twelve or thirteen. Competition, you know." Cynthia wiggled her cleavage, two melons in a halter top, to underscore her point. "And she sure as hell knew what my brother Tucker was up to."

Ashling stared. Cynthia meant some kind of sexual molestation. She wasn't sure which was more shocking to her—the fact of it, or Cynthia blurting it out like that to a complete stranger. Ashling's own string of memories drowned her in shame and had become attached in her mind with the secret shames of countless Irish girls who might whisper but would never shout their stories. But maybe they could and should.

"Your own brother…?" Ashling didn't know how to phrase it.

"Yep. Tucker Fucker. You Irish?"

Ashling nodded yes.

"I suppose Ireland is too holy for that kind of shit?"

Ashling gulped her coffee. "Well. No. It's just that people don't talk."

"All that Catholic repression?"

"I suppose. And family loyalty, fear…stupidity."

Cynthia chortled. "I always knew I'd cut loose soon as I hit eighteen. What about you?"

"I'm only in the country a little over a week. And just got myself fired from here."

"Good riddance. You'll find something else." Cynthia checked her watch. "I'm back. This was an illegal break." And she was gone.

Ashling poured another cup of coffee. She opened her letter. Brona had written on behalf of the family.

We miss you already, girl. Colm and Breda are doing okay, but the Ashling Accounting Plan is just a wee bit shaky without your supervision.

Ashling pictured her sister and brother hunched over the oak desk in the corner of the kitchen puzzling over the bills.

Thanks be to God you were wise enough not to entrust me with anything other than my own mini plan. I'm struggling with that as it is. Dermot is doing better than anyone. I know you can't tell as he's only six, but I'd put money on him being the one to inherit your maths' brain. We all know it didn't come from our dear, darling parents.

We have your return date marked in RED on the calendar.

Ashling gulped a mouthful of coffee.

Dad's woodworking is slowing down a bit. He says it's the economy. Hoping he doesn't have to take a shift in the factory. We all know the black moods he gets into then.

Mam reminds us we'll have your teacher's salary come autumn.

Ashling scrunched the letter into a ball. She banged her mug onto the table, splattering the notepaper. She had already spent years giving her parents space to be artists in their own right. It didn't seem to occur to any of them that she had a right to pursue her own dream as an artist. Let alone have autonomy as a fully-fledged human being.

Feck the convent, and feck her family.

She wasn't fecking chattel!

Ashling counted out her room fee to the clerk at the Y.

The sour faced manager came striding towards the front desk.

"This will be your last night. Starting tomorrow, all our rooms are booked. This is one of the most popular Ys in America, you know," the manager said.

"Okay…may I still work with Jorge in exchange for judo classes like you said?"

"I don't see why not. Come first thing in the morning and last thing at night. The doors are locked at midnight."

Ashling thought of the dark storage room. She swallowed the lump in her throat and silently accepted the receipt for her payment.

At first light, Ashling checked out of her room. She slipped over to the corner store and bought a sturdy combination lock. After choosing her locker in the women's restroom, she deposited her backpack there. Her heart was doing a treble jig. She picked the numbers for her combination using the date she left the convent six months ago, 15/12/81. Liberation Day.

At the far corner of the storage room, she slipped her portfolio between the piled-up mats and the wall and set up the gym for the morning judo session. When Jorge arrived, he didn't seem to notice her nervousness. Afterwards she put away the tatami, showered and dressed, using her locker just as all the other women did. She retrieved her portfolio and set off. All went without a hitch.

On her way to the Rosen Gallery, Ashling stopped at several bakeries that offered samples. A low-grade hunger headache hovered at the base of her skull. She was managing to live on one meal a day plus freebies.

Shelley explained her tasks—she would mainly be cataloguing the paintings that were to be hung that Friday for the debut show of a local artist. Shelley also gave her phone numbers to check on delivery of flowers and wine for the reception.

Charlie was in his office, apparently interviewing a silver-haired woman in a navy pants suit. After about twenty minutes, he showed the woman out. He greeted Ashling, but his eyes were glazed over.

A half hour later another woman with cropped grey hair and a buttoned-up shirt approached Shelley's desk. "I have an appointment with Mr. Rosen, Sally Trimbal," she said.

Ashling wondered if all the new artists were female, middle-aged, and buttoned up like Mother Theresa—this was the third woman of that ilk she had seen in Charlie's office.

"Shelley, is Ms. Trimbal an artist?"

"No. Charlie is interviewing for a job."

"Oh. I thought you hadn't any openings."

"What?" Shelley looked at Ashling, and into Charlie's office. She smiled. "It's not connected to the gallery at all. Charlie and I have talked of creating a position though, possibly in the fall. Ideally someone artistic with a penchant for figures."

Ashling shot her hand straight up in the air. "*Moi!* I'm right here."

"Aren't you going back to Ireland at the end of the summer?"

"Not if I can help it."

"Okay. Cool. Keep us posted." Shelley returned to her work.

Ashling looked around at the expanse of glass and light, stratospherically different from the cubicles at the temp job. She glanced over at Charlie and wondered if he had a different Italian suit for each day. She turned back to her lists.

Mid-afternoon, Charlie emerged from his office.

"Ashling. I was thinking you might like to come to the gala."

Ashling's eyes widened.

"It'd be a chance to meet artists, and local gallery owners," he said.

And maybe re-meet some of the people from the sixty-three galleries who had rejected her.

"I'd love to. That's fab." Ashling said.

"Heading out for my espresso. Can I bring you ladies back something?"

"I'll have my usual—latte, please," Shelley said.

"Is that like a tall *café au lait*?" Ashling said.

"Steamed milk and a shot of espresso, and Gino's espresso is a thunderbolt." Charlie slapped his palm to his chest.

"I'll definitely have the thunderbolt," Ashling said, smiling.

"*Molto bene*." Charlie flashed his smile and headed out the door.

That evening Ashling flowed through her judo warm-up, her mind lingering in the gallery of glass. She moved into the zone where all seemed slow motion and her thoughts were free to roam.

She thought of the letter she would write home. She'd put a good face on things—let them know about exploring San Francisco, meeting people, getting an invite to a fancy gallery opening.

She teamed up with a partner. They were evenly matched, and she could afford to keep a parallel line of thought going.

She needn't worry the family about Majella disappearing and leaving her stranded. Or that she'd jeopardized her chances with a good employment agency. And she certainly needn't mention that she wasn't going to Mass and had said "Feck off" to religion. They wouldn't recognize this new girl at all.

She breathed in, and in one circular motion Ashling swung her judo partner around, drew her legs from under her with a sweep of her leg, and propelled her to the floor. She dropped to the mat, her body at right angles to her opponent, one leg swung to the side, the other to the front alongside the woman's ear. She encircled her neck with her arm. Her partner struggled. Ashling shifted her weight across the woman's chest, strengthened the arm lock, and held tight.

She wished her parents would loosen their stranglehold on her.

Then she'd finally be free.

Ashling rotated the dial on her lock in the Y ladies' room, smiling to herself at the significance of the numbers. A pair of women, applying make-up, chattered to each other, then said goodnight and left. A cleaning lady in a powder blue coverall swished her mop in one of the stalls.

The wooden handle of the mop clattered to the floor and the woman darted to the sink and threw up with choking sounds. Ashling dropped her toilet bag and sprinted over. The white porcelain sink was splattered with blood. The metallic smell stung Ashling's nostrils, a memory flash of her grandmother who died of tuberculosis.

"I'll get the front desk to ring emergency."

"No!" The woman flailed her arms.

"You need a doctor," Ashling said.

The woman joggled her head back and forth and wisps of hair escaped from her headscarf. She clasped her stomach and dropped to the floor. Ashling crouched beside her.

"We need to get help," Ashling said.

The woman grasped Ashling's hand and dug her nails in. "No doctors." She was wild-eyed. Ashling wondered if she was unhinged.

Springing up, the woman heaved a lumpy clot into the sink. "See?" she pointed. "Better."

"But you might have something seriously wrong," Ashling said. Her grandmother had deteriorated rapidly, both of her lungs riddled with T.B.

The woman's eyes strained from their sockets. "Your accent from Ireland, yes?"

Ashling nodded. "I'm on a student work visa."

She pointed to herself. "Polish. No visa."

"And you can't see a doctor?"

"Yes. But expensive. And if need tests, much money. I have a daughter, four years. I save my money for her."

The woman wiped her mouth. She jerked forward to vomit again. Nothing came. Ashling filled a paper cup with water and raised it to the woman's cracked lips.

"Are there any cheap clinics?" Ashling asked.

The woman's face was parchment, her eyes so watery the blue was almost invisible. "They want much information. I'll go see my friend; she knows some nursing." She sipped the water, faltered, and slipped. Ashling grabbed her waist and supported her until she found her feet.

The Polish woman reached mechanically into her cart for a tin of bleach. Ashling helped her to a bench and sat her down. Ashling took the bleach and put all her strength into scouring the stains. Her grandmother had coughed up blood in starched handkerchiefs. Crimson on white.

The woman stared into space and murmured a phrase in a language that sounded Polish. She repeated the bitter refrain over and over. Ashling shivered. If she herself overstayed her visa, is this what it'd be like—so terrifying you would risk your life not to be found out? Was America really so special? Was it the only place to fulfill your dreams?

When the porcelain was gleaming Ashling helped the woman up and led her towards the door. She grasped Ashling's arm and held her gaze. "So good. Such a good girl." Her eyes had regained some of their blue.

Ashling smiled. "Mind yourself."

The woman shaped her mouth into a smile. She pressed her first two fingers on Ashling's heart. "And good heart," she said, and inched out, pushing her cleaning cart before her.

Ashling fumbled with the controls on her clock. She had to be up well before everyone else. She set the alarm for 5:30 a.m.

She tip-toed across the gym in the eerie stillness. Light from the streetlamps filtered in and danced on the polished floor. She entered the back room. The blackness engulfed her and set her head spinning with the sensation of falling. She groped for the mats, and using them as a guide, felt her way to the back.

Ashling climbed onto the stack of tatami, sure she was out of sight in case anyone came in. She rolled up her judo jacket to use as a pillow. An oily rubber smell crept into her nostrils, and the pile creaked and squished as she shifted from side to side, trying to get comfortable.

As soon as she closed her eyes the dark became that of the confession box where at age fourteen, she sought out a strange priest to confide in. The wooden panel scraped when the priest slid open the grille.

Bless me, Father. He was a barely discernible shape on the other side of the lattice, his head bowed. She forced herself to form the words. *My dad, my father…he touched me. He hurt me. I said "no" but he did it anyway.*

The priest shifted and cleared his throat. *You must have tempted your father to provoke such unholy thoughts and actions, my child.* She recoiled from the whiskey fumes on his breath. *For your penance say ten Hail Marys and devoutly contemplate the purity of Our Blessed Virgin.*

He slid the panel closed and plunged her into complete darkness. She bloodied her bare legs on the wooden kneeler in her scramble to escape.

The dark of the night with her father was compounded by the dark of the confessional, and later of Father Dempsey in the dim convent parlor. The blackness took up residence in her heart.

Now that she sought to escape it, the blackness surrounded her. Only this time would be different. She had a few short months to chase away the dark.

CHIAROSCURA

June 11

Flickering candles prismed rainbows across the Rosen Gallery and the air was redolent with the aroma of tiger lilies. Ashling paused at the entrance. To the right of Charlie's office, a jazz quintet jived on a platform stage. Guests meandered about, balancing plates of hors d'oeuvres with champagne flutes, and poring over the paintings. Ashling knew all the titles from her cataloguing. She liked the boldness and raw energy. The abstract expressionism. The jagged shapes.

She noticed she was one of the few women in the room not wearing black. It was like the convent, but with a lot more flesh on display. She had tried to gussy up her blue dress by winding a navy cotton sash around the waist. When she designed it with Mam, their inspiration had been the swirly dresses in Renoir's paintings—whimsical, mid-calf length in a twilled blue cotton. It fit snugly at the bodice and then flared out at the waist in a gentle billow. Ashling already felt like she had moved beyond its romanticism, just like she wanted to do in her painting—push out, push back, push through.

Charlie, looking debonair in a white tuxedo, stood near the musicians in conversation with a young couple. He beckoned Ashling over and introduced her to Kelly, and her boyfriend Cliff. Of course, Kelly was wearing a black cocktail dress.

"Ashling is a new arrival, and a fine painter," Charlie said, and offered her a glass of Veuve Clicquot. She knew from the party list that each bottle had cost nearly $40.

Ashling said hello. She took a gulp of the pricey champagne, and a lovely halo fizzed around her head.

"Kelly is also an artist. I'll leave you to chat," Charlie said. He touched Kelly lightly on the shoulder and left. Ashling thought she noticed Cliff's face darken and tense, and something pass between him and Kelly.

"That's some compliment from Charlie," Kelly said, in a bright voice.

Ashling tried to mimic the confidence she did not feel. "Thanks. You had an exhibit here, right?" She remembered the name from one of the posters in Charlie's office.

"About two years ago. I've gotten some other showings based on that. And a commission. Charlie's a good person to have on your side."

A waiter sailed up with a food tray, and Kelly's fuchsia nails popped a stuffed mushroom into her mouth. Ashling accepted a square of toast topped with caviar and the salty orbs exploded on her tongue. It was the first thing she'd eaten since breakfast.

"Do you have a day job, too?" she asked Kelly.

"I teach art at a Waldorf school. And Cliff has a good job, so that helps."

"I'd love to have a job connected to art, be able to make my living from it," Ashling said. "Did you go to graduate school, Kelly?"

"Yes, I got my MFA at the College of Art. They've become popular here in the last few years."

"We don't have MFAs in Ireland..."

"Master of Fine Arts," Cliff said.

Another waiter appeared and offered to top up their champagne glasses. Ashling's head was pleasantly jazzed. The Frida Kahlo look-alike at the Museum of Modern Art had said a graduate degree was needed to work there. She chatted on with Kelly and Cliff, and new ideas for her future began to interlace with the conversation, weaving a silent warp to the weft of the spoken words.

Throughout the evening, music and talk floated through the air, and the room hummed with energy. Ashling mingled with other guests. She saw Shelley and met her husband Anthony, who was relaxed and easy to talk to, and they exchanged stories about Ireland.

Ashling wandered from painting to painting. The champagne was a rush to her senses. The glass walls and windows glimmered in the candlelight, and passersby glanced in. She liked the sensation of being inside these walls as opposed to the brick fortress of the convent. In a few years perhaps, if she could manage to stay in the U.S., it would be her art on display, her art which proclaimed her truth, exposed shameful secrets. She might also be a curator or an art historian so she could have the space and time to paint. The details weren't clear, but the desire was fierce as the hunger in her belly.

She watched Charlie from time to time as he passed from one cluster of guests to another. She noticed how respectful people were, and how women looked at him. It wasn't just his good looks—like some Italian film star—but his sense of style and an easy charm that made him magnetic.

She remembered her Irish art teacher Brendan, and his easy charm. Ashling was nearly thirteen when she started taking weekly lessons with him and continued throughout her five years of secondary school. He was known and respected as an artist throughout Ireland and only took on occasional students. He was quite blunt about not wasting time if he didn't think someone had talent. He was very generous about loaning her art books, and she devoured them greedily in the week between lessons. Ashling resumed her art training and work with him when she left the convent just six months prior and needed to rachet up as many paid hours as she could so she could get out of Ireland. He knew of her fierce determination to escape, and she wondered if he assumed it granted him permission to rub up against her in the supply room, to push in just a bit too hard when demonstrating a technique over her shoulder, to rest his hand on her thigh for a few seconds too long. Separately the incidents were minor enough that Ashling even questioned herself as to whether they were intentional or not. If she spoke up, she doubted anyone would believe that a person of his reputation would act in a way that was inappropriate. He was a man with power. His Irish gallery was Ashling's bread and butter, her ticket to America. She couldn't mess it up, so she put up with it.

As she wandered through Charley's gallery in San Francisco in the present she wondered how if at the age of twenty/ twenty-one in the closing decades of the 20th century, she didn't have the power or courage or ability to articulate what was going on and hold her teacher and employer responsible for his behavior, then how on earth could eleven-year-old Sheila stand up to a powerful priest like Father Dempsey, a supposed prince of the church? It was truly an ungodly mess.

Charlie's voice called out her name and broke through her reverie. His eyes swept over her dress. "You look lovely, *bellissima.*

Makes your eyes look turquoise." His words buzzed a warning. Why was he being so charming? Or was she being paranoid after just now mulling over her Irish art teacher's sly indiscretions? Charlie took her arm and navigated their way through the buzzing crowd. "I want you to meet someone—a gallery owner."

Ashling inhaled deeply. She relaxed.

The gallery owner, Sophie, looked like she was in her late 30s, and with her ultra-short coiffure and svelte figure draped in a backless dress, could easily have been a model.

"Have you been to our Museum of Modern Art?" she asked Ashling. Sophie had a hint of an accent that might be French.

The exhilaration of that visit came back to Ashling and she relaxed. "Yes, the beautiful Matisses. Magritte's *Les valeurs personelles* still makes me giddy when I think of it." She hoped she wasn't slurring. Her French accent sounded *très bon* to herself.

"Sophie's specialty is European women painters," Charlie said. "Ashling was telling me about an Irish painter, Mainie...?"

"Jellett," Ashling said. "She studied with the Impressionists. To Irish people, the very notion of being able to paint *en plein air* is just so outrageous that it's irresistible!"

"Didn't she become known for her Cubist work later?" Sophie asked.

"Yes. She caused pandemonium in Ireland at the time. Such daring!"

Sophie smiled. Her blonde hair and flawless skin gleamed in the candlelight. She looked like the kind of woman Charlie might be attracted to, yet Ashling didn't sense a frisson between them.

"Do you know Mary Swanzy?" Sophie asked. "She died a few years ago. In fact, I just returned from Dublin—the Municipal Gallery had a centenary exhibition of her work. She was a habitué of Gertrude Stein's salons."

"I read that Matisse's *Woman with a Hat* which I fell in love with at the museum was originally acquired by the Steins," Ashling said. She allowed a passing waiter to refill her glass.

"Imagine the ruckus in those early days," Sophie said, laughing. Even her laugh had an accent.

"Irish female artists. A good thesis topic, Ashling?" Charlie said, and turned to the waiter who had appeared with a tray of desserts.

It was as if Charlie was reading her mind. Ashling reached to the dessert tray and chose two miniature puff pastries, hoping they might soak up the alcohol. She needed to stay alert.

"I was saying to Ashling that some of her paintings have a Fauvist feel," Charlie said.

"I've always had a fondness for the Fauves," Sophie said. "They appeared in a blast of color, then poof! Remember I had that Fauvist-inspired exhibition a few years back, Charlie, in my Napa gallery?"

Charlie nodded. "You had some unusual work by that young woman from New Zealand. You remind me of her a little, Ashling. She had your kind of spunk."

"Isn't that the girl that disappeared off the face of the planet?" Sophie said.

Ashling looked to Charlie for his reaction. He appeared not to have heard, and instead of answering, accepted a champagne top up from a waiter.

Sophie mentioned her interest in local female artists, and that she was fond of series. She handed Ashling her business card and said goodbye with a blackberry lipstick smile. She said she hoped Ashling would stay in touch.

Ashling thought of asking Charlie about the New Zealand girl, but when she stole a peek at her watch, she saw it was 11:20 p.m.

"Charlie. Sorry, I have to go right now—the Y closes at midnight."

"I'll call you a cab."

She opened her mouth to protest. She couldn't afford a cab.

"My treat. I'll call from the office."

Ashling was aware of shapes milling around the gallery, slow motion and silent, like an old movie. Her head was a shambles from the champagne. A sip of altar wine at Mass was the extent of her drinking to date.

Charlie touched her elbow. He steered her towards the door. His body was a bulwark, as she planted one foot deliberately in front of the other. She told herself that the champagne was making her paranoid. It wasn't right to conflate Charlie with certain Irish men and their squelched sexuality and delusions of power. Those were problems created by the deadly grip of the Catholic Church and exacerbated by years of punishing poverty and domination. She was in a new country now, a free one.

The yellow cab pulled up to the curb, and Charlie paid the driver fare and tip. Ashling managed to fold her body into the seat. With a superhuman effort her leaden arm rolled down the window.

"The party was magical. Thank you."

"*Ciao*, kiddo. See you Monday." He waved.

From the taxi, Charlie was a prince outlined against his glass-walled palace, illuminated by flickering candles. She was the pauper, whisked from the glimmering gala back to her den.

That night, lying on her bed of mats in the dark back room, Ashling tried to trick herself to sleep by counting all the no responses she was accumulating from galleries. It was all well and good to go to one glamorous party, but she needed money, and quickly. She willed herself to push past the blinding pain in her skull.

When her head sank into the makeshift pillow, her mind unleashed a movie, dark and shadowy like a Bergman film. Her fourteen-year-old self, with the purity of a figure in a painting by Vermeer, stood trembling in a white chambray nightdress with eyelet embroidery fashioned by her mother's hands. She had just turned off the kitchen light at the moment her father came in from a late shift from his hated job at the factory. Her brother and sisters were safely tucked in their beds, asleep. Their mother was far away in a hospital about to give birth.

Her bare feet were clammy on the cold stone slabs. She stared into the eyes of the father she adored. Eyes which were pools of black in the shadows.

His arm reached out towards her. She shook her head like a person in a dream. The moment absorbed all the half-whispered secrets she had gathered in from other girls about fathers, uncles, brothers.

"Who has a better right?" her father said and shattered her young world.

It took every iota of courage she could muster to formulate the no. He kept on reaching. He traced the outline of her breasts. His breathing was heavy. She stepped back but he was too quick. He grabbed her waist and slid his other hand beneath her gown and plunged it upwards between her thighs. She gasped. His fingers seared her flesh. He pressed himself against her and moaned.

Ashling stood frozen in shock. Her night dress was damp, her thighs sticky. She turned and raced from the room.

Afterwards, it was as if it never happened. Her mother came home with baby Dermot. Her parents returned to being their own self-enclosed unit, and Ashling eased it for them by doing their household jobs—as if the encounter had been her fault.

For Ashling his arm was continuously outstretched, forever reaching, forever touching. The darkness of him mashed with the blackness of the confessional and of Father Dempsey's robes. And the trembling girl in the nightdress was not just her but held the breadth and heft of all the hurt of Irish girls before and since.

ALCATRAZ

June 14

Charlie emerged from his office around noon as Ashling was saying goodbye. Working alongside Shelley on post-party accounts made her feel like she belonged in the gallery. Charlie had interviewed two other women who looked like Mother Theresa. Ashling was curious what post he was trying to fill. In between appointments he fidgeted with his pen, tap-tapped his notes and flipped through his Rolodex.

"How's the job search. Any luck?" he asked.

"*Nada*. I had this mad idea of starting walking tours of San Francisco with a focus on art. I've worn out so much shoe leather that I know the routes."

Shelley smiled. "That might actually be viable. What do you think, Charlie?"

"Who knows? You could make an arrangement with the galleries and museums." She wondered why his eyes looked sad.

"And combine with a short art class...in sketching, maybe?" Shelley suggested.

"Brilliant idea! We'd travel on the cable car, see the Golden Gate Bridge, the crookedest street, Telegraph Hill, Coit Tower.

They probably have similar set-ups in Florence and Sienna, why not here?"

"Maybe a day on Alcatraz, sketching the city from there?" Charlie offered.

"Yeah. I seem to see it everywhere. Dying to visit."

Charlie turned to Shelley. "Do we still have Alcatraz passes?"

Shelley rummaged in the desk drawer. "You're in luck. One left."

"Thanks!" Ashling stashed the pass with her precious documents. "I'm going to hit the bookstores now. I'm down to tier two in the job search."

"Try City Lights. Have you been to North Beach yet?" Charlie said.

"I've ambled through and inhaled. Kind of fallen in love."

"I'm heading over that way. Let me give you a ride?"

Charlie eased his Astral Silver Mercedes convertible up to the edge of the sidewalk. Ashling's eyes popped. He walked around and opened the passenger door. Her dress shimmied up her thighs as she slid on to the coolness of the dark blue leather interior, and she noticed Charlie's eyes lingered a moment on her hemline. She made no effort to pull it back down. Charlie was clearly single, and it was nice to get attention from someone so debonair.

Ashling slipped on her sunglasses and breathed in the earthy leather smell. They cruised up and down hills, Charlie smiling as he pointed out a landmark here, a street or alleyway there. The wind swept through her hair and the sun flirted with her bare shoulders. Heads turned to look at them. She was tempted to wave. She felt like Jackie Onassis.

Charlie parked on Columbus Avenue. Espresso and sweet bakery smells wafted from store fronts as they strolled. Ashling's stomach grumbled so loud she sneaked a glance to see if Charlie had noticed. Just past Greenwich, he paused at a doorway with the inscription *Italian Harvest*.

"I always feel happy coming here," Charlie said, and Ashling noticed the clouds had lifted from his face. "Good luck with City Lights."

She sighed without meaning to. "I need to get something, and fast," she said.

Charlie's eyes flickered. The sunlight played on his dark brown hair, teasing out golden lights.

"Ashling. Could I take you to lunch—say Thursday? Here in North Beach?"

"Okay." She wasn't sure if this was a kind of date, or if he was just being nice because he knew she was broke and starving.

She could feel Charlie's eyes on her as she walked away. She was aware of the soft fabric of her lilac dress nestling on her contours and rippling with each shift of her thighs.

Ashling spent the afternoon furiously adding to the art gallery mountain of rejections. Back in Ghirardelli Square, she gazed across the bay at the sun glinting off the stones of Alcatraz. The rocky terrain with seagulls careening overhead reminded her of the cliffs by her home she had haunted when she needed to calm her heart.

On the ferry, the tour guide told the group the history of Alcatraz as a high-security prison. She strained to hear him over the splash of the waves against the side of the boat. The sky was robin-egg blue and the water a sheet of glass.

They toured the former prison—three stories of steel and concrete fortified over the years to house the most dangerous prisoners. Ashling listened eagerly to the day-to-day details of the lives of famous people like Al Capone, Mickey Cohen, and the Bird Man of Alcatraz. There were no cold water taps in the showers, only hot, so the men couldn't get acclimatized and thus train their bodies to escape by swimming in the icy waters of the bay. Ironic—keeping those hardened men softened.

The tour guide offered people the chance to be locked in a cell and experience solitary confinement. Some said yes and bounded in. Ashling wavered, and then said yes, too. The second the guide locked the door behind her she knew she'd made a mistake. The cell was miniscule, black as pitch. Her skin prickled with terror. Her head spun, and she plunged through circles of darkness.

Her own screams brought her to her senses. She was pounding on the door demanding to be let out. The guide probably couldn't hear her—too busy locking other eejits like her in similar cells.

After a hellish eternity, the man turned the key and opened the door.

"Are you okay, Miss?" From the concern in his voice, she guessed she looked green. It was her own fecking fault.

She shivered and stepped into the light.

Ashling explored the wild beauty of the island. Pink fuchsia, purple heliotrope, tall bearded irises, lavender roses—runaway plants from gardens abandoned by former warden families. She conjured an image of the prison as it must have been in its darkest days, jammed with men condemned for life to this patch of land. She thought of Shelley's comment about giving painting lessons and imagined herself with a group of jumpsuit-clad men in ball and chains, standing before a slew of easels lined up along the island shoreline facing San Francisco. In the fantasy she saw herself wandering from man to man—observing, offering a suggestion about depth, or tone, or perspective. And noticing maybe one or two not painting just the landscape before them but breaking through the surface and infusing the work with their desperate longing for freedom. Her gut told her this was where she needed to go with her own painting. She needed to push past the representational, and crash through the surface to the turmoil below.

The tour guide announced the last boat was departing. Gulls screeched, cormorants and egrets soared overheard, and the ghosts of her imagined prisoners dissolved into the effervescent waters of the bay.

That night, Ashling's eyelids snapped awake when the storage room door swung open, and light streaked in from the gym. A male voice muttered under his breath. Her heart thrummed so loud she was afraid he would hear it. If he attacked her here in the dead of night, no one would know. She tensed, mentally preparing a judo offensive. A belt buckle jangled. Was it a yoga belt or was he opening his trousers? Could he know she was here? After endless fumbling, the man grunted, dragged an object from a box, pulled the door shut, and his footsteps receded across the gym. Ashling's chest convulsed with relief. She smashed her face into her jacket to smother the whoosh of her breathing.

That night she woke up every hour on the hour in a cold sweat. She could have been raped. She could also have been discovered and thrown out on the street. The manager would definitely report her to the police. What if she was deported and never allowed back in? She couldn't return to Ireland now. She couldn't bear to face the nuns, the priest, her family, the country. And she couldn't forge an expression of abuses while on Irish soil. She would redouble her efforts at finding a place to stay.

When she finally fell into sleep in the early morning hours, she dreamt she was struggling to climb a vertiginous hill and kept losing her footing. She plunged to the bottom and sprang upright from the mat stifling a scream, a second before her alarm clanged in her skull.

SALMAGUNDI

June 15

The cheapest hostel on her list was a backpacker's place on Derby, off Geary. The young man at the front desk handed her a key and pointed her up a narrow flight of stairs to the dorms. A sour smell escaped from his armpits.

The stairs creaked and the odor of stale urine stung Ashling's nostrils as she passed the bathroom. The frayed carpet smelled musty and was speckled with brown stains in a dull map of Africa. Ashling unlocked the door to the dorm and stepped in—the room looked like it had been upended by a herd of bullocks. She drew closer to the rows of bunk beds and saw the messy sheets were gray and threadbare. She heard a scratching sound from the closet and inched open the door. A family of cockroaches feasting from a half-full can of Spam scurried in all directions. Ashling sprang back and nearly tripped over her feet in her rush to get back down the stairs.

"Thanks." She handed the key over to the clerk.

He made no move to retrieve it but ran his eyes up and down her body and smiled a crooked smile. "You're welcome to hang here. I like to fill the place up with whites."

She laid the key on the desk.

"Greasers have an oily smell." He picked up the key and dropped it in the cubby behind him. "And don't get me started on chinks and wetbacks."

Ashling had no idea who the terms referred to, only that they were derogatory. "And you stink yourself, you feckin eejit. Your own skin might be white if you could see through the grime." She spouted it out in her best Irish brogue, pivoted on her heel and quick-marched across the entryway.

"Didn't peg you for a Mick." His voice followed her out.

"Feck off," she said, and slammed the door behind her.

Ashling looked at six other cheap hostels—none as bad as the first, but all grungy in their own way, with dark cramped rooms and soiled sheets. All of them left lingering smells of stale alcohol, vomit, and cigarette smoke, and a patch of anxiety around her heart. It was getting late, she hadn't eaten all day again, and her stomach was hollow. She passed a restaurant on Geary, saw a long food bar through the plate glass window, people who sat on two tiers chatting and eating in the warm light, and prices that were affordable. The name above the door was Salmagundi.

Ashling ordered Mulligatawny soup. It looked exotic and smelled spicy. Then again, most soups were exotic if you were only acquainted with oxtail and mushroom. She paid, and as she waited for her food, rummaged through the brochures on the shelf behind her. There were leaflets for classes at the American Conservatory Theatre, others for acting and music lessons, and brochures for the San Francisco Art Institute and the College of Arts and Crafts. She picked up the art brochures, found a table, and sat down with her soup.

The Indian spices made her eyes water. Voices bubbled over from the next table. "Have you taken the monologue class yet?" a woman said. "I'd like to start auditioning and getting experience." Ashling opened one of her brochures: *Study relationships among art, exhibition spaces and audiences.* Her heart beat faster. She glanced at the three friends at the nearby table, leaning in towards each other, faces bright and urgent. "I might try Improvisational Theatre, it helps with spontaneity," the young man said. Ashling leafed through the shiny pages—*Do what you love for a living.* She had studied and practiced and read about art since she was twelve years old and only wanted art books and supplies for birthdays and Christmas presents. She had pursued primary school teacher training while in the convent because it was a sensible career, and when she disappointed her parents by leaving, she felt honor-bound to finish her teaching diploma. But it felt all wrong. Art was her love. Father Dempsey's smirk coupled with the red stain on Sheila's yellow dress were never far from her mind. She had to develop her skills so she could express what no one would believe. She'd relinquished religious rituals she no longer had faith in, now she'd have to discover her own meanings.

The soup warmed her throat and fired her belly. Her mind sparked. She wondered how it worked with visas. The fees listed for California residents were considerably less than out of state, or foreign. All of them said financial aid was available. How great it would be if she could get the job in Charlie's gallery, accumulate savings and experience, send money to help out at home, and in a couple of years apply to graduate school. She could make a whole new life here. Start all over again in a place where no one knew her. Find the courage to express what she had to say. Through her painting shout out what she'd seen and heard.

She lingered until the day turned to dusk, reluctant to skulk back to her tatami throne in the Y. She glanced around at the Asian, African, Latin, and white faces, wondered if some were illegal, and if so, how could you tell? She stuffed the art school brochures into her purse, bussed her bowl, and headed out into the night.

A few short blocks from the bright lights of Geary and the theatre district, Ashling was suddenly back in a neighborhood which smelled of decaying garbage. She had passed Jones and Leavenworth before she realized she was heading in the wrong direction. She backtracked. She heard a voice below her and jumped—a man in a sleeping bag was mumbling nonsense to himself. On the next block, a painfully thin man wearing the remnants of a moth-eaten suit was helping a woman tie a plastic strap on her upper arm. He yanked it tight. Her yellow flesh bubbled around it and she jammed a needle into her vein. They paid no heed to Ashling.

She picked up her pace. She had just crossed Jones on Ellis when she felt a tug at her shoulder. She snapped her head around and caught the outline of a figure jerking her purse. Quick thinking told her she should give it up, but her whole life was in there—Social Security card, passport and every scrap of money saved by half-starving herself and sleeping in a creepy black room. She pried his fingers loose, held tight to her purse and raced on. She heard footsteps following her and got a whiff of boozy breath. She catapulted 'round and found herself face to face with a stocky man, bigger than she had intuited, with an unkempt beard and dull black eyes.

"Leave me alone," she screamed.

He made a lunge for her purse strap. "Come on, little lady, just fucking give it over."

His sneering tone flipped a switch in her brain. He wasn't going to screw up her new-found future. She grabbed his lapel and jerked it forward to take him off balance.

"What did you say about little?" She hooked the man's ankle as it lifted, turned on her hip, dragged him in the same direction as his foot, and flung him to the ground. His jaw slackened. "Fucking cunt." He shifted his thigh to help himself stand. Ashling swooped down alongside him, gripped his neck in an arm lock, and tightened. She flinched at the stench. He choked and gurgled and kicked his legs like an upside-down sheep. "What was that?" she said. She didn't loosen her grip. "Fuck…mistake…let me…" he croaked. She tightened her clinch.

"Big feckin mistake. I'm a black belt in judo."

"Okay…okay…shit…" His face was scarlet. She had a momentary panic she had gone too far.

"I loosen my grip, you vanish. Understood?"

The man spluttered. Ashling let go, bounced back up and assumed a combat stance—shoulders square to hips, feet apart and grounded, knees bent, arms raised and ready. Her attacker dragged himself upright, wavered, regained his bearings, and disappeared into the shadows.

The Mulligatawny soup rose up in her throat. She was stunned by her own strength and foolhardiness. Her skills and her bluff had saved her, but if the man had a knife or gun or was sober, she wouldn't have stood a chance. Her stomach heaved, and she spewed her half-digested lentils all over the pavement.

VANESSI'S

June 17

Ashling glanced over Charlie's shoulder at the fog flitting along the North Beach fire escapes. From their outdoor table at Vanessi's she could see tourists and locals wend in and out of cafes and draw in their jackets to ward off the chill.

"Is this an old San Francisco institution?" she asked, hoping to nudge Charlie from his inertia. His eyelids were veiled, and he had hardly touched his food.

He nodded. "Founded by Joe Vanessi in 1936."

Ashling bit into the pesto gnocchi—potatoes never tasted so good. "So, Jack Kerouac and the Beat poets might have dropped by?" She had read some of the history at City Lights.

"Vanessi knew everyone. He was an ex-bootlegger—ran a speakeasy a few blocks away on Broadway. His real name was Silvio Zorzi."

"Sounds like a gangster. Or a film star," Ashling said, laughing.

Charlie smiled. "Both the politicos and socialites hung out here. I'm told customers used to line up to see the cooks in mock fights with cleavers."

The sun spiked through the fog barrier shooting glints of gold through their wine. In the café and on the sidewalk, everyone perked up like flowers stretching towards the sun. Charlie removed his jacket and rolled the bottoms of his shirt sleeves into an elegant fold. Ashling tilted her face upwards to catch the warmth.

"Isn't this the most beautiful city in the world?" she said.

"I'd say one of them, yes. Though Florence and Rome rank. And Paris is phenomenal."

"I'll get there someday," she said.

"Will any of your siblings leave like you, do you think?" Charlie asked.

"Brona, one of the twins, she'll hightail it out of timorous Timaleen the instant she turns eighteen. Her destination—a candlelit bistro in Montmartre where she will gain notoriety as The Trilingual—English, French, and Gaelic—*Chanteuse!*"

"She sounds charming." Charlie smiled. "Is she talented?"

"Definitely. She might need a bit of help with the business end, but Paris is firmly in her sights."

"And you? What are your plans?" Charlie raised his eyes to hers and a miniature portrait of herself reflected back.

"I'm mulling over ideas. All connected to art."

"Showing in galleries?" Charlie said.

"Eventually, I hope. And a way of making my living through art. I have to help my family first, though. Get them going in the right direction."

Charlie's eyes shone amber. "We have that in common, Ashling."

The waiter came out and topped up their wine. Charlie raised his glass. "To art." She lifted hers. Their fingers met, and a sweet shock coursed through Ashling's wrist. She caught Charlie's eye and he smiled. Maybe he felt it too?

"Ashling." His voice was almost inaudible. "I'm sorry I'm... I've been trying for weeks to find someone to take care of my sister. She's disabled."

"Oh. From an accident?"

"A stroke. July 4th six years ago. She's paralyzed from the waist down." Charlie raised his wine glass to his lips and paused. He was a study in sadness.

"Are you very close to her?" Ashling asked.

"Yes. She and her husband, Lionel moved here from New York to be near me," he said. She recognized the lost look she had seen in the past few days. "To the city?" she asked.

"No. Rose wanted the peace of the countryside." He tore off a corner of the Italian bread. "The last girl left without notice. Their insurance covers it, and the pay is really good—$900 a month, plus room and board. But I can't find a good match."

Ashling swallowed. That was an absolute fortune.

"What does the work involve?" she asked.

"It's a companion. Lionel looks after her. But he needs breaks, help with meal prep, some light housework. They have a cleaning woman who comes once a week, or so."

Ashling let an idea float in her brain.

From inside the restaurant, waiters and chefs called out to each other in punchy phrases. The strains of a mandolin struck up from a nearby café, and she recognized the tune—it was one her dad sometimes sang when he worked on his carpentry.

'twas on the Isle of Capri that I met her, 'neath the shade of an old walnut tree...

She remembered the buttoned-up women Charlie was interviewing. "Are you specifically looking for someone older?"

Charlie's mouth relaxed. "Well, I was. But that strategy clearly isn't working."

Ashling twirled her glass. The work sounded easy. The salary was huge, and accommodation included so she could save it all. If she stayed 'til the end of the summer she'd be able to send money home, and still have a down-payment for a room or apartment in San Francisco. If she could find a way to stay on.

And maybe that job in Charlie's gallery would come up.

And she could paint.

And start her life for real.

She was sweet as a rose in the dawning….

Ashling searched out Charlie's eyes. "Would you be open to someone doing it short term?"

Charlie's eyes widened. "You mean you? You'd be interested?"

She nodded. "My visa expires in a little over two months, August 31st."

"If you want to renew… I have a pal in Immigration who I could ask about options."

Her heart surged. She hoped she was right to consider this.

"Well. It's not as if I have anything wildly exciting going on in San Francisco at the moment."

A light went on behind Charlie's eyes. His face came alive. "And by then something may come up for you here."

She wasn't sure if he was alluding to the potential job at his gallery, but she'd have two months to show him how suited she was for it.

Ashling swallowed her last bite of gnocchi and dug into her salad. "A few of the places that took a peek at my work asked about a series. Sophie, too."

Charlie picked up his fork. "And we sometimes get clients who like a particular painter or style and want more—want to group paintings together."

The next-door singing voice wafted over. *Blue Italian sky above…* Charlie and Ashling's eyes met, and they both looked up at the blue San Francisco sky. A smile spread over Charlie's face. "Days like this, it's just as nice as Italy."

Charlie ate with gusto. Ashling finished her salad. She leaned back and sipped her wine.

"The job with Rose could be a bit like a retreat," she said, smiling.

"A rural painting odyssey." Charlie raised his glass and smiled back. They toasted.

"Speaking of art. Let me see if Arturo will rustle up a zabaglione for us."

Ashling raised an eyebrow.

"It's an amazing dessert. Egg yolks, sugar, and a liqueur beaten into a mouthwatering experience."

The plaintive voice from the nearby café continued to sing along with the clear strum of the mandolin.

I said lady, I'm a rover, can you spare a fine word of love?

During the judo work-out at the Y, she bowed to her partner and they both advanced towards each other. Ashling was caught off guard and thrown to the ground, pinned down but managed to wriggle free. The match resumed. It heated up, both players working hard to stay on their feet. Ashling was thrown suddenly, pinned, escaped, threw her partner, pinned him down and managed with great effort to hold him there. He worked up the strength to break away and get the better of her again. Her breath caught in her throat. It turned dry as dust and her eyelids hardened. This was the third time she'd had these strange symptoms. When she got back to San Francisco with some money, she'd see a doctor if it happened again.

She thanked Jorge for giving her work and helping her with judo. "I'll miss it here. It's like having my own private dojo," she said. Jorge told her he was leaving too. When she asked him why, he confided that he was worried about Immigration.

"But aren't you born here? Your accent, it's American," she said.

"My parents brought me here when I was eighteen months old. I've never been to Mexico, but my parents are undocumented, so I could be sent back if they catch up with me."

"But why would they send you back? You went to school here, right? And you have a good job, you're a martial arts instructor..."

"I thought I was safe, but now I'm not so sure. And if I'm caught, they could have my parents deported too—even though we have nowhere to go back to."

"So, where will you go?"

Jorge shook his head. "I don't know yet. I'll lay low for a while, then I'll see."

The Immigration system was looking more and more ominous by the minute.

Ashling tramped along the weathered boards of the pier by the Y. Old fashioned streetlamps illuminated the space, and sea gulls skimmed the cast iron grating scanning for scraps. A couple seated on a bench gazed into the water. A man wearing a Giants' cap leaned over the edge, his fishing pole a dancing arc.

Over the past few days Ashling had transported her belongings to the Rosen Gallery. Charlie had her backpack and portfolio, and she had kept a small bag with bare essentials for her final nights at the Y.

She stopped at the far end of the pier where the pilings faced the darkening waters. Placid palm trees lined the Embarcadero, and Coit Tower was a squat smokestack on a hill. In the distance a sea lion squawked. She breathed in. She breathed out. She hoped she was right to trust Charlie and leave. This ocean, this city, judo, art—they filled her with a bursting kind of prayer.

II: COUNTRY

IN BOCCA AL LUPA

June 20

They drove along the Embarcadero in the early evening light. Through the tinted window glass of Charlie's Mercedes Ashling saw the Ferry Building, Coit Tower, and the red brick of Ghirardelli Square, flashing their reflections in the hood as if saying *arrivederci*. See you back here soon.

The expansiveness of the view from the Golden Gate Bridge made her giddy. The blood orange steel was the only barrier between them and the darkening ocean.

"Down over there." Charlie pointed. "That's San Quentin, the maximum-security prison."

She thought of Alcatraz. The incongruity of the light of the evening and darkness of the prison.

Charlie headed north towards Highway 101, and they passed places with unusual names—Sausalito, San Rafael, Larkspur. They crossed into Napa, where rows of vines receded in the waning light. Charlie talked about the wine country, how Napa and Sonoma wines were famous worldwide. He spoke of the droughts. As the terrain became more rural, she saw the parched yellow fields—the price paid for abundant sunshine and not enough rain. The flip side of the green, saturated Irish landscape.

The day shifted to dusk. Ashling fought her tiredness. At the Y she had risen before daybreak for two weeks, filled with dread that someone would discover her tatami lodgings. Charlie pushed the button to close the roof and it crept up and enclosed them in a cocoon. She had a rush of panic, a terror of being trapped. She stole a glance at Charlie. He was quiet, focused, lost in thought. The radio was tuned low to a jazz station.

They drove through the country into the night. Occasional headlights flitted across the interior. They passed wood-frame houses with porch lights on, but beyond the houses was darkness.

"It's cozy in a Norman Rockwell way," she murmured.

He smiled.

"How long more do we have?" she asked.

"About another hour and a half. It takes a tad over four hours, if I don't miss the turnoff." Charlie grinned. "There are no houses or markers for miles, and I often screw up when it's dark."

"Looks like we're deep into farmland."

"Yeah. Rose wanted to bury herself in the country. It's about as far from Manhattan as you can get."

"Must make it hard for you to visit?"

"Yep." His lips were tight.

"Isn't it lonely with just her and her husband?"

"Wilfred—Rose's son by a previous marriage—lives with them too," Charlie said.

Ashling turned towards him in surprise. "You didn't mention him before." Did Charlie deliberately withhold the information, and if so, why? Here she was in a car in the dark, driving to who knows where, and not one of her family or friends had a notion where she was. And suddenly a son dropped into the equation.

"Didn't I? He works as an accountant about forty minutes away. He gets rides from neighbors."

"He doesn't drive?"

Charlie shook his head. "Neither does Lionel. New Yorkers. Never needed to and now they won't."

"How do they get groceries?"

"I bring up most of the supplies, and Wilfred picks up milk and produce and such."

They were now on a narrow country road and hadn't passed a car for ages.

"Do you come up much?" she asked Charlie.

"About every second weekend. I have a room there, but rarely stay over." He glanced at Ashling. "At least, I haven't in the past."

She was glad it was dark, so he couldn't see her blushing. It sounded like Charlie was flirting with her.

"You must be exhausted with all the driving back and forth," she said.

Charlie chuckled. "Let's just say I'm campaigning for them to move to San Francisco. Or Marin County."

Ashling's panic receded. Charlie was a well-connected gallery owner. Shelley knew about his sister, and that Ashling was going to work there for a while. It would all be fine.

Now, there were no houses at all in sight, just narrow roads, and fields. Charlie turned up the radio and jazz rippled in her brain. A deer flashed across the road and disappeared.

Inside the house, Ashling absorbed the nocturnal scene—brother and sister in chiaroscuro locked in an enigmatic embrace.

She held her breath. She was still. Excluded.

Charlie disengaged. He stood up. "Rosie, this is Ashling,". She extended her hand to shake with Rose.

Rose's grip was weak, her palms clammy. She indicated that Ashling should sit opposite her. Charlie pulled up an overstuffed chair and sat by his sister's side.

"I assume you drink tea since you're Irish. Lionel is making it." It sounded like an order.

Ashling laughed. "You must know us well. Not too many people here drink tea this late at night."

Lionel entered carrying a tray. He was about 50, small and wiry, with a band of thin brown hair circling a small head. The tray was meticulously arranged—china teapot, cups, milk jug, sugar bowl. Even the cookies, black and circular with a white creamy center, were lined up symmetrically on the plate.

Lionel peered at Ashling through dark-rimmed glasses and nodded. She said hello. The light glinted off his monk-like tonsure. He served tea.

Rose nibbled around the edges of a cookie. "When I was in London for a dance recital I learned about the rituals of tea. We intended to travel to Ireland, but never did." She lifted the teacup with her thumb and index finger and took a delicate sip.

"That happens a lot, people plan to visit but don't make it across the channel." Ashling would have liked to dunk her cookie in the tea but decided that would be gauche.

"When we were little Chas and I had an Irish nurse, Annie. She stayed with us for years," Rose said.

"Where was she from?" Ashling asked.

"Was it Cork, Chas?" Rose had shaped her cookie to a tiny circle and deposited it on her tongue like a communion wafer.

"Not sure if it was Cork or Kerry," Charlie said.

Lionel fussed with Rose's lap rug, straightening it out, tucking it around her slippered feet. He needlessly rearranged the pillow behind her back. Charlie glared at him. Ashling gulped tea. Rose seemed oblivious.

"Annie must have been only seventeen or eighteen when she came to us. We'd cuddle up in her lap and soak up her stories." Rose took another cookie and nibbled like a chipmunk. Charlie smiled. "Mother worried we'd pick up her accent and rough manners."

The skin prickled on the back of Ashling's neck. Had she landed in the Mad Hatter tea party? They didn't seem to realize this talk might offend her.

"Were you a fan of dance?" She looked at Rose.

"Rose was a prima ballerina. She danced all over the States, and Europe and Asia," Lionel said. He pointed to a display cabinet in the adjoining dining room, packed with framed photos. Ashling's eyes widened in surprise. To be paralyzed was a horrific thing to happen to anyone, but to have it happen when your whole career depended on movement was monumental. The cookie morsel in Ashling's mouth slid down the wrong way. She coughed and they all turned their eyes on her. She took a swallow of tea to cover her embarrassment. Rose picked up another cookie and began her circular nibbling.

"You were a professional dancer, before...?" Ashling said.

Rose shaped her mouth into a fake smile. "Yes. Before." She shook out a half-eaten packet of M&Ms on the table to her right and swallowed a mouthful.

"The closest I've come to dance is judo," Ashling said, trying to smooth out her faux-pas.

Rose shot up straight. "Martial Arts, my goodness! Well, maybe you can teach me some moves."

Ashling wasn't sure if she was making fun of her.

"How long have you been doing judo, Ashling? Charlie asked.

"Since I was about fourteen. A retired black belt from Dublin moved to Mayo and started up a club in the town near where we live. I'm a blue belt."

"I have no idea if that's high or low, but have a feeling you are very competent," Rose said, swallowing another mouthful of M&M's.

Ashling laughed. "The next level up is brown, then black is the top. At some point I'd like to get there."

"Have you ever used it for self-defense?" Charlie asked.

Ashling shivered, remembering her encounter in the San Francisco Tenderloin. "I've occasionally said I was a black belt to try and avoid a confrontation," she said. She wasn't sure why she didn't tell them about the drunken man who tried to steal her purse and scared the living daylights out of her.

The TV hummed. It grated on Ashling's tired brain and an ache crept into her temples.

"I doubt you'll have any need for judo all the way out here. We're pretty isolated," Charlie said, chuckling. He stood and stretched.

"I really better get going. I'll get your things from the car, Ashling. And bring in the groceries."

Ashling stood up, too. She couldn't wait to escape—maybe it was first-time strangeness with Rose and Lionel and this dark house.

"Are you sure you want to make that long drive in the dark, Chas?" Rose said.

"I have to. I need to be at the gallery early tomorrow morning."

Lionel stood up and inclined his head in Ashling's direction. His movements were robotic. "I'll show you your room."

She followed him back into the dark hallway. He pointed to their right. "That's the kitchen." It had sliding pocket doors which were open, and everything looked neat and perfect. Lionel plodded down the hall and indicated a door on the left. "That's our bedroom, we keep the phone there." He looked sideways at Ashling. "The last girl ran up the phone bill—calling Sweden at all hours."

"We don't even have a phone at home," Ashling said.

Lionel nodded. He pointed. "Bathroom across the way, and your room is here, next to ours." There was another room opposite hers with a closed door, but he didn't refer to it.

Lionel flipped on a light switch and Ashling stepped into the bedroom. The thick carpet was avocado green, the weighty curtains a greenish brown, and the bedspread a non-descript beige scrawled with dun-colored leaves. She remembered reading somewhere that in Persian, the word for green meant dark or black. This house seemed all greenish black and reminded her of the convent.

When she looked back Lionel was gone. She hadn't even heard him leave. She retraced her steps down the hallway to the living room and stopped outside the door when she heard her name spoken.

"Sweet name. Very clever of you to find me a lovely Irish girl, Chas," Rose said.

"Anything for my Rosebud," she heard Charlie reply.

Ashling's stomach roiled—their words made her feel like merchandise. She tiptoed back to her room. She propped herself on the edge of the bed and massaged her temples to quiet the rising headache. Was this all a big mistake?

Charlie knocked on the open door, laid her backpack on the floor and her jacket on the bed.

"You look worried, Ashling. I know what you're thinking, but you'll get on great. I'll be up next weekend, and I'll check at the Y for mail."

"Thanks. If anything looks important you might forward it."

Charlie laughed. "It'll get here a lot faster with me. We didn't even bother with an official address—the mailman won't venture up that driveway."

"I must have been fast asleep. I don't remember the driveway at all. What address will I use when I'm writing?"

"Use my P.O. Box, and I can take care of all your outgoing correspondence."

Their fingers touched as she took her portfolio. Ashling's tingled. He smiled and was gone.

Ashling closed the door. Maybe if she unpacked it would make the room feel more friendly and dispel the sinking feeling. She slid open the closet door. All of her muscles tensed when she saw a shape, a Chinese red silk robe suspended on a wooden hanger and the sash gathered in at the waist making it look like a headless human. The folds of the fabric were meticulously arranged, and revealed shimmering patterns of lanterns, blossoms, and pagodas. It could have been an earlier incarnation of Rose.

She used the other hangers for her dress, her skirt, and her tops. She draped her judogi over the back of the chair—this room would be her new dojo. She unfolded her easel and chose a painting to put there—the one Charlie said reminded him of Diebenkorn. Her first attempt to depict a dark force lurking beneath the surface of her country, and it being connected to the church, to repression. Sheila's face came to mind. Her yellow dress. The crimson stain. Again, she felt the urgency to get to a place where she could help, through her art.

She glanced around. At least the room looked inhabited now. She picked up her jacket from the bed and underneath saw an oversized book on Modern American Painting. She turned to the fly leaf which was inscribed: *Ashling, to new beginnings.* It was signed *In bocca al lupo! Charlie.* Bocca—mouth, lupo from the Latin for wolf—In the mouth of a wolf? Why would he write such a strange phrase?

She slid to the floor, leaned against the bed, and turned the pages. She skimmed through, her mind skipping along as she glanced at the luscious reproductions of works by DeKooning,

Rothko, Thiebaud, Warhol, Georgia O'Keefe, artists she had only mostly heard of or seen just one or two reproductions of their work.

She heard a muffled noise in the hallway and snapped her head up. Her door had swung partially open, and a hulking shape materialized outside—in the dim light she could just make out a very large man carrying what appeared to be a gigantic pizza box. She pressed the book against her chest to muffle the pounding. The man opened the door to the room opposite and disappeared inside without noticing her. Wilfred.

Ashling got up, tiptoed to her door, and closed it softly. Her fingers shook as she slipped the knob of the lock. It didn't engage. She listened for sounds, wondering if she was in danger here. She heard none and hurried to get herself ready for bed.

As she drifted off, she had an image of herself kneeling in the dark of a confession box. The priest slid back the grate and the bars were made from wolf fangs. Terrified, she flung up her arm to protect herself. Before her hand fell back on the bedcovers she had slipped into sleep.

BELLS & WHISTLES

June 21

Ashling shot up in bed. On the headboard a miniature bell jingled madly. The clock on her nightstand read 2:22 am. She heard a knock on the door, and Lionel stuck his head in.

"She usually sleeps right through—must be the excitement of you coming," he said.

Ashling clasped her head to contain the pain. "You need me?"

"To help lift her to the commode. My back is giving out from doing it on my own," he said, and padded off.

Ashling trundled out of bed and wrapped herself in her judo tunic. A colony of bellringers had taken up residence inside her skull. She felt like Alice following the White Rabbit when she saw Lionel disappear into the bedroom next door.

Ashling entered the room. The only illumination was from a nightlight in a wall socket and a patch of yellow spilling in from the adjoining bathroom. Each piece of furniture cast a distorted shadow. She could make out Rose's shape in the bed, Lionel poker-spine stiff beside her, and the commode close by. Lionel motioned Ashling forward. He directed her to hook her arm up and under Rose's shoulder, and as he did the same on the other side, gently hoist her up, then when she was swiveled, facing away from the bed, to slip arms around her waist and maneuver her to the commode. Lionel took most of the weight. Ashling was needed for ballast and pivoting.

Rose's face in the dim light was expressionless. Once on the commode, Lionel dealt with the rest. Ashling was bewildered. Charlie hadn't mentioned that dealing with bells or bedpans where part of her duties.

They returned Rose to bed. Lionel angled his chin towards the door to indicate Ashling could leave. She noticed a thin needle of light underneath Wilfred's door and wondered why they didn't ask him to help his mother. Judging from the outline she had seen; he was plenty big enough.

Next morning Lionel guided Ashling through a shining display of pots and pans. She was grateful for the dimness of the kitchen—a factor of the dark wood cabinets, low-level track lights, and greenish linoleum tile. A headache clasped the rim of her head like a suctioned-on skull cap.

Lionel opened a drawer lined with row after row of meticulously arranged towels.

"Cotton for dishes, linen for glasses, terrycloth for hands."

Next was a cutlery drawer where each piece was polished and perfectly aligned. The symmetry was blinding.

The sound of Rose blowing a shrill metallic whistle from the direction of the living-room spiraled through Ashling's head. Annoyance rose in her chest—Charlie had also neglected to mention whistles. Lionel shoved the drawer closed and shuffled off, his velour slippers flapping. Ashling grabbed the kettle, put water on to boil, found a teabag.

Lionel bustled back in—there really was something of the White Rabbit in his hasty movements, one leg shuffling to keep up with the other.

"Two eggs over-easy, two slices of bacon lightly cooked, two sausages, and two slices of toast," he said in a non-stop stream.

"Over-easy is flipped over once?" Ashling asked.

"Yes, and less than 25 seconds on the second side. A large glass of orange juice. I've put the coffee on."

"Okay." Ashling opened the refrigerator. Items were lined up like in advertisements. Leftovers were stored in plastic containers and stacked with ones of similar size. Fruits and vegetables were arranged as if for a still-life painter with a neatness obsession.

Lionel demonstrated how to crack an egg exactly down the middle with a knife, pour it onto a saucer to examine for clarity, and slip into the hot pan. He showed her how to soak up the bacon grease with paper towels. White bread toasted at number four, buttered to the edges, and spread with an even layer of raspberry jam. He called it jelly, though to Ashling jelly was a dessert.

Ashling sipped her tea—it helped to ease the skull-cap grip on her crown. She picked up the breakfast tray. It could have been a model for one of the Wayne Thiebaud food paintings she had seen in the art book the night before. Simple geometric shapes isolated from each other and symmetrical—a still life of daily food rituals.

Lionel followed her into the living room. Rose sat in her wheelchair, dressed exactly as she was the night before, an unopened packet of M&Ms on the table by her coffee mug, her eyes riveted on the television. The curtains were still drawn, the room somber.

Ashling arranged the tray across the arms of the wheelchair and tucked the napkin under Rose's chin. She got a whiff of stale sweat when she leaned in.

"Thank you, dears." Rose never took her eyes off the screen. "Sit by me, Ashling."

Lionel disappeared. Ashling thought her stomach might cave in and she was gasping for a that cup of tea sitting on the kitchen counter, but this was her first day on the job, so she felt compelled to do as she was told.

"The soap stars are my favorites." Rose picked up a knife and fork.

"Why are they called soap stars?" Ashling asked.

"I think it's something originally to do with advertising for soap," Rose said. She carved her bacon into tiny strips. "*As the World Turns*, *Days of our Lives*, *All My Children*. Do you have them in Ireland?" Her eyes never wavered from the screen.

"We didn't have television in our house. But I think it might be like the English drama, *Coronation Street*, or the Irish one, *The Riordans*."

"I know everything that's going on in their lives. I get to live in all these different worlds," Rose said in a wistful voice.

"They're company?" Ashling said.

Rose darted her eyes sideways towards her, then back to the TV.

"Without the inconvenience of having to go out and meet people."

Ashling looked at the buttery square of toast in Rose's hand and it made her even hungrier. "Like reading books?"

Rose shot Ashling another sideways glance. "I packed away all my books—or Lionel did—in the attic. It hurts my eyes to read now."

"I could read to you," Ashling said.

A woman on-screen began to sob, and Rose leaned in closer to the TV. "What kind of books do you like?" She carved up her 25-second egg.

"Art books, novels," Ashling said.

Without shifting her gaze, Rose pointed to a magazine on the side table. "We'll start with my *Soap Opera Digest*."

Ashling glanced at the magazine. The soap opera on the T.V. sounded sappy, and she didn't relish reading about the lives of these spoiled rich Americans. The whole exercise was a waste of precious time and she didn't have time to waste.

Later, Ashling walked back to the kitchen with the tray. Rose's voice trailed after her in a whisper. "I used to like the Brontë's. Maybe in the future." Ashling looked back at her in profile, all Rose's energy focused on a heated onscreen quarrel. She couldn't be sure she had really spoken.

Ashling turned from the hallway into the kitchen, and thought she saw Lionel appear from the other direction and dart into the living room. She shrugged off her suspicion that he was monitoring her, gulped down a bowl of corn flakes, and retreated to her room with a fresh cup of tea. She drank it while thumbing through her new art book.

The lonesome station attendant in Edward Hopper's *Gas* and the characters in *Nighthawks* looked like they were in a fishbowl, being observed. In Hopper's paintings she saw a striving to express the loneliness and isolation you could feel, even when surrounded by people. In her home, and later in the convent, she was always surrounded by people, but realized now that she herself had still felt lonely and isolated then.

Now she was in this fishbowl of a room, in this house, in the middle of a forest, somewhere in California, in the Western USA. In the past, wrapped in the mantle of religion, she believed that on the outer layer of everything was a beneficent God who looked down on and protected her. That mantle was threadbare now. Through her art she would explore her inner and outer worlds and carve out fresh meanings.

In the afternoon, Lionel handed Ashling a chamois cloth for dusting the dining room, and he retreated to the kitchen. She could see Rose in the adjoining room, laying one M&M at a time on her tongue as she absorbed the soaps. Rose had the air of an Edward Hopper subject—isolated, intent, marooned.

Ashling could hear Lionel's kitchen sounds. The pop of cabinet doors, the splash of water on the stainless-steel sink, the scouring of the already spotless countertops. A faint odor of ammonia stung her nostrils. She wasn't sure yet what to think of this peculiar family she had landed in. She felt like a floating squiggle in a Miró painting.

A solid mahogany table occupied the center of the dining room—the chairs neatly arranged. A red, silk table runner with Asian tassels and curlicues was shockingly bright in the low-key room. Like the robe in her closet, this probably came from Rose's travels in Asia. Ashling trained her soft cloth on the fine layer of dust nestling along the periphery of the runner. She dusted the rose inlay on the backs of the chairs and wondered if all this old-world furniture had come with the house—it didn't seem like it belonged in a stylish Manhattan apartment.

"It's my mother's." Ashling jumped. Rose's voice was thick, as if traveling through silt at the bottom of a pond. She had her back turned, facing the television, and couldn't see Ashling. Had she read her mind?

"From her brownstone on Riverside Drive. All brought over from the old country," Rose continued.

"From Italy?" Ashling said. The furniture didn't look Italian.

"Rosenzweig? Hardly! Our grandparents were Eastern European Jews."

Ashling was gob smacked. Charlie and Rose were Eastern European Jews? She had assumed Charlie was Italian-American.

All of her associations with him—his gallery, Italian Harvest, Vanessi's—were light-filled, what she imagined to be continental, not gloomy old-world tradition. Although Dublin had a Jewish Lord Mayor sometime in the 1950s, and Leopold Bloom in *Ulysses* was Jewish, Jews were foreign to her.

"Are your parents, dead?" Ashling asked.

"My father has been gone ages. Mother…she died six years ago." Rose's voice lost all affect. "Just a few days after the big ships sailed in for the July 4th bicentennial celebration."

Ashling remembered Charlie telling her that Rose was paralyzed on Independence Day, 1976. How strange that her mother died several days later.

"I thought her furniture better suited to my new life." Rose turned her eyes back to the screen.

Ashling dusted in a trance. She removed the dust particles from the crevices in the ivory border of the towering display cabinet. She turned the key in the miniature brass lock. She picked up a photo of a younger Rose, resplendent in a blue sequined costume. She dusted it carefully and replaced it. The next one was of Rose dancing with a partner—her costume was fiery red and her *joie de vivre* palpable. Row upon row of pictures celebrated her success.

"I looked well then, didn't I?"

"You look beautiful, Rose. Like a dream."

"Aaah." Rose's inbreath was a sigh caught in her throat. Her eyes stayed focused on the screen.

Ashling polished a large silver plaque framing a dance award, and could see her own distorted image, as in a fun-room mirror. On the next shelf, she dusted a photograph of Rose in a black lace tutu. Her back was arched, one black-stockinged leg outstretched behind her, chin jutted upwards, thigh pressed against the thigh of her partner—brimming with passion.

"What age were you when you started dancing?"

"Six. It seems like centuries ago."

"That's a long time to dance."

Rose swiveled around and glared at Ashling. "It may seem like a lifetime to you, but I had a promising career as a teacher and choreographer ahead of me."

Patches of heat spread up Ashling's neck to her cheeks. "I'm sorry. I didn't mean it that way. I think I'd go crazy if I couldn't paint."

Rose's eyes bulged. "One could paint from a wheelchair."

Ashling breathed in. "And teach?" She watched the trail of white saliva dance on Rose's lips. "Couldn't you teach from your wheelchair?" Ashling said, astounded at her own boldness. All of her dread of wasting her own life by getting stuck in a mindless job was causing these words to tumble out. Her parents still expected her to be teaching in a primary school classroom in Mayo in three months' time. It was almost as bad as being stuck back in the convent.

Rose spluttered. She swerved herself back towards the television and grabbed the controls. "*Oy vey ist mir*! I can't tell if you're plain impertinent or just innocent." She dropped the remote and grabbed the whistle. The shriek careened through Ashling's skull. "I need my coffee. And I've missed the ending—you'll have to read it to me tomorrow."

Ashling worked alongside Lionel preparing dinner. The spaghetti Bolognese involved gobs of butter, cream, and olive oil. Lionel put her in charge of making the salad, with instructions to tear the lettuce into uniform bite-size pieces. He opened a can of tomatoes and thawed something from the freezer.

They sat with trays on their laps and watched *Little House on the Prairie.* A thrum started up in Ashling's head in protest. She had only a few months left. She had come to America to live fully and didn't have time to sit here night after endless night, shut in, staring at a screen.

Rose curled the strings of spaghetti around her fork in a tidy package, and despite her neatness she added another stain to the robe. Ashling copied Rose's technique but ended up with a massive amount of swirled spaghetti, so resorted to knife and fork. She could only stomach a few bites—it tasted like glue. From the TV world, each good-natured "ya betcha" and "ya know," struck another chord in her rising headache. By the time everyone was finished eating, she had a full-blown cacophony in her skull.

They ate their dessert of ice cream and tinned peaches, while watching MASH. A key turned in the outside door. Ashling saw a shape enter the hallway and head for the kitchen and knew it must be Wilfred. She heard the moan of the refrigerator door, and footsteps heading towards the living room.

Wilfred entered, balancing a large pizza and two Pepsis. Rose's eyes lit up and a smile grew from pale cheek to pale cheek. "Sweetheart!" She extended her arms in the gesture of a mother calling a small child. He crossed over and kissed her softly on the forehead.

"Wilfred," Rose waved her arm, "this is Ashling."

Ashling tried not to stare. Wilfred was the largest person she had ever seen. He was mid-twenties, six feet tall, and weighed about 350 pounds of soft flesh. His dark brown hair was pulled back in a ponytail, and his face was nestled inside another face.

"Hi." Wilfred's finger pads were soft as butter when he shook her hand. When he sat down, the chair creaked.

Wilfred munched his way through the pizza and washed it down with soda. He offered his mother a slice, and she accepted.

He offered Ashling one, and even though she was hungry, she declined. The pizza had a fishy smell that made her stomach somersault and a gloppy taste rise in her throat. Wilfred didn't offer his stepfather any, and Ashling realized that the two of them hadn't exchanged any form of acknowledgment.

Ashling escaped to the kitchen with the dirty dishes. She loaded the dishwasher, careful not to let any item touch another as Lionel had instructed. From the living room, their three discordant laughs jumbled around. Rose's was a sharp, spasmodic chortle, Wilfred's a hoarse cough, Lionel's a low reluctant exhale. They laughed like people who had forgotten how.

When MASH ended, Lionel came into the kitchen and put on water to boil. Wilfred arrived, scrunched up the pizza box and dumped it in the garbage. He snatched a pint of ice-cream from the freezer.

"You're from Ireland?" He turned to Ashling.

"Yep. And you're from Manhattan."

He sneered. "I'm now a rural Californian." He dug his spoon into the ice-cream.

Ashling arranged the cups on the tray. "Are you having tea or coffee?"

"No." The elbow of his spooning hand was an automatic swivel—carton to mouth to carton.

"Charlie said you're an accountant," Ashling said. She opened a packet of the same cookies she had tasted the night before. The label said Oreos.

"It's a paycheck." Wilfred gobbled. A chocolate stain smeared his upper lip. "I spend my day poring over ledgers, trolling through spreadsheets."

Ashling busied herself with the tea preparation and Lionel fussed with the milk jug, sugar bowl, spoons. Ashling thought

Lionel looked like a hedgehog, all bristly, and she wasn't sure if he was mad at Wilfred for being there in the kitchen.

"I thought of becoming an accountant at one time," she said. "Or my mother thought I should because I was good with figures. It's called bookkeeping in Ireland."

"Why didn't you?" Wilfred's eyes were a nice greenish brown. They were so deep set with fat that in the dim light he looked like a raccoon.

"I don't really have the heart for it. I had a couple of friends in school for whom maths is an art form," Ashling said.

"Maths? Oh, math." Wilfred scraped the bottom and sides of the carton. He filched an Oreo from the plate and Lionel shot daggers with his eyes. "I must have missed that part of the course." His mouth curled at the corners in the beginning of a smile.

"The music of the spheres? Wasn't it Pythagoras who came up with that concept?" Ashling said, smiling.

Wilfred's mouth dropped open in surprise, as if he wanted to say something, but didn't know what. He looked at her out of his raccoon eyes. "I think I'll have tea."

Lionel's bald pate turned pinkish. He fiddled with the bridge of his eyeglasses and plunked down another cup on the tray. Ashling held the tray aloft and crossed towards the door, with Hedgehog Lionel and Raccoon Wilfred trailing after her into the living room. She had a notion she was in an absurd version of someone else's life. She hadn't felt like herself since she left San Francisco. The second she walked into this bizarre household; her whole blooming universe had tilted.

YINYANG

June 22

It was like being back in the two-room primary school saying her multiplication tables, terrified that if she missed, she'd get whacked by Sister Ignatius. Reciting in her head Lionel's detailed instructions on how to shake and stretch each laundry item for maximum drying, Ashling transferred the washing to the dryer. The teacher used to make her drape her hand palm down on the desk, fingers spread, and then she raised her ruler in the air like a conductor positioning a baton and swung it down with all her might. The moments of anticipation while the ruler fluttered in the air were almost as terrifying as the crippling pain afterwards.

She set the timer for the dryer and went back when it dinged. She removed the clothes one by one and replayed Lionel's script, worrying she might be forgetting something—he'd made a huge fuss about the minutiae of the task.

Lionel entered. He glared at her. "What do you think you're doing?"

Ashling searched his face for a clue to her transgression. "Folding laundry?" Her heart beat faster.

"Look where you're putting it." His face turned pink.

"In the laundry basket?"

"Smart ass! Didn't you just take the dirty laundry out of there?"

Ashling struggled to keep her voice calm. "Yes."

"And now you're p-putting the fresh laundry back into the same b-basket that had the dirty clothes in it. It's just not hygienic."

"Sorry."

Lionel gestured to an almost identical white plastic tub on a shelf above the dryer. "See the letter C on the side?"

Ashling instructed her heart to slow down and transferred the laundry.

Lionel's eyes popped. "You can't do that." Particles of sweat danced on his nose and the salty smell mingled with the scent of the laundry detergent. Sister Ignatius used to sweat when she slapped, even her milky blue eyes perspired.

"You've contaminated it." Lionel's glasses slipped down the bridge of his nose. "It all has to be washed again."

Time slowed down. Two tiny blacksmiths with sharp hammers were using her temples as anvils.

Lionel removed a white handkerchief from his pocket, unfolded it, laid it over his face, and pressed. When he lowered the cotton square his features were imprinted like the Shroud of Turin. He folded it in quarters, returned it to its pocket, swiveled on one leg, and quick-marched out.

Ashling pushed against her temples to compress the pain. The place was a feckin madhouse! She flung the laundry back into the washer, dumped in the detergent, and began the cycle again. The machine roared to life and agitated, mirroring the turmoil inside her head.

She ran to her room and slammed the door shut. She executed controlled sweeping motions of a judo throw, skimming the ground with her foot, hooking rapidly onto an imaginary ankle. She repeated the moves, over and over, honing her balance and technique, and then, with a bow, began a match with an imaginary Lionel. She slammed him to the floor, burning her elbows on the carpet, and threw him into a neck grip. She squeezed tighter and applied a stranglehold.

"Oh, sorry Lionel. Got a bit carried away."

She hopped up and bowed as if ending the session.

Ashling opened the dark curtains and let the filtered daylight stream into her room. The glass was thick and frosted, and she could see vague shapes of trees and shrubs outside. She walked over to her easel and set up a new canvas. She painted a scene of Lionel presiding like a schoolmarm over rows of unruly students. She made him a nun in full regalia. She gave him Sister Ignatius's milky eyes and a wimple, which tore into his neck and left a bright red ring.

She remembered the day Sister Ignatius had boxed Majella's ears and knocked her to the floor. She remembered little Sean Keogh who was taken out of school because he was having nightmares and waking up screaming every night. She remembered countless cruelties physical and psychological, Sister Ignatius and other nuns had inflicted on children and gotten away with. Just like the priest, Father Dempsey, and surely, he wasn't the only one, was getting away with abusing girls practically in plain sight. What was wrong with the adults, the parents? Why weren't they shouting out and protecting the children? The whole bloody country was either oblivious or playing deaf and dumb.

As Ashling painted she grew more engrossed. Beads of sweat bubbled at the base of her neck and her hairline dampened. She pulled at the neck of her t-shirt for ventilation and crossed over to open the window. She turned the lever and pushed. Nothing. She examined it, pulled, but still couldn't get the window to budge. She gave up. She painted until she had reclaimed the integrity of her hands, and partly rescued her spirit from Master Lionel and Sister Ignatius.

Ashling entered the darkened living room to find Rose in her usual position watching TV and ingesting sweets. She had asked Ashling to read a summary of the programs she missed.

"Your timing is perfect, dear—this just finished."

Ashling crossed over to the window and reached up.

"What are you doing?" Rose snapped.

Ashling was startled. "Opening the curtains."

"Well don't. You can read by the lamp."

Maybe they were they all blooming vampires.

Ashling read about the love affairs, the betrayals, the murder plots, the weddings, the divorces. Rose knew all of the characters and made happy little "mmm" and "ah" sounds. From the little Ashling knew about Irish programs in the same category, *The Riordans*, which was set on a farm, and *Tolka Row*, set in inner-city Dublin, the American episodes were much more glamorous. Everyone was wealthy and beautiful. In the bits she'd seen at a friend's house in Ireland, the Irish characters were gritty—more like real people.

Ashling finished up and Rose's eyes fluttered half open.

"Beautiful voice." Her own voice was dreamy, bringing her back from a faraway place. "Very soothing. Did you ever think about going on the stage?"

"I'd be an awful actress. Besides, I've found what I love."

Rose kept her lids at half-mast, as if even the partial light was too strong for them.

"What if it didn't work out—your painting career?" Rose asked.

"I'll always paint, but I might work in a gallery or a museum. Maybe become a curator."

"It's good to have a backup plan," Rose said.

Ashling glanced over at her, crouched in her dingy robe. She noticed the tea stains shaped like tears.

"Did you have one?" Ashling thought of the beautiful photographs, the grace and motion. "A backup-plan?"

Rose's eyes widened. She opened her mouth, but no words came.

"I'm just asking about your life," Ashling continued, "like you're asking about mine."

"The difference being that you, my dear, have a life." Rose turned away.

Ashling imagined she was in a psychic judo match. She parried. "There must still be plenty you can do. Working with your hands?"

Rose snapped. "The chutzpah!" She spun herself close to the TV and snatched the remote control. "It's time for *As the World Turns*."

Ashling guessed that "huts paw" was a bad thing.

Rose leaned in towards the screen—her back shaped in a curve. Ashling stood up. The forward bow of Rose's spine reminded her of its mirror image, the arc of her back in the ballet pose. She thought of the yin yang symbol of the divided circle. The light and the dark.

"Rose?"

A smidgeon of a shoulder shudder indicated to Ashling that she had heard her.

"Would you let me paint you?"

Rose swiveled her head around and narrowed her eyes. "Why would any young girl want to paint an old hag like me?"

The idea was forming in Ashling's mind. Notions of spiraling, division, expansion, and contraction. "I could do a series, starting with your photographs."

Rose's eyes softened, and Ashling caught the barest glimmer of the woman in the dancing photos.

"Where would you paint?"

"In here. If I can open the curtains." She held her breath.

"Those drapes are not to be opened. You may take the photographs into your room."

Ashling's mind flew through the gallery of photos in the cabinet. "And, when I get to you as you are now?" She made it soft, inviting.

"I told you, I'm not for display." Rose's voice was flinty again. "I don't want to be seen, so why would I let you paint me as I am now?"

Ashling's attention was drawn towards the cabinet and its treasure trove of images. "Unless you need me at the moment, I'll get started."

Rose retreated behind her armor and resumed her television pose.

Ashling selected some early photos from the cabinet, turned the tiny key, and walked to the door. She paused and looked around at Rose's taut back.

"What is it now?" Rose said.

"You're not a hag."

Rose hesitated a moment, lifted her chin, and eased up the volume.

Ashling arranged the photos on the empty bookcase in her room. The first painting would be of six-year-old Rose in tights and ballet slippers.

She glanced towards the window to check the light, and crossed over to adjust the curtains. As she approached a shape shifted outside. Her whole body prickled, and she heard herself shriek. Lionel appeared almost immediately from the hall. Ashling stood frozen by the window, pointing.

"There was someone or something out there," she said, trying to keep her voice steady.

Lionel crossed over and looked out. "An animal, maybe." He adjusted his glasses. "We get a lot of deer out this way."

He trained his hedgehog eyes on the window lock.

"I tried to open it earlier…for fresh air," Ashling said.

"We keep them locked. Makes Rose feel safe." He drew the curtains and sauntered off, his heels stepping out of his soft felt slippers, his slack-muscled arms swaying like a monkey.

Ashling sprinted to the door and shut it tight. The place was a bloody prison. It was starting to feel like what she had left behind in Ireland. She clasped her temples. After just a handful of days she could barely remember what it was like to be pain free and have a clear brain. She had little appetite and could already feel her ribs starting to protrude. What kind of household had Charlie signed her up for? Lionel was an evil schoolmarm, Rose, a lumpen shape with a twisted view on life, and Wilfred was a weird and humongous glutton. And now she was barricaded in because of those mysterious shapes outside.

Her nerves were shot. She would be strict about her judo practice and build her stamina. She needed to make this work. She was tough. She stuck things out.

FIRST POSITION

June 26

Still enshrouded in sleep, Ashling threw her judo tunic over her nightie, and wandered into the kitchen. The countertop was cluttered with grocery bags, the coffee machine gurgled, and a caramel smell permeated the air. Seconds after she heard his voice in the living room, Charlie swept in and gathered her up in a hug. He smelled like North Beach. When the lump formed in the back of her throat and the tears surged, she realized how much tension she had been storing. She resisted the hug and pushed back from his chest.

"You never warned me about the weirdness." She pitched her voice low so that Rose and Lionel wouldn't hear.

Charlie's eyes flickered. He looked hurt. "Do you mean Lionel?"

"Mainly—he's a maniac. And what's with Wilfred?"

"I suppose I'm used to them. I know Lionel is fussy."

"It goes beyond fussy. Everything has to be absolutely perfect."

"He does like order, it's true." Charlie was crafting his words, and Ashling restrained her impulse to elaborate.

"I know Wilfred has some problems," Charlie said. "But. Are you okay with Rose?"

Rose could be excused for acting strangely. "I like her a lot. I don't like the curtains always closed. But I like her."

Charlie held her gaze. "And with Lionel, is it the obsessiveness that bothers you?"

"He's so…he's a dictator. Doesn't he work outside the house at all?"

Charlie opened his lips, closed them, opened them. "Since Rose's…he's an electrical engineer, but he gave up his job to devote himself to her… I'm grateful to him."

Ashling could tell by something held back in his voice that Lionel annoyed him too.

Charlie looked at her. "I think it might be the first week, getting used to you. I'll have a word with him."

"And they don't seem to be on speaking terms, Lionel and Wilfred," she said.

Charlie skimmed his fingers over the tops of the paper bags. "Yeah. Some family thing. Long ago." His eyes were sad.

"I thought Ireland had dibs on those simmering family feuds," Ashling said, her voice light.

"What about your family?" Charlie asked.

"No. We're really close knit." She caught herself—her automatic response. Of course, it was true, mostly.

Charlie picked up one of the bags and crossed over to the far side of the counter.

"I thought you came up Sundays?" Ashling said.

"Usually. But I was able to slip away today and wanted to see how you were doing." He flashed his smile and her edges softened. Life had come back into the house.

"I'm sorry you had a hard week." Charlie donned a navy and white striped chef's apron and stepped briskly behind the counter. Ashling moved instinctively to help, but he placed his hand gently on her wrist.

"It's your day off, so I'm going to serve you." He pointed to a high stool by the counter. "Your throne, *signorina*."

He peeled open an oil-streaked bag. "Do you like lox?"

"It's one of my favorite foods." They could rarely afford it at home.

He opened the bag of bagels, releasing an aroma of warm dough and sesame seed. Ashling let her shoulder blades slide down her back. For the first time since she arrived at the house, she felt hungry.

Charlie sliced oranges in halves and squeezed the juice. He removed four tall, fluted glasses from the freezer and a bottle of champagne from the fridge.

"Mimosa," he said.

"What's the occasion?"

"You. My sister is happy. I can tell she likes you."

"She's only had a week of me." Ashling was glad she hadn't breathed a word against Rose.

Charlie popped the cork, an explosion of air and sizzle. "She's picky." He mixed the champagne and orange juice. "And so am I," he added with a wide smile. He poured for them and raised his glass in a toast.

A shower of sparks shot through Ashling with the first sip. Charlie was definitely flirting with her. She thought she liked it.

"Mimosa is sometimes called the sensitive plant, its leaves snap closed when touched," Charlie said. "May I eat in here with you?" He made it sound like they were in a private booth.

"Not with Rose?" Ashling said. Her tunic slipped off her shoulder revealing the slim strap of her nightgown.

"I'll visit with her later." Charlie's eyes landed on her exposed shoulder and lingered. "You've probably noticed the fare here isn't scintillating."

"Yes. I have." Ashling looked at him looking at her.

"Did you have any plans for your day off?" His voice was liquid.

"I was going to paint."

"You're getting work done, then? I'm so pleased."

"Yes. I've got a flow going." And inside a glow going.

She didn't want to tell him about her Rose series yet. She was formulating a notion of it being her ticket to getting a showing in a small gallery somewhere. But she wanted to earn it. To make sure it was excellent.

"How about after brunch we take a walk, then you paint for a few hours, and later I'll make dinner. I have a pasta dish I want to try out on you."

"Sounds perfect." And it did—Charlie's presence transformed everything.

The shuffle of Lionel's slippers announced his arrival. He picked up the tray Charlie had prepared for them, mumbled thanks, and disappeared back to the living room. The familiar low TV sounds blipped through the silence.

Charlie topped up their mimosas with champagne. Ashling bit into the layer of salmon, and some tangy green pellets that he said were capers.

He took an envelope out of his breast pocket and handed it to her. "Your salary. I put in a little more than we discussed. I do know this isn't the easiest household."

Ashling peeped in the envelope and saw three crisp one hundred-dollar bills. She had never seen any denomination above a twenty. "Wow. Thank you, Charlie. It can be your absolution for sins of omission!"

He smiled. "I have more painting supplies for you, too—maybe that will further obviate my transgressions! By the way, save room." He pointed to several paper bags on the counter. "I brought a special dessert for you, and I have bear claws for the others."

Bear claws reminded Ashling of "huts paw," and she asked Charlie what it meant. He threw back his head and laughed, freely and openly. He told her how it was spelled. "It's Yiddish, it means gumption or courage, and the meaning depends on the tone."

Ashling remembered Rose's tone very well. "I think it might be like when in Ireland we say someone is 'bold.' It means brave but can also mean a bit cheeky."

Charlie nodded. "Same with 'chutzpah.' My mother used it a lot." He got quiet. Ashling felt she couldn't ask, not yet, about the strange coincidence of their mother's death and Rose's paralysis happening within mere days of each other.

Charlie served her a tiny pastry dusted with white powder. "There's a hint of gruyere and parmesan."

Ashling took a bite. "Oh, boy!"

Charlie laughed. "Now, gallery news. Nothing to report yet but we're all keeping an eye out in case there's an opening."

Ashling thought of all her fruitless traipsing around the city.

"Shelley keeps her ear to the ground. And we have you squarely in mind when we talk about the possible fall position in my gallery."

Ashling's chest rose and fell. "Wow! Thank you. You know I only have a little over two months left on my visa." The expiry date of August 31st was etched on her brain.

"I've put a call into my contact in Immigration—see if we can't get an extension. I hope that's okay?"

Ashling's head spun pleasurably with the news and the mimosa. Her ever-present headache was morphing into a fizzy halo. "Will you need my visa info?"

"Let's wait and see what he says, and then come up with a plan?"

Ashling nodded. Charlie cleaned off the counter. "Ready for that walk?"

"I'll get dressed." She swayed and held on to the countertop as she negotiated her descent from the stool.

Ashling stepped out the front door onto the gravel. Beyond the narrow clearing, the house was surrounded by a solid wall of evergreens which extended in all directions into a forest. It was like stepping from one fishbowl into another.

"Where's the driveway?" she asked Charlie.

He pointed to an opening in the trees that she hadn't noticed. The entrance was camouflaged with branches and twigs forming a fine curtain.

"How does anyone find it?" she said.

Charlie laughed. "The people who built this house clearly liked their privacy. And it was exactly what Rose was looking for."

Charlie led her through the wall of trees opposite the driveway entrance, and instantly they were in a densely wooded area. It was dark and shaded—just like the interior of the house. Ashling shivered. Charlie offered his arm, and she happily slipped her hand into the crook of his elbow.

The forest seemed devoid of normal life—small animals, birds, even insects. Except for a faint low rustle of leaves, all was silent around them. When Ashling looked up, the tree cover was so complete she could barely see the sky.

They walked on, winding their way through the dappled patterns of leaves and branches. Her head was spun sugar from the champagne.

Under the canopy of trees Charlie's voice was hushed and private.

"What did you think of that art book?" he said.

"I love it. I'm absorbing the images."

"Good." He gave her hand a gentle squeeze.

"I like Edward Hopper. I feel like I'm spying on the characters in his paintings," she said.

Ashling and Charlie were pushed together as they moved through a narrow space between two tall trees. He slipped his arm around her to guide her through, her hip brushed against his thigh and lit a flame in her center. As they emerged through the archway, Charlie didn't loosen his grip, though now there was plenty of room.

Ashling was afraid Charlie could hear her beating heart—a mix of terror and anticipation. She searched for words to quiet it. "These woods remind me of what Jackson Pollock does, the dripping, dancing canvases."

"Yes. He's daring. And passionate." Charlie's fingers were fire on her shoulder.

They had to turn sideways again to enter an even narrower opening between two trees. Their bodies swiveled towards each other, and their hips collided in a pulse of heat. When Charlie's arms encircled her waist, the movement lifted Ashling like a ballerina *en pointe*. Their lips blazed when they met.

After the kiss, they held hands and walked on, and soon emerged into an open hilly area. The earth was scorched at the base, but as it rose was covered with tall coarse grass.

"It's like stepping onto the moon." Ashling ran ahead and raised her arms in the air like a bird flapping its wings. Charlie laughed and followed her. He took her in his arms and kissed her again, and again.

"This place has a strange beauty," she said.

The pale, yellow grass extended endlessly.

"Isn't it funny there are no animals?" Ashling's voice echoed, bounced, disappeared.

"We get an occasional deer. And there's the mountain lion," Charlie said.

"You're joking?" She searched Charlie's face, but he wasn't smiling.

"Lionel saw one down in front of the house about six months ago," he said.

"I thought I saw a shape outside my window. Could it have been one? I had no notion there were lions in the wild in the U.S." Ashling conjured up the image of a fierce lion she had seen in the zoo.

"It might have been. You hear of them closer to the city too. Every so often a hiker will get attacked in Marin County."

Ashling scanned the meadow of straw for signs of life.

"They're scared by deep voices and large shapes, so we're okay," Charlie said.

The grass scratched Ashling's elbows. "Doesn't look like I'd stand much of a chance alone, though." She meant it as a joke, but her voice cracked. "Speaking of wild animals. What does *In bocca al lupo* mean? Your inscription on the book. I think it's literally 'in the mouth of the wolf?'"

"Yes. But it's an Italian expression for good luck."

"Okay. So, it's the opposite?"

"Something about not wanting to tempt fate by being too positive."

"That's sounds very Irish—not tempting fate," she said.

Ashling could see that in another few minutes the grass would be up to her shoulders. Even now, if she fell, she would be invisible.

"Ready to head back?" Charlie asked

She nodded and turned.

Charlie laughed. "Wrong direction." He took her arm and guided her back into the maze.

Ashling painted in her room, working from the dance photos of Rose. The memory of the foray into the strange outdoors faded, and the jolt of Charlie's kisses lingered. Just thinking about it made her quiver. Her mind raced ahead. Would it lead to a romance? She thought of him in his tuxedo, charming and debonair, drinking Veuve Clicquot. Imagined them together in Europe. On art trips. Her paintings in his, and other galleries. Here, inside her room she felt safe and important, like an artist in her own studio. She knew she was ready to let go of the strictures of Catholicism regarding sex before marriage, just like she was letting go of the rest. Maybe she had already let go of that, knowing that it was only girls who were punished for transgressions. Charlie could be her patron and her lover—it sounded very Renaissance.

She sashayed her wrist, trying to capture the flow of six-year-old Rose's ballet pose—her slender arms curved and apart as if holding some very wide object. Rose had told her this was first position. Ashling was struck by the elegance and strength, and especially by the determination in the face of the little girl. A wave of recognition coursed through her, reminding her of herself. Young Rose was trying to grasp the whole world.

She heard a noise and jumped. Her eyes sought the window first, and then she saw that her door, which she had left ajar for air, had swung open further. A shadow fell across her threshold, and Wilfred, in pajamas, balancing an entire cheesecake and a six pack of Pepsi, stopped outside her door. He glanced in. His eyes met hers for a second. A cold shiver ran down her spine. He swiveled towards his own room and turned the door handle, releasing a blast of TV rumble. Ashling rushed over and shut her door, muffling out the sounds. Could Wilfred have been the one outside her window earlier? If she had to defend herself would her judo skills be enough to counteract his sheer size and weight? She practiced several rounds of kicks and jabs, then slipped back into her painting world.

As the evening drew in, Ashling's nose was tantalized by the smell of oil and garlic emanating from the kitchen. There was a tap on her door, and Charlie, in his chef's apron, held aloft a glass of straw-yellow wine in a frosted goblet. The color made Ashling think of the lunar grass on their walk.

"A glass of Pinot Grigio for your delectation, *signorina*."

Their fingers touched on the frosted stem and lingered. "*Grazie, signore*."

"*Prego*." He bowed. "Dinner will be served in approximately ten minutes, family style, in the living room."

Ashling could hear Rose and Lionel's voices in the background. Charlie leaned in closer. "We probably won't have any private time before I leave, but I'll be back next Sunday, and the following weekend I might try to get up Saturday evening and stay over."

Ashling's eyes widened. Charlie laughed softly. "I do have my own room—it's upstairs." He lightly brushed her scalding cheeks with his fingertip and slipped away.

She decided to wear her velvet skirt and the green filmy blouse that accentuated her eyes. She examined herself in the mirror. Her skirt slipped off her waist where it used to fit snugly. Her face was angular and her cheekbones more prominent—she thought she looked much older than when she boarded the plane in Ireland less than four weeks ago. She had journeyed light years away from that girl in novice whites.

IMPROVISATION

June 29

Ashling demonstrated a judo technique to Rose in the living room. "You maintain the pull to the front, hook the ankle, drive your left hip back, and then you make the throw."

Rose's eyes glinted amber. "So, it's about sustaining equilibrium, throwing the other person off balance?"

"Right." Ashling went through the movement again in slow motion. "You have to be focused." She swiveled slowly away from Rose and spoke over her shoulder. "One moment of distraction and you can be caught off guard." She inched back around and caught a movement in her peripheral vision—Rose had begun to spin herself slowly in her wheelchair.

"It's similar to dance in some regard, but in dance you're not fighting, you have to flow," Rose said. She operated the chair with one hand and let the other soar, as if floating onto the shoulder of another dancer. "Be as one with your partner." She swayed with her upper body, undulating her neck and shoulders, gliding through space. "But you need the same focus and sense of rhythm."

Ashling's lips curled in a smile—she had never imagined Rose having such range of motion. She crossed over to her, lightly touched her fingers to those of Rose's upturned hand and followed her lead.

Rose hummed at a barely audible level. The tune was familiar to Ashling, though she couldn't name it. Rose waltzed them around the perimeters of the living room, her movements jerky as she dodged the TV and chairs. Ashling drew her breath in sharply as Rose headed for the side table and swerved just in time to graze it with the wheel. She reoriented herself, raised the level of her hum a notch, and swept towards the dining area. Ashling wondered if Rose would be able to navigate the furniture there in the tight space, or whether she'd crash into the cabinet.

Rose danced on, shifting counterclockwise, turning continuously left and right, gaining confidence, as if it were perfectly normal to dance around table and chairs in a wheelchair. Her hum grew loud and clear and Ashling joined in. She imagined she was in Charlie's arms, spinning, turning, twirling, melting.

Rose came to an abrupt halt directly in front of the display cabinet and stared at the photographs inside staring back at her. She dropped her arms.

"Out of shape." Her voice was a rebuke.

Ashling ignored the edge. "We'll have to practice then. Doesn't a dancer practice for hours every day?"

Rose narrowed her eyes. "A dancer does." The d's were hard as diamonds, and Rose swiftly maneuvered herself back to the TV. Ashling followed at a safe distance. "What was that step?" she asked. Rose was flirting with the remote control on the coffee table—touching it, withdrawing her hand, touching it again. "The Viennese Waltz," she said.

"Do you have the music?"

Rose hesitated, then her fingers fluttered like ribbons, suggesting it was somewhere behind her.

"Next time we'll use the music," Ashling said.

Rose manufactured a reduced version of "harrumph," chose her whistle in lieu of the remote, and blew softly. Lionel entered immediately, confirming Ashling's suspicion that he lurked.

"I'll take my coffee a little earlier today, dear." Her voice was soft. Still in the dance, Ashling thought.

Lionel's eyes narrowed, and his hand jerked up to adjust his glasses which lodged perfectly on his nose. Ashling moved towards the music console, and out of the corner of her eye saw him lay his fingers on Rose's forehead. "You look flushed, and you're a little warm."

"I feel just fine."

Lionel fussed with a cushion at her back. "You're late tuning in to *Donahue*, do you want me to turn it on?"

Ashling peeked over and noticed Rose's eyes were shining. "Maybe I'll read instead. Lionel, would you get my books down from the attic? Start with the As and Bs."

Lionel opened his mouth and closed it again like a fish. He glared at Ashling. She swiveled back to her search.

"I might like to have you read to me, Ashling," Rose said.

"Grand." Ashling aimed her register low, not wanting Lionel to sense any excitement. He shifted his eyes back and forth between them, seeking the formula to solve this puzzle. Then he removed his glasses, wiped them with a miniscule cloth, and shuffled off to make the coffee.

Ashling entered the living room and saw an Asian woman in white coveralls whom she assumed was the housekeeper, vacuuming the carpet. She reached out her hand. "Hi, I'm Ashling."

The woman nodded, "Chen, yes." She resumed her work.

Ashling crouched down by the console to look through the records and tapes. Straining to read the titles in the dim light, she saw Chen also peering into the dark corners as she tried to clean them. Ashling glanced towards the hallway, crossed to the windows, and swept the drapes open. She played with the window lock. Chen made a noise and Ashling turned around—she was shaking her head wildly from side to side.

"What? You don't want them open? But..."

Lionel's voice belted out from the hallway. "What's going on?"

"I'm just trying to get some air and light in here." Ashling heard his footsteps jogging towards them, then he ran in, balancing a wobbly pile of books. "You know it's forbidden." He dropped the books, raced to the window, and snapped the drapes shut.

Forbidden was one of Sister Ignatius's favorite words.

Ashling took advantage of Lionel's spluttering. "I know Rose likes it dark for the television, but she's taking her nap now."

Lionel's eyes were about to pop out of their sockets. "N-none of the windows open in this house. We have an excellent air c-conditioning system." His hair was doing its wispy dance. "You can d-do what you want in your own room, but the rest of the house is to be kept dark."

"But why?" Ashling said.

Lionel's stare could have sliced her in two. "It's…the…way...she…wants...it." Each word dropped like a lump of lead. Ashling flung the lumps back at him. "And you play into that. You encourage it."

"How dare you!" Lionel's arms shot out with clenched fists and he sprinted forward. Ashling thought he was going to hit her. She stepped out of the way, grabbed his sleeve as he continued his forward motion, and swung him past her with all the force she could muster. He caught himself just before he fell, and Ashling turned and faced him, feet apart and planted, ready. Lionel straightened himself up. His face was purple, and his eyes were fogged over. He puffed out air, once, twice, three times. Ashling thought he might explode. The word that came to her was 'apoplectic.'

His mouth opened. "I'm her husband, I d-do what's best for her," he said.

"You act like her jailer." Ashling's voice sounded calm, but her legs quivered. She knew she was crossing a line but didn't know if she could or even wanted to uncross it. The veins in Lionel's neck bulged like earthworms. He grunted, waved his arm to signal Chen to continue working, knocked his heels together, and strode out of the room in a military march.

Ashling turned back to the music console. A wave of fear washed over her that she'd be fired. What then? She'd land back in San Francisco, if she could figure out how to get there. She'd forfeit the opportunity to save money, lose the valuable connections to the art world, lose Charlie, and maybe lose the chance of getting her immigration status sorted. This was probably why women kept quiet, so as not to lose things—jobs, connections, relationships. She rummaged through the records. The jacket cover of Gershwin's "Fascinating Rhythm" caught her eye. It sported a picture of a young woman joyfully riding a bottle of champagne as if it were a bucking bronco, with tiny tuxedoed men flying behind trying to grab on. There would likely be a price to pay for speaking her mind, for taking the reins of her life—but she refused to be muzzled.

Later on, Ashling curled up on the sofa and read *Wuthering Heights* aloud to Rose, who sat across from her in her wheelchair, eyes closed, listening. Gershwin's "Fascinating Rhythm" played softly in the background. It seemed to Ashling that she wasn't going to be fired, yet, and could only assume this was due to Rose's influence. Rose hadn't mentioned their Irish nanny, Annie since that first night, but Ashling wondered if that long-ago connection was part of the reason Rose was willing to open up, little by little.

Ashling read on. Rose's eyes fluttered like butterfly wings, and gazed way beyond to an unseen horizon. She shuddered—a chrysalis about to emerge from its cocoon—and began to sway back and forth hypnotically, in tune with the music.

Ashling lowered her book. She watched Rose ease her wheelchair into the center of the room and sashay from side to side, eyes half-closed, shoulders softened in surrender. Rose engaged more and more of her upper body, swayed her arms and neck in a sensuous circle, then parted her lips and emitted a voiced breath. They sat there together, soaking in the jazzy rhythm.

I have to be inside the house—sort of on call, but it means I get plenty of time to paint. I'm working on a series about Rose and might show the paintings to Charlie when he comes this weekend. It's not very glamorous here—but I suppose it's real life. Am enclosing some money. Ciao!

It gave Ashling a sense of power to put thirty dollars in an envelope. She had come to this country a month earlier with less than three times that. Charlie's bonus and her earnings she was stashing away towards the rent on her first San Francisco apartment. In a month she'd have well over a thousand, and if she stayed one month more, she'd have a nice cushion. Charlie would help get her legal status arranged. And she could keep on painting.

Ashling browsed through her art book and found a section on Norman Rockwell. She knew he was mostly an illustrator, but that he was considered iconic. She had seen copies of some of the famous illustrations from *The Saturday Evening Post*—the happy, whimsical images. She hadn't seen *The Problem We All Live With*, where a young Black girl is escorted to school by officials in arm bands against a background of racial slurs. She was amused by *The Connoisseur*, where a white haired, white gloved, suited gentleman examines a Jackson Pollock canvas.

She had thought of the illustrator Rockwell as belonging to the 19th or early 20th century and the painter Pollock being of an entirely different, ultramodern era. She flipped to the section on Pollock and discovered they were contemporaries. If the figure in *The Connoisseur* was not the artist, it was certainly a Norman Rockwell man facing a Jackson Pollock world. Ashling admired the precision and detail in Rockwell's work, and felt the lure of the improvisational chaos in Pollock's. The former suggested that the world could be framed and described literally, the latter, that what's beneath the surface of that order is chaotic and can't be. It felt like her world right now. The corner of Ireland she came from, with its neat stone cottages, whitewashed school building, and perfectly appointed convent could be mistaken for a Norman Rockwell world. She had glimpsed the drips seeping from beneath the façade and knew in her gut the effort it took to push that Pollock chaos back inside. She had to find her way of expressing it. For Sheila, for Majella, for all the girls and women. For herself.

EN POINTE

June 30 - July 3

Rose and Lionel hunkered in close to the TV watching *Magnum P.I.* Ashling sat at the back of the room and sketched but couldn't help her eyes wandering occasionally to the buff, half-naked Tom Selleck.

When Wilfred came in, Lionel didn't even shift his eyes from the screen. Rose flashed a quick smile. "You're home early, dear."

"Less paperwork than usual." Wilfred slumped into an easy chair next to Ashling. It squeaked like a giant mouse, and his thighs squirted out the sides. She dragged her eyes away.

"Pepsi?" He pointed to his signature six pack.

"No, thanks."

The silver foil crinkled as Wilfred unwrapped an enormous burrito, unleashing an aroma of cilantro, beef, and grease. Ashling's stomach lurched. He chomped. She felt it would be rude to go back to sketching so she turned to him. "Do you work close by?"

He laughed, deep in his throat. "The nearest town is over thirty miles away. My buds pick me up at the end of the driveway."

"I thought you didn't mind the commute, dear." There was a quake in Rose's voice.

"Only job I could get." He sank his teeth into the fast-disappearing burrito.

Rose glanced back at Ashling. "Wilfred has a great many gifts but doesn't develop them."

Wilfred swiped at the juices on his chin and slid deeper into his chair.

"You have very gifted hands, Wilfred." Rose turned her attention fully away from the Hawaiian beach on TV.

"Which I use for crunching numbers," Wilfred mumbled into his burrito.

Ashling squirmed but kept her silence. The sketchpad remained on her lap, and she wished she could dive back in and escape.

"As a boy he could make anything." Rose's voice was rising.

Ashling put down her pencil. "What did you make?" she asked Wilfred.

"Things from wood mostly—whatever I could get my hands on. Just fooling around."

"I have an exquisite coffee table in my room that Wilfred made when he was just a teenager." Rose's voice lilted. "And there was that lovely wooden compass that we lost somehow..." Her voice trailed off.

Wilfred tilted back the can and gulped down the remaining Pepsi. He burst open another, releasing a sucking air sound, and thrust it to his lips. Ashling had seen chain smokers, but never chain soda drinkers, and wondered if all the rubbish contributed to his weird depressive state.

"You could always start again, dear," Rose's voice had an edge of anxiety and wanting.

Wilfred finished his burrito, bunched up the foil, and molded it into a ball. He tossed the silver orb back and forth from palm to palm, as if preparing to pitch. Then he poured the last drops of Pepsi down his gullet and propelled himself up from the chair. "Too late." He sounded old.

He gathered his cans and lumbered from the room. Moments later he passed the doorway carrying a tub of ice cream. His footsteps faded down the hallway, and his bedroom door opened. *Magnum P.I.* erupted with a sudden blast from the TV in his room, so that the drama played briefly in stereo, then the door closed.

Rose sighed and switched her eyes back to the screen. "I wish Wilfred would meet some nice girl." She shook her head as if shooing away a fly. Ashling recognized the voice with the spine of steel that her own mother used when hinting at something she wanted. Rose's shoulder muscles were clenched. Lionel was still and expressionless, and his shoulders were also in a knot. Ashling checked her own. The same.

She made an effort to lower her shoulder blades, but the pinching lingered. She stared at Lionel and Rose's stalwart backs in chairs facing the television set, acting as if all were normal when in reality they existed in a kind of stasis. It would be a perfect subject for a Hopperesque painting.

Ashling closed the door to her room. She slipped a tape into her Walkman and The Pogues screamed from the machine. She leveraged the player into her belt and launched into a series of vigorous judo kicks and swings. The judo segued into dance, and she improvised until she was performing some hybrid dance/martial art—legs and arms swirling in circular patterns through the air, hips swaying, feet in constant motion. She let her body go where it led her. The way The Pogues mixed punk and traditional Irish sounds challenged her to mix and mess. She grabbed her brush and started to paint.

She began from a photo of Rose at the age of twelve or thirteen, *en pointe*. Rose said the decision to go *en pointe* was a threshold one—she was making a commitment to devote herself to dance. As Ashling worked, her own body in motion, her wrist alive with the energy of the music, she remembered her own apotheosis in the museum in San Francisco when she fiercely renewed her commitment to make a life with her art. She realized that, like Rose, she had also dedicated herself heart and soul to visual art at the age of twelve or thirteen, but it was beyond her ken to imagine a career as an artist. In her room, as she painted, the smell of turpentine and oils pleased her nostrils and her paint strokes came out fluid and free. She glopped paint onto the canvas, and the splashes of color released the potency of the adolescent Rose making a monumental decision about her life—the terror, and also the terrific joy. Young Rose was recognizable, but the lines were undefined, and everything pulsed with energy. Ashling continued to paint way past midnight, her whole body radiating with exhilaration. She had landed on an undiscovered shore.

Charlie greeted Ashling in the kitchen and pressed her close with a hug. Lionel and Rose were close by in the living room. She absorbed the heat from his body, and then perched on her stool at the kitchen counter. She was so happy not to have to cook here, though it meant she ate Lionel's tasteless fare. It was nice to be waited on. All her life she was the one who did the serving.

Charlie cracked eggs for French toast. Ashling sipped her coffee.

"Charlie, I'm ready for you to see what I'm working on." Ashling's voice was a sunny extension of her North Beach dream.

"I'd love to."

She glanced at the local paper Charlie had brought. She noticed the name Ukiah, and a reference to Mendocino County. It was her first inkling of where she actually was, though the names meant nothing to her. She flipped through the pages. The news was mostly about crops and logging. There was a column about some county official caught stealing, and one about a Peeping Tom.

"Charlie. It says here there's a guy who's been seen spying on women. Could that have been the shape by my window?"

Charlie paused. "I doubt it. No stranger would ever find his way up this driveway."

Exactly what Lionel had said. "I suppose. And then there are all the locks. Are we in some kind of fortress?" Her laugh caught in her throat.

"It makes Rose feel safe." Charlie cracked an egg cleanly on the side of a bowl, and the golden yoke stretched and glopped downwards.

Just like Lionel again, Ashling thought. They think it's normal.

She glanced at the center pages of the paper and saw advertisements for the 4th of July.

"Looks like a lot of local Independence Day celebrations around. Do you do anything here?"

"It used to be a big deal for us as kids growing up. But I think I mentioned Rose had her stoke on July 4th, so that's put the kibosh on that holiday," Charlie said.

Ashling nodded. "Of course. I remember now."

Charlie pointed to the pile of mail. "Did you see you have a letter from Immigration?" Ashling's heart tripped. She saw the official stamp, ripped open the envelope, and scanned the page. Her body sagged. "They rejected my extension request."

"Dammit. I was afraid of that. Remember I told you I was meeting with my buddy, Bill? Well, he told me they hardly ever give extensions on student visas."

Ashling slumped. "I'm not sure what to do, what options I have."

"I'll give Bill a call when I get back and ask him what the next step should be."

Ashling mustered some heft into her voice. "Thanks. Let me know what it costs."

Charlie glanced towards the door. "My treat." He leaned over the counter and kissed her quickly on the lips. "I have very selfish motives." Ashling felt giddy and taken care of at the same time. It was lucky that Charlie had a pal in Immigration. The excitement over her painting was pushing out through her pores. She was exactly where she needed to be right now.

The pan hissed and released the scent of cinnamon, and Charlie moved back and forth from stove to melon-slicing in a culinary dance. With the flip of his wrist, he delivered the French toast onto plates. "I'll get details from Bill and report next weekend. Okay?" Ashling nodded. She elongated her spine. She breathed in the musty scent of cantaloupe. It was the first food to tempt her since Charlie's linguine with clams the weekend before.

After brunch Charlie visited with Rose, and Ashling decided to take a short walk. She crossed to the outside door and turned the knob. They usually kept the key by the window ledge, but it wasn't there. She ran her hand along the small table, bent down and looked under the mat.

"Going somewhere?" Lionel's voice startled her, and she jumped.

"I wanted to step outside—get some fresh air."

He disappeared into his bedroom, returned with a key, and unlocked the door.

Ashling shot him a laser glance. "What if there's an accident, a fire?"

Lionel's hair quivered. "I'll leave it here, under the planter."

Ashling escaped and shut the door behind her. Maybe they were all psychotic in addition to being vampires.

She breathed in the strangely odorless atmosphere and circumnavigated the house, tromping on the gravel. This was where she came for her daily helping of fresh air, but it was clearly not meant for strolling. Her judo practice gave her a hardy workout, but now she felt like a long brisk walk.

She looked to the place where she thought the driveway was but couldn't see it. She turned towards the woods, searching for the trail she had walked with Charlie, picked a direction, and started out. She kept looking back to remind herself of the way she came, as she dodged in and out between the tall tree trunks—a crazy temple of columns.

I'm like Gretel in the Grimm fairytale, she thought, or Little Red Riding Hood whose grandmother had a house deep in the woods. They all went to houses deep in the woods where they encountered witches or goblins or wolves. Or mountain lions? The hairs on her arm stiffened. She instructed her internal compass to remind her of the way she came, but after what seemed an endless trek, she was still staring at trees that all looked identical.

Breathe. Pause. Orient.

But there was nothing to orient to. The tree cover was so dense she couldn't see the sun, though it was noonish and should be overhead. She trudged on. Her whole body was seeping sweat. Globules swelled and dripped into her eyes and she wiped them away and pushed her legs forward. What did Charlie say about using a low voice if she came face to face with a mountain lion? The cinnamon and eggs rose in her throat along with the panic, and she heaved, landing the whole breakfast at her feet.

It felt like light years later when Ashling spotted the house through the trees. She tried to swallow the sickly taste on her tongue and scrambled into the clearing. Maybe she had never been more than fifteen minutes away in any direction. Her eyes were wide with terror and she pushed back tears of frustration.

Lionel didn't seem to notice her distress when he opened the door. She heard Rose and Charlie's voices in the living room as she slipped down the hall and into the bathroom. She wondered how long she'd been gone. She brushed her teeth until her gums hurt. She stumbled into the shower and let the needle-sharp jets lash the sweat and panic from her body. She thought of the Alcatraz prisoners, deprived of cold water, and finished off her shower with a punishing icy splash.

Ashling was expecting Charlie to come to her room, but her heart still leapt when she heard his tap, tap. She reminded herself it was a professional visit. She opened the door, and he stepped inside, leaving the door ajar.

Ashling led him to her easel with the work in progress of Rose, and then moved away. She dug her feet into the carpet to stop the tremble.

Charlie looked. He was silent. He mustn't like it, she thought. He moved in closer, as if examining the brush strokes, and moved back, continuing to gaze. Ashling stood like a concrete block in the center of the room. Maybe he absolutely detested it. Or it was so boring that he was neutral. His eyes flitted to the bookcase and the line-up of dance photos. His face was pale. Maybe he found it insulting, or intrusive.

Finally, he took a step back, released his breath, looked over at her with lidded eyes. "You're planning a series."

Ashling unfroze. "Yes."

"It's wonderful. I can see you delving, getting at the layers." He swiped the corner of his eye. "Rose was so young, and… alive." His voice was low and private.

"Yes. I still can't believe she's letting me do this," Ashling said.

Charlie's eyes were drawn back to her painting of Rose *en pointe*. He kept glancing at it, then away. "I remember this moment—the endless discussions with my mother."

"Was she against it?" Ashling thought Charlie must have been young if Rose was thirteen.

"I think it was so far from her experience. The idea of her daughter as a professional ballet dancer."

"I know what that's like." Ashling felt that icy tug at her center. Her family hooking her with their idea of what she should be.

Charlie looked at her. "Your art?"

Ashling nodded. "Yep. It's a bit of a stretch for my mother, too."

Charlie glanced back at her painting. "Having some time to experiment can do wonders."

"Away from the hustle and bustle of city life?" A smile wriggled on Ashling's lips.

"Do you miss it?"

"I wasn't in San Francisco long enough to have much of a social life—your gala event was the highlight. That and trekking out to the Avenues on a foggy night to see a brilliant Bergman film. I look forward to going back though when it's time."

Charlie laughed—clear and open. "It can be overwhelming at first. Finding an apartment, commuting to work—all that everyday stuff."

"Are you saying this is a good career move for me, Charlie?" Ashling said in a teasing voice.

"May not be as absurd as it sounds. You've already taken a big leap in your work." His eyes twinkled. "And she told me she danced with you."

"Shh. Big secret!"

Charlie eyed the open door, then crossed over and eased it closed. His hand was warm and firm as he led Ashling towards the bed. An electric jolt shot through her as his lips met hers. When he slid his hands underneath her shirt and up her bare back, her rational mind pulsed a no, but every nerve ending in her body felt ready to fire.

Rose's voice sounded out from the entrance to her bedroom next door. Charlie and Ashling pulled apart, froze, listened, their eyes met and smiled. Lying on the bed, fully clothed, she could still feel every inch of him, and the imprint of her own body on his as they pressed together. She tried to banish thoughts of her father's body pressing hers as a panic raced through her. A sudden terror of being more intimate.

Rose's whistle for Lionel cleaved through her skull and they pulled apart.

After Charlie left, she stood at the easel. The light and shadow they had lain in recalled some Bergman films she loved. If they were in a film, the intervening sequence with Charlie would have been removed from public viewing, but each of their faces was brighter than in the prior shot, as if the cinematographer had given them a wash of warm gels, soft back light, and a rim light of silver. The Bergman shadow was the wound in her core. The not knowing if she could ever bear to make love.

SLIPPING AND SLIDING

July 6-8

Rose had let slip that her birthday was the next weekend, and Ashling volunteered to make a cake. Lionel came in as she was melting butter, sugar and chocolate in a pan, and inhaling memories of all of her family birthdays at home in Ireland. She cleaned up meticulously as she went along, soaking measuring dishes in the sink, and chasing down stray beads of sugar. She didn't want to give Lionel anything to complain about.

The kettle hummed on the stove.

"Lionel. I'd like to give Charlie a call," she said.

Lionel swiveled his head around like a monster in a movie. "Is something wrong?"

"It's not urgent—"

"The phone is strictly for emergencies." He adjusted the kettle and centered it perfectly on the gas ring.

Ashling paused the spoon in the midst of her chocolate swirl. "Don't you ever call out?" she said.

"No. Rose likes it that way."

The pan sizzled and Ashling gave a quick stir. "You're letting her turn into a hermit. No light, no air, no address, no communication."

Lionel straightened his already straight glasses and trained his eyes on her. "Well, you're trying to change her." He made it sound like she was slowly poisoning Rose.

"I'm just being who I am," Ashling said.

"And that changes her."

"What if it does? You said yourself she'd come out of her shell."

"But is that best for her?" Lionel swirled boiling water in the teapot and tipped the water into the sink.

"How could it not be?" Ashling said.

He measured out the tea leaves. "She has nothing to look forward to."

His calm infuriated Ashling almost more than his previous storming. "You talk about her as if she were dead." She brandished her spoon in the air and a splash of chocolate glopped onto the counter. "You can't be happy to see her so—"

Lionel poured the boiling water steadily into the pot. He paused the kettle in mid-air and burned his eyes into hers. "You know nothing about it. You didn't know her—before."

Ashling shrunk back. She looked at his steamed-up glasses. "She must have been magnificent. From her photos I can see—"

"She was my whole life." He strung the words out like heavy pearls.

Ashling stepped quickly out of the way of the still suspended boiling kettle. Lionel snapped his attention back to his task. He glanced at the chocolate spot on the counter, and before he could revert to complaining codger, she grabbed a sponge and wiped it off. She got a whiff of burn, and barely got the heat lowered in time to save her chocolate melt from ruin.

Rose let Ashling brush her hair after her bath. She had taken to getting dressed rather than staying in her robe and nightgown all day, and the stale odor was gone. Ashling didn't ask what age she was turning on Saturday—she already looked years younger than when she first laid eyes on her. Her skin was clearer, her hair shinier, her posture more alert.

"What are we listening to now?" Rose asked.

"Van Morrison."

"I like him, he's very...soulful." Rose closed her eyes.

Ashling wove the brush through Rose's fine shoulder-length hair. She could see now that the grey was only at the sides in two streaks, and the rest was a rich brown like Charlie's.

"Have you ever worn a French braid, Rose?"

"Not in eons." Rose opened her eyes. "Show me."

"You take a small section here on top." Ashling demonstrated. "Then you gather in pieces from each side and add them one by one to the basic braid." She held the hair in place and peeked around at Rose's face. "It's lovely, it suits you. Hold this a minute." She placed Rose's hand on her hair and headed to the door. "I'll get a mirror, so you can—"

Rose tensed. "No."

"A hand-mirror. I have one in my room."

Ashling disappeared and reappeared a few moments later with the mirror. Rose was in the exact same position. "I don't use one." Her voice was winter ice.

Ashling paused. "Ever? You mean never? But how..."

"Lionel takes care of everything for me. And you too, now."

"Yes, but...aren't you curious? Even a little?" Ashling moved towards her and surrendered her mirror face downward on the table. She reached for Rose's suspended hand, gently pried her fingers open, and released her hand onto her lap. Rose breathed. Ashling resumed braiding. Van Morrison crooned on.

...Hiding behind a rainbow's wall,

Slipping and sliding, all along the waterfall, with you

My brown-eyed girl...

Rose lowered her lids and hummed to the music.

Ashling stepped back to examine her handiwork. Rose's arm floated up and touched the braid. "It ripples," she said in a little voice.

"*You, my brown-eyed girl,*" Ashling sang, laughing.

Rose raised both hands to her head and, working backwards from the crown, traveled strand by strand along the ridged hair. Her fingers quivered. She brought her fingertips to her face and let them slip down over her glowing cheeks. She looked up at Ashling, a half-smile on her lips. Ashling gave her the thumbs up sign.

Rose laughed, high pitched and giddy. She stretched her hand towards the mirror. She raised it high, so she could see the top of the braid, but not her face. Then, little by little, she shifted the mirror back and forth to allow a small part of her face to be visible at a time, dividing it into segments like a Picasso. When she had peeked at every portion, she held it away and finally let in the whole picture. She gasped, as if she were a girl discovering a new version of herself—realizing she had just become an adolescent, or a young woman. Ashling moved behind her and bent down to fix some straying strands, and Rose's deep brown eyes beamed at both their reflections in the mirror.

Ashling knew she was developing a fear of going outside because of the mountain lions, and of getting lost in the maze of the forest. It was bad enough to be terrified of the dark, lots of people were. But she had to conquer this other tendency before it got hold of her.

She stepped out and looked back at the house. She had an impression of it suffocating, of not having enough air around it to breathe. She looked up. She had forgotten there was a second story. The upper area was a lot smaller than the main house, and she remembered Charlie mentioning he had an attic room. She wondered where the stairs were.

Ashling took a deep breath and plunged into the forest. She picked up leaves and twigs and pebbles and set them down at intervals of a few feet. She played with the shapes, making little mounds, or stars, or squiggles. She looked back every so often to check her trail, like the long tail of a kite. She felt like a child in a fable. She was pleased with herself for being so resourceful, and the bending and arranging lent her walk a dancelike rhythm as she pressed on, deeper into the woods.

Ashling bent down to get a fresh supply of pebbles and felt a stab on the back of her neck. She lunged forward, caught herself, stared behind, heard a rustle, abandoned her trail, and ran. Someone had struck her with a sharp rock. Her neck pulsed, and an ache spread upwards to the crown of her head. She heard more rustling among the leaves and raced wildly, dodging in and out through the trees. A dryness crept into her throat and a heavy numbness attached to her eyelids. Her breath came in darts, each one harder to haul up than the one before, a wheeze like a deathly keening.

She ran madly, leaping over twigs and thickets until she couldn't hear the rustling anymore. She slowed down and listened. It was gone. She stopped and let herself fall to the forest floor. Her breath still came hard and sharp, and her eyelids were hardening like plaster. She saw the leaves through a fog. She tasted damp earth.

Easy does it. Breathe in. Breathe out. Rest.

Ashling lifted her face from the ground. Little by little she raised herself up to sitting, and then slowly to standing. She wiped the dirt from her face and looked around—so much for her trail.

She picked a random direction and walked. She wound her way through the trees and after maybe half an hour, she turned and picked another direction. And then, another. She forced herself not to cry. She could barely see the sky, just a glimpse of blue here and there. Time lost all meaning. She pushed on. Her swollen eyelids pressed against her eyes and she coughed to try and clear her chalky throat. Finally, she stumbled on a dirt mound and saw it was one of her markers. Tears of relief pressed against her leaden lids and stung in streaks down her cheeks.

Lionel stared at her when she opened the door. She heard Rose's voice in the living-room and stumbled in.

"I got hopelessly lost." Ashling said. Her voice was a croak.

Rose stared at her too. "What's wrong with your face?

"I'll get a washcloth," Lionel said, and left.

"Your lips, eyes. And your skin, it's like parchment," Rose said, with worry in her voice.

"Someone hit me with a rock," Ashling said and collapsed on the sofa.

Lionel returned and handed her a warm facecloth. "Who? No one comes out here."

"I don't know." She rubbed the back of her neck. Lionel inspected. "You were dive bombed," he said. Ashling stared at him through half eyes. She kicked off her sandals.

"By a crow. It's happened to me. Did you see any crows or hear them?" he asked.

"I don't think so, I was terrified, I was racing. There was a rustling." She pressed the cloth to her face, onto the swollen lips and eyes.

"Looks like poison oak to me, dear," Rose said. "Wilfred got a bad dose when we first came here."

"What's poison oak?" Ashling asked and lifted her legs onto the sofa. Like a figure in a Seurat painting, she was made up of a million dots slowly separating.

Lionel peered into her face. "It's a plant that grows here. I'll show it to you—you have to avoid it."

She thought of the other times she got these symptoms. In the gym at the Y, on the street in the city. There were no plants around then.

"The swelling will go down. But you should take some aspirin for your headache," Lionel said, and off he went.

"Make a cup of tea for her too, dear," Rose called after him.

Ashling's puffy lips curled at the corners. "Cures everything."

She let her head sink into the softness of the fabric. Her eyelids snapped shut, and all the Seurat dots dissolved.

MOONDANCE

July 10

Charlie assembled hors d'oeuvres in the kitchen for Rose's birthday celebration. This gave Ashling a chance to be alone with him, glance through her mail, and catch up. She fancied she could feel the heat coming off his body and wondered if her desire was detectable. From the way his eyes danced when he looked her way, she had a hunch that it was.

She noticed the address on the top letter, grabbed it and ripped open the seal. "It's the Compton Gallery," she told Charlie.

"I know them—they're small but good." Charlie arranged smoked oysters on a silver plate.

"It's one that looked at my portfolio." Ashling scanned, "... liked your work...later when..." She let the letter drop on the counter. "A big no."

Charlie paused and wiped his hands. "Here, let me have a look." He glanced over the letter. "They're actually very encouraging...interested in seeing more of your work at a later stage...particularly a series."

"So, that's genuine?" she asked.

"It's great. And you're working on a series which is really, really good." He touched her fingers lightly and passed a current through his fingertips which set her heart floating. She relaxed. Everything was converging. Her San Francisco dream was inching closer—a month and a half and maybe she'd be back there, if she could solve her visa dilemma.

She watched Charlie's fingers as he wrapped a slice of melon in a pink, paper thin slice of meat. "Prosciutto," he said, when he saw her looking. He made it sound sexy.

Ashling slit open another letter, one from Ireland.

"I wanted to ring to ask you to pick up something for Rose's birthday, but Lionel…discouraged the use of the phone," she said.

Charlie chuckled. "I think Inga and maybe one or two others really racked up the bills."

"But they were probably ringing Sweden, or wherever they were from. I just wanted to reach you in San Francisco!" She knew Lionel was really trying to control the communication.

Ashling scanned her letter and drew a sharp in-breath. Charlie immediately looked over. "What is it?"

She hauled her eyes away from the page. "Family stuff." She shoved it back in the envelope.

Charlie touched her hand. "You sure?" Ashling nodded. She stood to get a drink of water and hide her face from Charlie. She gulped the water down and cleared the lump in her throat.

Charlie pointed to a package on the counter. "I got you something to give to Rose." He handed her a gold box and Ashling lifted out a long silk scarf in varying shades of shimmering blue. "Oh, I have good taste!" She smiled. "It's perfect—like something Isadora Duncan would have worn."

"And thanks to you, Rose may even wear it." Charlie resumed his preparation. "You'll join us, of course, for our little celebration?"

"Unless you want it to be just the family." Ashling refolded the scarf.

"I consider you one of the family now." He planted a quick kiss in her hair. "Rose wouldn't have even mentioned a birthday if it weren't for your influence."

Ashling's shoulders drooped, and her head pounded despite the lovely compliments. She finished her water. "I might go lie down for about ten minutes—I have a bit of a headache."

Charlie's brow furrowed, and she thought it made him look even more darkly handsome. "Are you sure everything is okay?"

She managed to squeeze out a smile.

Ashling lay on the bed and read the letter again.

...so, the money you sent came just at the right time. Poor Colm is awfully depressed. He mopes around with his pals from the factory. He says that if he has nothing by Christmas he might have to go to England—please God, it won't come to that. We're blessed to have you helping us, Ashling. And of course, we'll have your steady salary come autumn.

Her mother had flung a fishing line and attached a hook right in her center. They wanted her to keep sending money from America, and then when she came back, to lay claim to her salary. The headache rimmed her skull and clenched.

They all sat around the dining room table, like a family. Ashling had changed into her Renoir dress and the billowing blueness of it made her feel more cheerful, though a tiara of pain still pinched her head. Her chocolate cake sat on a ceramic dish in the center of the table, and Veuve Clicquot cooled in a golden bucket. She smiled inside as Charlie popped the cork and captured the bubbling cascade in slender flutes.

Rose draped the Isadora Duncan scarf around her neck. "It's exquisite!" She attempted to tie it. Lionel and Charlie had a go but got the scarf knotted, and Wilfred didn't even try. Ashling undid the false attempts, doubled over the soft fabric, slipped one end through the loop, and let the other fall over Rose's shoulder, a complement to her royal blue blouse. Ashling had arranged her hair, and her cheeks and eyes were shining. She doesn't look much older than Mam, now, Ashling thought.

Rose opened another present from Ashling. "A painting?" She peered at the image. "No, it can't possibly...from a photo of myself and Wilfred...on the carousel." Her eyes filled with tears, but she laughed. "I'm verklempt. I haven't seen that photo in years."

"It was sticking out from behind one of the others in a frame," Ashling said. "I hope you don't mind. You both looked so carefree."

"I'm flattered." Rose's voice cracked, and she laughed at her own emotion. "I don't think I was ever this young or pretty." She handed it to Wilfred. "Look at the expression on your little face, Wil."

Wilfred accepted the painting as if it were a hot plate. "Central Park. I must have been...seven or so?" His deep-set eyes looked soft and open. "Same age as your little brother, Ashling."

Ashling couldn't believe that Wilfred had paid enough attention to remember her brother's age, and it was startling to hear him say her name suddenly in a personal way. Wilfred passed the painting to Charlie, who admired it awhile, and passed it to Lionel. Lionel's eyes clouded over, and he quickly passed it back to Rose.

"You're giving us back our youth, Ashling," Charlie said, the softness of his voice warming her heart. Rose was cradling the painting in the crook of her arm like a baby. "She's a sorcerer." She smiled broadly. "A good one—with a magic wand."

"Magic paint brush," Wilfred added. Ashling felt her cheeks had been brushed with a warm splash of pink.

Lionel and Charlie passed around the champagne and they all raised their glasses and clinked. Rose opened another gift—a wooden compass. She gasped.

"Wilfred. It's exquisite. And there's a rose carved in the center."

Wilfred smiled. "The compass rose."

Rose ran her fingers over the grooves. She pointed to the pivot hole in the center. "Is that an actual diamond? What do you call it, the jewel bearing?"

Wilfred nodded. Tears formed and ran down Rose's cheeks. "My dear. I don't know what to say. It's absolutely the most perfect...the fact that you made it. When did you get time?"

"Late night TV." He laughed, shy and self-deprecating.

Rose passed the compass around to be admired. "This house has turned into a hive of industry—everyone working away behind closed doors like busy bees."

Lionel lit the candles, and they began to sing.

Happy birthday to you, happy birthday to you,

Happy birthday dear Rose, Mom...and Charlie,

Happy birthday to you!

Ashling froze when she heard Charlie's name. She couldn't stop her eyes from bulging. "It's your birthday, too?"

He nodded and laughed. "I don't like gifts."

Ashling was grateful when Rose chimed in that they had a gift for him whether he liked it or not—it gave her time to release her jaw and tone down her gaze. Her cake was passed around, and all of them swooned over the intensity of the flavors. Ashling remembered her altercation with Lionel while making it and was glad it turned out sweetly.

Ashling volunteered to help Charlie clean up. He washed the champagne glasses by hand and passed them to her to dry. She listened until she heard both bedroom doors close.

"Why didn't you tell me it was your birthday, too?" she burst out.

Charlie laughed. "I didn't know we were going to celebrate until last week. We haven't had any kind of marker since Rose's stroke."

"What a coincidence that you were both born on the same date." Ashling carefully dried the long stem.

Charlie paused in his sudsy washing. "Ashling, we're twins."

The glass slipped from her hand and she grabbed it just in time. "What? No, you…"

"Rose didn't like me mentioning it, since…well, she aged a lot."

"So, before, she…?"

"Yep. She looked like a lovely thirty-six-year-old the day she had her stroke."

Ashling did a quick calculation and deduced they were both forty-two, same age as her parents. She had assumed Charlie was about thirty-seven or -eight. She rubbed the glass, over and over, polishing it inside and out. "I think she looks years younger than when I first met her. Maybe she'll get back to looking her age if she keeps getting better in her mind."

Charlie's eyes gazed into the distance. Ashling's thoughts flew back to the trouble her family was in six thousand miles away. It was as if the parent had left home, rather than the child.

"Ashling." Charlie's voice careened towards her and snapped Ashling out of her mind travel. The glass slipped through her fingers, fell to the floor, and shattered.

"Jesus! What…? I'm sorry."

Charlie immediately moved to get a broom and garbage can and Ashling bent down to pick up the larger pieces.

"Be careful. Don't cut yourself." He swept up the shards.

Ashling dropped to her knees. "Lionel will kill me."

"He'll get over it. Even Lionel has eased up, thanks to your influence on this household." Charlie knelt opposite her, the remains of the glass between them. "There's something wrong in Ireland, isn't there?"

Tears welled up. "My brother Colm lost his job—the factory closed down. And business is slow for my dad."

She picked up needles of glass and dropped them in the garbage bin. "I did all the household budgeting since I was about twelve. I set up systems for them when I was away, and I tried to organize it all before I left to come here." She licked the salty tears and wiped her face with the back of her hand. "I suppose I can't control the economy."

Charlie slipped out his wallet and peeled off several twenty-dollar notes. He moved so swiftly she hardly realized until the money was under her nose.

"No Charlie. I can't." She pulled back.

"Please." He held out the bills. "It's well earned."

She shook her head.

"I'm not sure if you have any idea what you've done here. No doctor, nurse or social worker has been able to help Rose the way you have."

"I'm glad—but it's still not enough reason to take all that extra cash."

"It is to me. I have plenty of money and only one sister. My twin. Please?"

The strangeness of that concept washed over Ashling—Charlie having a twin, and it being Rose. Her twin sisters Breda and Brona had a special bond. There was an overlap in their relationship, some unspoken and maybe inexplicable tie that was theirs alone. She saw, now, that was there for Rose and Charlie too.

He offered the money again. "Say it's a gift from me."

She wavered. "All right. I'm going to put all of it in with a letter and specify that it's from you. Thank you." Ashling swallowed her tears and turned her attention back to the few remaining pieces of glass. "What was it you wanted to ask me before?"

Charlie emptied the dust pail. "Well, it's a proposition. From me, but from Rose too."

"What kind of proposition?" She picked up a shard of glass.

Charlie cleared his throat. "We would all like you to stay on here."

"But I said I'd stay for two months, 'til the end of the summer." She stopped. She stared at Charlie. "You don't mean indefinitely?" Her hand closed over the glass and pressed it into her palm. "Jesus Christ!" Blood dripped onto the floor.

Charlie grasped her hand. "Put pressure here—I'll grab the first-aid kit."

He rushed to the bathroom. Ashling stared down at the blood as plop by plop it dripped onto the spotless tiled floor. She was fragile as the glass, and the hammering in her head was steady as a metronome. She wanted to lie down on the bloodied tiles and bang her head until the pain dissolved. The floor was inviting her to give in. She used every iota of willpower she could muster to stay upright until Charlie returned.

In her bedroom, hand bandaged, painkillers ingested, Ashling played a Van Morrison tape and slapped paint onto the canvas. Charlie closed up the first-aid kit.

"I'm only twenty-one." She spewed out the words.

Charlie circled around her. "You have your whole life ahead of you. What about Rose?"

"She's only forty-two—she's not about to drop dead." Ashling's painting hand had a life of its own.

"We don't know that." Charlie paused by the window. His voice dipped. "The paralysis puts a strain on the vital organs."

Ashling glanced over at him. "I'm very fond of Rose, you know that. And I really appreciate how generous you've been. Anyway, staying isn't even an option unless something changes with my status."

"I'm still working on the visa; we'll figure it out." Charlie's voice was heavy and sweet as molasses.

Ashling stared at her canvas. "And there's my painting—"

"Which has developed enormously since you've been here." Charlie moved closer. She felt his force field.

"I suppose." Her eyes bore into her painting. She didn't quite recognize it—it was as if an unknown part of her was emerging through the canvas.

Charlie moved even closer. The force field grew stronger. "And you'll never make the kind of money you get here—be able to help your family."

She examined the lines and shapes and colors and textures as if the answer might lie there.

"It's a onetime opportunity—a chance to get a head start, save, build your portfolio."

His words were a chant, forming a nimbus around her head. "I still hope to open up a place for you in the gallery, and when the time is right Rose might even move closer to the city."

Charlie was beside her now. It was hard to think. Her insides zigzagged like the shapes in her painting. Ashling steeled her eyes on the canvas, purposely not looking at him. She was making up her mind—not just whether to stay in the job, but whether Charlie was the one she'd make love to for the first time. She was deciding whether to choose him.

She could feel him a few millimeters away. What did the age gap matter? He was gorgeous.

His breath was on her neck now. "You know I want you to stay." His words like silk.

Her arm came to life, and she splashed on more paint. She stood back to look. "Not bad—for a damaged hand painting!" she said.

Charlie put his arm around her shoulders and moved closer. Her knees turned to jelly. He looked at the canvas. "It's wonderful," he said. He crossed in front and kissed her. A bold, messy Jackson Pollock kiss. She encircled him with her free arm—the other still held the paintbrush.

"Okay. I'll stay on—at least for a few more months—if you can get my visa renewed."

They drew apart, and her new painting came into view. She leaned in and looked closely. "I didn't use red there…or there. It's blood!"

Charlie lifted her hand. "The bandage leaked, but the bleeding seems to have stopped now. I'll get you a large Band-Aid."

He found a soft cloth in the first-aid kit and offered it to her. "Do you want to clean the canvas?"

Ashling looked at her painting. "I think I'll leave it. I like it."

"Good. I agree. Mixed media."

Ashling laughed. Her head was shrouded in layers of muslin, soft like a wrapped-up baby.

Charlie led her to the bed. "I'll dress your wound."

She swayed as she sat down. Charlie's arm on her waist steadied her. He sat beside her and unwrapped the bandage. He wiped the cut, rubbed on gel, and applied gentle force to a huge Band-Aid.

"How do you feel now?"

"A little queasy. My hand is fine, though."

He gathered up the used bandage and cloths. "I'll get rid of these and wash my hands. Do you want something for your stomach? Tea? Brandy?"

"Brandy sounds nice. Our mam used to give us warm milk with a splash of brandy when we were sick as kids."

"I'd be happy to add milk if you like."

"No. I'll have the grownup version."

He flashed his Brando smile.

The Van Morrison tape ended as he reached the door.

"Can you flip the tape, please, Charlie?"

He clicked the machine open, reversed the cassette, and slipped out.

Ashling scooted up on the bed and leaned back against the headrest. She had to think. Everything had happened so fast. Charlie and Rose were twins. The whole family wanted her to stay, and she had agreed to—for a while at least. Charlie hoped eventually to move the household to the city. He was working on her visa.

Her brain wanted to melt to mush but she made herself go through the steps. She was accumulating money rapidly and had no expenses, so could save. She was able to help her family without going home. And she was advancing her goal of deepening as a painter and getting her internal world on the canvas. She had imagined having the courage to create art from what she had seen and half-seen in Ireland. The way girls and women were treated, the things the clergy got away with, the way everything was hushed up and made to disappear. Surely it was worth it to incubate here for a while, even if Rose was prickly, Lionel obsessive, and Wilfred strange. Rose was shifting, she had seen a hint of Lionel's vulnerable side, and even Wilfred had astounded everyone by tapping into his creativity. Maybe all that would be more bearable. She was piling this up in her head, chunks of information like bricks in a wall she was constructing. A wall of reason.

Well, it's a marvelous night for a moondance, Van Morrison crooned as Charlie tap-tapped, and entered carrying two snifters of brandy.

With the stars up above in your eyes...

He handed her a glass, and she scooted over so he could sit beside her on the bed.

Charlie swished the brandy, savored the aroma, sipped.

A fantabulous night to make romance...

He intertwined his fingers with hers and glanced over. "Okay?"

She smiled. She inhaled the smooth vapors. The liquid rippled sweetly across her tongue and down the back of her throat. Charlie's fingers traced a path up her inner arm and just under the fabric of her party dress. She was a conduit of tiny vibrations. She sipped some more.

Van Morrison sang on. *And I'm trying to please to the calling, Of your heart-strings that play soft and low...*

Ashling and Charlie turned towards each other. They drew close and kissed, lightly, on the lips. They set aside their brandy, and Charlie encircled Ashling's face with his hands and drew her in for another, deeper kiss.

"It's been a big day for you," he whispered in her ear. "Dramatic." His breath on her earlobe, whistling inside, her whole body a conch shell suffused with his magic.

"You're the one who had a birthday. And I never gave you a present," she whispered, smiling.

He gathered her body close and they lay, facing each other on the bed.

Well I wanna make love to you tonight, I can't wait till the morning has come...

Charlie's laugh was a soft caress. "I don't need to speak. I'm channeling Van Morrison." His kisses were magnets, drawing her in.

And I know now the time is just right, And straight into my arms you will run...

Is it? He asked with his eyes. The right time?

Her body said Yes. Her eyes said Yes. Even her big wall of reason screamed Yes. And Charlie's wanting her made her want to say Yes.

She wished she had gotten birth control when in San Francisco.

"I have protection," he whispered.

She looked at him, puzzled. "From what?"

He laughed. "From *les petits bebés*. I have a condom."

"Ha! 'Protection' makes it sound like I'm dangerous. That you've got your shield!"

"No shield, but a sheath. I can show you how to put it on if you like."

Ashling nodded. It made Charlie even more sexy.

"It's a marvelous night for a moondance," she murmured, her fingers flowing towards his shirt front.

"With the stars up above in your eyes..." He responded, slip-sliding off her dress.

A fantabulous night to make romance, and their skin was touching, tingling, trembling.

Ashling took in the whole sweep of Charlie's body—like a Roman god. He was looking at her, white to his bronze. "You look like a wood nymph," he whispered.

"Happy Birthday!" Ashling teased.

The Roman god and wood nymph ravished each other, both exploring, offering, taking, surrendering. The violence of the night of her father shot through her. She gasped. She pulled away. Charlie's eyes widened in a question. Father Dempsey and her father's actions, that was hate and wrong, this was love, and it was right, and she had removed herself by thousands of miles and a vast continent. Ashling flipped off her brain switch and abandoned herself to the dance.

FLORENCE NIGHTINGALE

July 12-16

Doctor Jeremy Talbot arrived to give Rose her annual checkup. Lionel introduced Ashling to him. Despite the heat, the doctor wore a suit and tie, and even tipped his hat when he said, "delighted to meet you." He could have stepped out of a Renoir painting.

Ashling went next door to her bedroom to paint. She was percolating with memories of her night with Charlie, the passion mingled with the pain of past memories, and an occasional pop of anxiety about agreeing to stay on. Her whole being was abuzz, and the energy sizzled into her brushstrokes. She started a new piece—and surprised herself that it was an abstracted image of Alcatraz. A starry constellation might be more appropriate, she thought.

Prior to this she had mostly stood in one spot as she painted, now her molecules jammed into each other, propelling her body into motion. She approached the canvas from every possible angle—high, low, extreme right, extreme left, above, behind, and in sweeping, panning curves. Just as she had been drawn towards Alcatraz, she now felt an imperative to paint it. The color palette was browns and grays and burnt amber, the angles skewed, compositions off balance. The painting was surging through her, bypassing her conscious mind. A whole cache of images based on memory flashes of her visit—the hot showers, ghostly prisoners painting in ball and chain, sightings of the fortress from the safety of the mainland—burgeoned around her like an invisible halo, waiting to take shape on the canvas. Maybe she'd end up with an Alcatraz series, too.

Ashling overheard Dr. Talbot's voice from next door. "I haven't seen you so well in a long time, Mrs. Cody. Something is agreeing with you." She heard him snap the clasp on his bag.

"My Ashling," Rose replied. Ashling smiled when she heard the smile in Rose's voice.

"I beg your pardon?"

"The Irish girl you met who takes care of Rose," Lionel said.

"A permanent companion?"

She heard no response and could only assume that it was nonverbal, or withheld, as the next voice she heard was Rose inquiring whether she still needed these checkups.

Ashling's inner balloon deflated. Did Rose think she was staying with her forever? Did Charlie tell her that? Did they think of her as the Irish maid? Or maybe she had just smiled at the doctor, and left the answer open. Surely Rose could see that Ashling couldn't devote her life to her. That she had other dreams and ambitions.

She plunged back into her painting world.

Ashling was awakened by the ringing bell over her bed. She sprang up, grabbed her judogi, and dragged her legs from the room.

In the dim glow of a tiny nightlight, she helped Lionel lift Rose out of bed and onto the commode. They were shadowy figures in the semidarkness. Rose coughed with a cry in her voice. Ashling slumped on a chair to wait, and her eyelids were tiny sandbags fluttering down. Lionel nudged her shoulder when he was ready, and they eased Rose back to bed.

Ashling stumbled to the bathroom. She gasped when she found herself face to face with Wilfred in the dusky hallway. She saw his eyes drop to her breasts, then away, and she pulled her judogi back around her nightdress. He signaled for her to go ahead.

Ashling returned to her room, closed the door, and stood there a moment, listening. She heard Wilfred's footsteps going into the bathroom and flung herself back into bed. She had never even thought of Wilfred as a sexual being—his body buried beneath layers of fat. She did notice that his trips to the kitchen were less frequent, and the chairs complained less under his weight. She tried to banish the imprint of his gaze but lay on her pillow, wide awake. To coax herself to sleep she tried a technique she'd read about where you turned both of your closed eyes inwards and upwards towards the middle of your forehead to strain your eyes and tire them out. It didn't work.

Rose wasn't feeling well enough for reading, so took up her television-watching position. Her cough was ragged. Ashling, her head fuzzy, her eyes gritty from lack of sleep, was dusting a framed photo when it slipped from her hand. The glass broke, and she glanced towards the kitchen to check whether Lionel had heard. She bent down and saw that another photo was tucked in behind the main one. It was of Lionel and Rose fourteen or fifteen years earlier, and Wilfred aged about nine or ten. The boy was slender, with a soft open face, and Lionel's hand rested on his shoulder in a gesture of affection. Rose held a little girl, aged about three, in her lap.

"I'm sorry, I broke the glass. I don't think the photo is damaged though," Ashling said.

"It's not serious." Rose blew her nose and coughed. "Which one is it?"

"The main one is of you—but the other is of Lionel and Wilfred and a little girl."

Rose held out her hand. It quivered. "Let me see." Her lips moved as if she were praying. Ashling handed her the photo and left to get the vacuum cleaner. When she returned, Rose was feasting her eyes on the picture.

"Ashling, come sit by me." She was barely audible. She set the photo on the side table.

Ashling sat on a low stool and Rose gestured her to lay her head on her lap. All was moving in slow motion. Ashling was so exhausted that she surrendered her cheek to the soft velour of Rose's robe. Rose ran her fingers through her short locks and sound waves whooshed inside her head. The sweet cherry smell from the cough medicine tickled her nose.

"Ava would have been just a few years younger than you if she had lived." Rose sounded underwater.

"Who?"

"My little girl. Mine and Lionel's." Her voice broke.

Ashling, her head still on Rose's lap, reached over for the photo. Rose continued to stroke her head, tracing lines with her fingertips.

"That must have been taken a few months before she died." There was a catch in Rose's throat.

"Was she sick?"

Rose shook her head. "An accident. She and Wilfred were playing with a rubber ball on the sidewalk, and it rolled onto the street. Ava scrambled after it. There was a car. She was rushed to the hospital, but it was too late."

A teardrop splashed on Ashling's cheek.

"Wilfred never forgave himself for not stopping her, though he was only a child, too."

"Is that why Lionel and Wilfred don't speak?"

Rose nodded. "We tried for another child over the years. My stroke was the final nail in the coffin. All the old resentments resurfaced."

Rose recommenced raking her fingers through Ashling's hair. Ashling let her head sink deeper into Rose's lap. The TV flickered on her face. She dozed.

When she emerged from sleep Ashling still held the photograph. She wondered if Wilfred's weight gain was related to this horrible accident in the family's past.

"I wish I had been able to monitor his eating," Rose said, as if reading her mind. "But I was…numb." Ashling was still. "Wouldn't it be convenient if we could go back and fix the past." Her cough was a scraping inside her chest.

Ashling stirred herself and propped up the pillow behind Rose's neck. "Did he, Wilfred…get better as time went on?" she asked.

Rose cupped Ashling's hand in hers. "In his teenage years, as all his peers were growing pimply, Wilfred blossomed. My career was blossoming too." She looked up at Ashling. "You may find it hard to believe, but Wilfred was very popular with the young ladies then, handsome and dashing—like his uncle."

Ashling's face bloomed hot. Did Rose know about her and Charlie? She freed her hand and fiddled with the cushion at Rose's back.

"And then, after my stroke, the bingeing started again." Rose reached back and patted Ashling's arm. "However, since you came there have been changes. Maybe some things can be fixed."

Ashling's face was scalding. Thoughts of Charlie were racing through her mind, and she hoped Rose didn't mistake her embarrassment for liking Wilfred. She rearranged the shawl on Rose's shoulders. She meted out a helping of cough mixture and spooned it into Rose's mouth.

As the week progressed, Rose's condition worsened. She now made a wheezing sound as she struggled to draw breath, and Ashling was awakened at least once every night by the jangling bell. The sounds of Rose hauling breath resonated through the house day and night. Lionel, Wilfred, and Ashling tip-toed around. Rose was adamant in not wanting the doctor, and Lionel and Wilfred complied.

Ashling continued to paint for several hours every day. The photos of Rose were arranged in chronological order on the bookcase in her bedroom. Since finding the secret photo of Ava, she now removed each one from its frame and searched to see if another was hidden behind it. In most cases she found one—a recording of the past that the family had tucked away. She didn't paint directly from these hidden ones but used them to inform the shadow regions of Rose's life and her trajectory as a dancer.

Ashling matched the photos of Rose dancing with the approximate time that Ava died and thought she could trace the pain in Rose's face and body, and the efforts to cover up that pain. Her dance schedule was already demanding, but she seemed to apply herself with even more fierceness. Ashling also noted Wilfred's growth, his childhood, his devastation over his sister's death, his gradual maturing, and the happy debonair teenage phase that corresponded with Rose's high point. The bookcase transformed into a gallery of their lives.

Her painting was humming along so nicely that Ashling decided she might be ready to work on what she thought of as her Sheila series. In a letter from home, she found out that Father Dempsey had moved to another parish. There were no details of why, and her family didn't indicate there was anything suspicious involved. A young curate just out of seminary had taken his place. At first Ashling felt relief and wondered if Reverend Mother had in fact acted on Ashling's account. Then she remembered how impressed the whole community was when they were assigned a wonderful priest such as Father Dempsey and Ashling now wondered if he had been sent down from a high-profile position in Dublin to their little backwater of Timaleen under some cloud. Sent to a place he wouldn't be noticed. Or a place they thought he could be cured. It made her blood boil. They were playing Russian roulette with children's lives.

She prepared her canvas and set it up. She looked over some sketches she had doodled. Ideas. Outlines. Sheila's Botticelli features. Her wide, sad eyes. Her yellow dress. She mixed paint, trying to find the right yellow. She hesitated. She couldn't find a point of attack, a way to begin. She pushed past this and splashed paint on the canvas, piled on an ochre tinge, sculpted shapes. Her anger surged through her arm and down through her fingers into the brushstrokes. Directionless, she muddled on.

Several days in a row she came back to the same painting, added to it, approached it from different angles, fretted over it, touched it up. Each time it receded, backing away from her, retreating rather than advancing. In frustration she realized she wasn't ready yet. For whatever reason she wasn't able to give form to this topic yet, to speak of Sheila and other girls through her painting, to find the right expression for that darkness. She folded up the canvas and dumped it in the bin.

Late one evening, after a wheezing session abated and Rose was breathing more comfortably, Ashling was seated on her stool on one side of Rose's wheelchair in the living room and Wilfred sat on a chair, on the other side, each holding one of her hands. Ashling felt Wilfred's eyes on her, and when she looked up, he flashed a smile. His glance swept over her. She dropped her eyes. Lionel arrived from the kitchen just then with a mug of steaming liquid, suffusing the room with the scent of freshly squeezed lemons and the sweetness of honey.

He looked at Ashling, glanced at Wilfred.

"Go relax…you two. I've got it covered."

Ashling scanned Lionel's face for a sign. She didn't know if that comment constituted Lionel actually speaking to Wilfred and pairing her up with him. Wilfred stared, like a patient having his eyes examined with a pin light. Lionel bent over Rose and offered the drink.

Ashling escaped to the far end of the room and sunk into the sofa. She snatched up a magazine and flipped through it, the pages making a slow tick, tick sound. The print passed before her in a blur.

Wilfred hoisted himself from his chair, crossed over and plunked down beside her. He also grabbed a magazine, opened, and ignored it. Maybe he too was wondering if Lionel had addressed him, Ashling thought.

Rose swallowed the beverage in soft gulps and sighed. She drew in breath with a whistle.

"You think she'll be all right?" Ashling asked Wilfred, after a while.

"We've been through this before—it's not as scary as it sounds, just a bad chest cold." He stared at his magazine.

"Shouldn't the doctor be called?"

"Mother has a terror of doctors. She puts up with that check-up once a year, but otherwise she avoids them like the plague."

"What if it's really serious?"

"Lionel..." The name sounded alien on Wilfred's tongue, "Lionel is practically a doctor himself at this stage. And Charlie and I have plenty of practice." He inclined his head towards her. "And then, there's you."

Ashling hoped that she wasn't releasing pheromones that were being picked up and misinterpreted by Wilfred. Her body felt porous, and she was powerless to control it.

"I know next to nothing about doctoring," she said. She noticed the magazine in her hand was of young women's fashion that she hadn't seen in the house before. She flipped to the cover—*Elle*. "Unless you count being big sister to four kids." And two parents.

Wilfred draped his arm around the back of the sofa. Ashling got a whiff of the starchiness of new clothes, and glancing down, saw that he was wearing brand new jeans and a fresh cotton shirt. He looked like he had shrunk a size.

"I don't know what we'd do without you here." His fingers danced within touching distance of her shoulder and made a gentle depression in the fabric right by her ear. She laughed, a nervous quiver, and shifted over. "I think I'll change my name to Florence Nightingale."

Lionel shot a sideways glance at Ashling and Wilfred and trekked back to the kitchen. Ashling catapulted from the couch to Rose's side.

AMORE

July 17-18

Ashling was in the kitchen making pudding for Rose when she saw the headlights flash in the window, and in an instant Charlie was in the hallway calling out hello. A tsunami of longing coursed through her. Anxious to be with him, she quickly served up the rice pudding. Charlie went directly to the living room and he and Rose were locked in a tight embrace when Ashling entered. More like lovers than siblings, she thought, and tried to tame her beating heart. When they pulled apart Ashling saw the concern in Charlie's eyes.

"It's just the same old trouble, Chas. My weak chest," Rose said.

He planted a kiss on her forehead.

"Ashling has made me some magical Irish remedies," she said, and Charlie straightened up and emanated a smile over Rose's head. "Here's one. Rice pudding with raisins and honey."

Ashling stiffened her knees to keep them from wobbling as she brought over the pudding.

Lionel shuffled in carrying a steaming mug.

"And another—hot lemon with floating cloves." Rose's voice was high and bubbly.

Lionel nodded to Charlie and retreated to the kitchen.

"Didn't Annie make rice pudding for us when we were sick as kids?" Charlie asked.

"You're right." Rose smiled. She tasted the pudding. "Annie was our Irish nurse, Ashling. I think we told you?"

Ashling remembered that their mother worried they might pick up her accent and manners.

"She would park us on her knee, and feed each of us a spoonful at a time," Charlie said. He sat by Rose and held her hand, and for a moment they were in a private universe. Rose looked up. "This is delicious, Ashling. You have to try it, Chas." She wiped her spoon in her napkin, scooped up another serving and eased it into Charlie's mouth. Charlie smacked his lips. "Better even than Annie's. You must have a secret ingredient, Ashling." He turned his lidded eyes to her and undressed her with his smile.

Ashling shot back a bold gaze. "I can get you your own serving if you like."

"Later." He made it sound like a promise.

Ashling instructed her legs to carry her back to the kitchen. Lionel stared at her as she rushed in. She buried her face in the cupboard to hide her flaming cheeks, putting away the rice, the honey, the raisins. Charlie had blatantly flirted with her in front of Rose, and he was the one who was so adamant about keeping it secret. How was that possible when it seemed like every raised lid, covert smile, and shaking limb betrayed her? She breathed a sigh of relief when Lionel said good night and vanished. She could hear footsteps and a wheelchair in the hallway, then quiet.

The minute Charlie entered the kitchen they kissed, a collision of desire. Ashling was fragile from lack of rest. Her skin was transparent. Charlie's body, electric. The pair spun towards his bedroom upstairs and into a whirl of loving.

Ashling glanced around at Charlie's room as she slipped her clothes back on. The disheveled sheets and streak of moonlight made her think of an attic apartment Balzac might have penned his novels in. The only furniture was a low bed, an antique wardrobe, and an escritoire. It was their secret hideaway.

Charlie's sleeping face was relaxed, his lips curled in a smile. Ashling wondered if she would ever be able to make love without being haunted by memory flashes—of her father, of the priest, sometimes of Sheila in that yellow dress. Her exquisite pleasure was braided with pain.

She planted the lightest of kisses on Charlie's lips, and stole away, down the secret stairway.

Poised on the barstool at the kitchen counter next morning, Ashling looked over the mail as Charlie ground the coffee beans.

Charlie had express-mailed her letter to Ireland with the money, and a reply had arrived.

...it seems like America truly is The Land of Opportunity. Please say a special thanks to your wonderful boss. I've never heard of anything like that—the generosity. I'd stick with that job, Ashling.

Ashling could picture her mother sitting in her slip of a room with the partial view of the high-stepping Atlantic waves. Her own mother had died at twenty-one when Mam was a baby, and her corset—pale pink with bones and antique lacing—hung above the sewing machine like a portrait. Mam's education had ended at fourteen when she went to work for a milliner, and in her mind, a job in a good house with extravagant sums of money flowing, and in a paradise, such as California would constitute the epitome of success, even if she was essentially a glorified maid. Ashling wondered if Mam would even sacrifice all that for having Ashling home and teaching in the primary school.

The steamer hissed and gurgled, and Ashling looked up as Charlie blended the milk and pungent coffee into a frothy beverage. He arranged biscotti on a plate and set a cappuccino in front of her with a heart floating in the foam.

"I got the guys to teach me," he said.

He was bringing North Beach to her.

Ashling dipped her biscotti, careful to preserve the heart. Her life was veering off in a whole new direction—Irish family being helped, love and career intermingled and soaring. She hadn't had a yen for a cup of tea in the longest time.

Charlie sat down beside her, and heat radiated from his thighs.

"Any word on the visa?" she asked.

His eyes clouded over, and he braided his little finger with hers. "I met with Bill. He was hoping to find a loophole in your renewal option—"

"But they're issuing literally hundreds of these lottery visas. Everybody knew about them back home," Ashling said.

"As far as I can tell that's part of the problem. So many Irish visas are going out by lottery that they're clamping down."

Ashling's body drooped. She fingered the edges of the notepaper. "I can't go back now. My mother—" She crinkled the letter. You, she thought.

Charlie rested her palm in his and stroked it as if tracing her lifeline. "There is an option Bill told me about."

He skimmed his finger over the pinkish indentation from the broken glass. "It's called a third preference visa. It's based on petitioning for immigrant status, then waiting for them to assign a number."

"Do you automatically get a number if they approve the petition?"

"Apparently it can take a while because the quota of visas available each year is limited."

"How long?"

"It could be fast, or it could be years. You have to prove that you can do a job no other American citizen can do."

"That must be for people with specialized skills in their fields." Ashling's voice cracked.

"You do have special skills. I've never seen Rose take to anyone the way she's taken to you."

Ashling searched Charlie's face for signs of levity. He was not smiling.

"But I don't have any skills that, for example, an American might not have."

"You have a connection with her." He planted a kiss on the zigzag scar. "She's transforming, Ashling."

A cool shiver ran up Ashling's spine. Being praised and elevated above and beyond her powers, and for something that meant little or nothing to her and her plans, was eerily reminiscent of her family in Ireland. She was happy Rose was improving. She felt a growing closeness to her. She just didn't want her whole worth defined by other people's plans for her.

"I'm not saying it'll work." Charlie slid his hand along her back. "But we all want you to stay. Rose, Lionel, Wilfred. Me."

"So...you would apply for me under this third preference clause. And in the meantime, I'm soon to be illegal. I could be deported and barred from returning." Ashling flashed on the Polish cleaning woman coughing up blood in the bathroom of the Y—afraid to go to a doctor. The English woman's boyfriend, Carlos, pounced on in the street, his retreating back on a one-way bus trip to Mexico. The judo instructor, Jorge, living in fear for himself and his family.

"There's no paper trail to this address since I'm using a P.O. Box. And you're being paid in cash." Charlie's voice was soft as he massaged her back in concentric circles. Ashling wondered if he was casting a spell on her.

"And if they come to you? After my visa's expiration date?"

"It's highly unlikely. But if it did happen, I would simply say I don't know where you are."

"What about Bill in Immigration?"

"Bill's good people. No worries there."

It all sounded vague. But she knew that hundreds of illegal immigrants disappeared into the crowds daily and made their way under the radar. She had no idea whether she'd want to be one of them, or whether it would be worth it.

"Do you really think the third preference thing could work?" she asked.

Charlie's lashes dipped. "It's a long shot, but we should give it a try." The massage circles on her back got smaller and smaller and he stopped his hand just behind her heart. "I have the forms. We'll fill them out."

The heat from his hand was spreading around her heart. In slow motion, Charlie tilted up her chin, and kissed her with anisette lips.

That evening the family had congregated in the living room, and Rose presented Ashling with a silver shopping bag. "I had Charlie pick it up for me," she said.

Ashling burrowed through the layers of tissue paper and lifted out a dark green mini-skirt with an embossed pattern and pleats, and a pale green top of crinkly cotton. She ran her fingers over the fabric and noticed the fine tailoring. Her mother's creations were lovely, but there was an aura of richness to these expertly designed items.

"Thank you, Rose, they're gorgeous. How did you choose them?"

Rose's face was split in a Cheshire Cat grin. "*Vogue*. I picked the designer and Charlie found the boutique. I think we guessed the right size."

Ashling pictured Charlie running his fingers over the clothes and deliberately avoided his eyes.

"I'll go try them on."

Ashling lingered a minute in front of the mirror in her bedroom. The clothes fit as if they had been custom made. The color turned her eyes a deeper green, and her hair a whiter blonde. She felt light and trendy.

She stepped into the hallway and stood a moment, taking a mental snapshot of the scene in the living room. The family was arranged in a Still Life—Rose leafing through a magazine, Lionel engrossed in an engineering journal, Wilfred working on a crossword puzzle, and Charlie at the table arranging documents. Vivaldi's *Four Seasons* played in the background. They looked like an ordinary family.

Ashling cleared her throat and four sets of eyes shot up to look at her. Rose gasped. "Oh, my! *Bubalah*! Very pretty."

Ashling crossed over and leaned in to kiss her cheek. "Thank you, Rose." She tasted a salty tear.

"*Bellissima*!" Charlie intoned, and it sounded like an aria.

Wilfred's eyes swept over her and he smiled shyly, lids at half-mast.

"It's Rose's good taste," Ashling said with a mock curtsy, and she crossed to the table to sit by Charlie. She could feel Wilfred's eyes trailing her.

Charlie had laid out the Immigration forms in order. He and Rose and Lionel had to supply names and details of previous helpers. There was quite a string of them, and none had lasted very long—Inga, the Swede, who ran up the telephone bill, Samantha, who acted like a bossy nanny, Deborah who was lazy, and so on.

"Ashling's got chutzpah. That's the difference between her and the others," Rose said.

"And how do we phrase that for Immigration?" Charlie raised an eyebrow.

"Moxie? Can you say that? She's got moxie, AND she makes the best rice pudding."

"I'm not sure either of those could be construed as unique characteristics," Ashling said, her lips parting in a smile. She did know that her boldness, along with caring, pushed Rose beyond her stubbornness. And it occurred to her that none of Rose's men challenged her much. Puppy dog Lionel, Big Bear Wilfred, and Sweet Brother Charlie all catered to her every whim—you couldn't put that on a form either.

They sat shoulder to shoulder conversing in hushed tones, creating a document aimed at securing Ashling's stay in the country. They had to present a detailed schedule of every task she performed for Rose, and Charlie testified to the improvements in Rose's health and well-being since Ashling's arrival. Ashling was moved by the strength of Charlie's interest in her welfare. The word love had not been spoken between them but was hovering. Ashling had never said the words to anyone, and not speaking them now exerted a powerful force. Sitting here in this room, surrounded by the constellation of Charlie's family, soothed by Vivaldi, they were all engaged in a collective application. They all had input—they all wanted her to stay in the United States.

When Charlie prepared to leave on Sunday evening to drive back to the city, Ashling felt as if she were fragmenting. Her body craved his and had become accustomed to his touch. His patience and understanding helped soothe her anxiety. She had told Charlie of her years in the convent and strict Catholic upbringing. She had not mentioned her father's violation, the whispers and innuendo she'd picked up from other girls, her certainly about Father Dempsey's molestations.

The need to keep their affair a secret added an extra layer of tension. Charlie said he wanted to wait a while before letting Rose and the others know. He said it might upset Rose because she was starting to see her as a daughter, and he didn't want to impede her progress. When she was stronger, he said, they could tell her. Ashling still found it hard to believe they all didn't pick up on the magnetic force field between them.

As he kissed her goodbye in her room, the completed application safely tucked in a manila envelope, she pushed back the word love which danced on her tongue.

"When Rose is completely over this episode, how about I bring you to San Francisco for a long weekend?" Charlie said.

Ashling's eyes widened. She had become so enmeshed in the household and the whirl of work and love and painting and immigration. The idea of being with Charlie as a lover in San Francisco was a huge white canvas waiting to be filled in.

They hugged and pried themselves apart. As Charlie disappeared through the doorway he turned around and blew her a kiss. "*Ciao…amore.*" He pulled the door to, softly. Ashling was fairly sure that *amore* meant love or lover. It was almost the same as saying I love you.

GUCCI

July 26-August 13

The curtains were open. And it was quiet. In a splash of light, Ashling saw Rose, fully dressed, sitting in front of a sewing machine where the T.V. used to be. James Galway's flute played Debussy in the background.

Rose greeted Ashling with a smile. "It's so much nicer in here with natural light," she said.

Ashling wondered if her weekend with Charlie had made her delirious, and she was hallucinating. She found her voice. "The usual for breakfast?"

Rose spun the handle on the sewing machine and lined up her fabric. "I've been up for a few hours. I had toast and coffee and feel fine."

Ashling realized there had been no bell ringing during the night, though the peals still resonated faintly in a chamber of her skull.

"I recovered a lot faster this time, thanks to you. Once a year right after that doctor visits I get this cold." She kept her eyes on the needle.

Ashling still stood just inside the doorway, feeling like an actor who had wandered into the wrong play. Seeing Rose active, and in light was so incongruous.

"One nice thing is that Charlie always stays when I'm sick," Rose continued, and she glanced up. Heat rose at the nape of Ashling's neck. She blushed pink.

"I'll just grab a coffee."

She escaped to the kitchen and poured the coffee as slowly as she could, taking the few moments to calm her churning insides.

Back in the living room, she fortified herself with several gulps of the brew. "What are you sewing?" she asked Rose

"I'm practicing on some remnants 'til I get back in the swing. I dragged out all my old patterns. I used to love sewing but was too restless when I was younger."

"My mam's a terrific sewer. As long as she has a pattern, she can make anything," Ashling said.

"Is she a professional seamstress?"

"Gosh no. But she does have a decent local business."

"You're very devoted to your mother." The tone was vaguely accusatory. Rose pressed a walking stick with a rubber shoe onto the foot pedal of the machine and it whirred. The sound coursed through Ashling's head as she replayed Rose's comment in her mind. She lowered herself carefully into a chair. "I suppose I'd do anything for my mother. Isn't that natural?"

"Up to a point." The fabric sailed along, guided by Rose's hand.

"Wilfred seems devoted to you."

Rose shot her a glance. "He's a wonderful son." Ashling averted her eyes and mentally threw frost over her cheeks. Rose reversed the fabric and began again.

"Maybe we just expect it of our own. Your mother sounds remarkable. All those children and a dressmaker too. And your youngest brother is still only six or seven?"

"He's nearly seven."

"And there's a big gap between him and the next?"

"Ten years."

"There's planning." Rose whirred away.

A chuckle escaped through Ashling's lips. "Family planning? My parents never heard of it. Well, they did of course but they were—are—devout Catholics."

"And the Pope frowns on contraception, doesn't he?"

"To put it mildly. In our family it was called separate beds."

"You mean your parents…? But they're so young."

Ashling nodded. "After me, Colm, and the twins." She remembered the double bed leaving and two singles arriving.

Rose gave her a sidelong look. "And your little brother?"

The sewing machine buzzed inside Ashling's head. She remembered the two slim beds placed chastely side by side in her parents' room like strangers.

"Dermot was a surprise."

"You said that you practically brought him up. You were fourteen, fifteen?"

"I did all the nappies and later the feedings. I didn't mind."

"But that's not your job." Rose turned her attention back to her sewing. Her hand was growing steadier, her hems becoming straighter, she zigzagged less.

"I was the eldest."

Rose's eyebrows arched to crescent moons as her eyes flitted over Ashling's face. She delved into her cavernous sewing basket and extracted a pattern. "Wasn't that when you started to keep the family budget?"

"A little younger. I was good at maths so it made sense." Ashling heard the defensiveness in her voice. The constantly letting her family off the hook. She was struggling to regain custody of her mind from Rose's laser beam. "I have my own life, now, I'm free."

As soon as the words were out, she began to wonder. The blackness in her heart released the image she tried to keep buried there. Her father's hand reaching towards her. The no forming inside her and filling her up. Him violating her regardless. The flying vestments of Father Dempsey, his cocky evasions, and her certainty of his guilt, all mashing another layer onto the black.

Ashling sipped her coffee. The bitterness punished her throat.

"You certainly have a free spirit, my dear." Rose's voice sung along with her machine's rhythmic whirr and pulled Ashling's attention from the other side of the Atlantic. "You've set me on fire, and it's rubbing off on the men."

Ashling turned to Rose. She really was on fire. She was alive and fresh and engaged—an entirely different woman from the one Ashling first met. She appeared to have aged in reverse, like in a fairytale.

"I wouldn't be surprised if Lionel and Wilfred actually speak to each other one of these days," Rose said. She was floating on a slipstream of bobbins and wheels.

It occurred to Ashling that this moment now, Rose's rejuvenating self, was an instance worthy of record in the dance series. The moment of Rose's stroke was, of course, cataclysmic, but maybe this one should be the conclusion.

"Rose, how about I sketch you here at the sewing machine, in all this light?"

Rose straightened her neck, held it erect as a swan. She paused. "I think that would be fine."

Ashling shot up and raced towards the door.

"Ashling. There's a robe in your closet—"

"Yes." She recalled her shock at the first sight of it. She had pushed it to the far end of the wooden rung so that it was merely a flash of red now when she opened the door.

"I want you to have it."

Ashling remembered the plush silk, the delicate embroidery, the aura of richness. The sense of the robe being inhabited.

"It was handmade for me when I danced in Hong Kong. It will be longish on you, but I think it would be a wonderful painting robe."

Ashling's lips moved to formulate an objection.

"No discussion." Rose shot her index finger in the air. Her voice was teasing, but firm. "It's a gift."

The robe that had frightened her less than two months ago now appeared radiant. Ashling slipped it off the hanger, fed her arms through, and let it fall. It draped over her frame, adjusting itself to her size and curvature. The sleeves came just above her wrists, the length was almost to her ankles, and the sash gathered in the extra fabric gracefully, as if it had been made for her after all. Gazing in the mirror, she experienced a jolt of non-recognition. She was bonier than when she first arrived, her cheekbones more prominent, her eyes sea-green glassy mirrors. The robe was merely the culmination of the transformation.

Ashling returned to the living room with a sketch pad held aloft. Rose's lips parted in a gasp.

"You look as if you just stepped out of an ancient Chinese scroll."

She stretched out her arms and Ashling slid into them. Rose held her tight for several seconds and Ashling thought of Ava, the lost daughter. Moist eyelashes brushed her cheek.

Rose released her, lowered her lids, and busied herself with unraveling a bolt of fabric.

"I've always had a fantasy of sewing costumes for musical theatre." Her voice was ebullient.

Ashling paced, searching out the best angle to sketch from. "Well, I'm going to document you. An official start to your career as designer."

Rose's laugh was clear water rippling over stones.

"Versace watch out!" Ashling said and laughed with her. Her new robe crinkled and whooshed as she raised her arm to sketch.

Wilfred had just come home from work that Friday when Charlie arrived with another package, courtesy of Rose. Rose's voice was jittery with excitement as she handed Ashling the gold paper bag.

"Let's see it!"

Ashling reached in through the crinkly layers and extracted a blue cotton dress with a pattern of huge black ovals of different sizes. The label said Gucci. There was also a fine black leather belt. Ashling found her breath and raised her eyes to Charlie and Rose, the co-conspirators.

"It's beautiful." She shuddered to think what it cost.

"I saw it in *Elle*," Rose said, and she reached out and caressed the fabric. "Would you wear it for dinner?"

"I brought a new Chardonnay for us to try." Charlie held up a black and silver wine bottle. "Worth dressing up for."

"I feel like I'm in a film." Ashling laughed and ran off to her room.

In front of the mirror, she slipped the dress over her head and it fell languorously onto her shoulders. The top was loose and V-necked, and just barely covered her breasts. She gathered it in at the waist with the shiny belt. It was casual, yet stylish—Rose knew what suited her.

She emerged from the room as if striding down a runway. Rose clapped her hands with a squeal of delight. Charlie stood behind Rose and sent Ashling a secret smile. Wilfred gazed a moment, then lowered his eyes and mumbled, "very nice." Rose looked at her son and beamed, and Ashling wondered if Rose was dressing her for Wilfred.

"Let us dine," Rose announced, as if it were a special occasion. "*En famille*," she added.

Ashling walked ahead to the kitchen to help Lionel with the food. She knew Charlie thought the dress was sexy. Rose thought it was stylish and attractive. Wilfred was hiding whatever he thought, and she remembered his eyes glancingly on her breasts. She was happy, for once, to escape momentarily to Lionel, who, as far as she knew, had no designs on her at all.

In the coming weeks Ashling accumulated work at a rapid rate. In the Rose series, she had interwoven the hidden photographs, used them as a secret lore to draw on to explore the inner emotions. She wasn't painting directly from them, but they informed the shadow regions of the story of Rose's life and her trajectory as a dancer. She sorted and shuffled, fitting the pieces together like a puzzle, finding the right sequence, balancing the shadow and the substance.

Ashling was never still in her mind or body, even in bed at night. The pain inside her head never fully retreated but swung back and forth mimicking a metronome, marking her minutes, her hours, her days, her weeks. She dreamed her painting while she slept; twitching, turning, processing, piling up images in readiness for her waking. She continued to practice her judo every day and to incorporate her moves into a dance motion.

She shimmied around her easel, finding new ways to approach with her brush, jutting in and out at various angles.

Her Alcatraz-inspired work was also emerging—ever more expressively abstract with its muted tones and skewed angles. She had a notion that there was a model here for an approach to painting about the sexual coverups in Ireland. Priests, teachers, fathers, brothers. When she was really in her stride, she no longer was aware of herself and the canvas as separate. She was deep inside the painting.

Time, too, had taken on a new dimension. Her days of working with Rose, interacting with Lionel, negotiating her way around Wilfred, and her sensuous dance with Charlie had assumed their own quality and value. Her body and mind were interwoven with Charlie in a similar way to her relationship with her painting. She was the vortex of a swirling tornado. Her Rose paintings spiraled irrevocably towards the moment of the stroke, her Alcatraz ones towards some notion of escape and freedom, and in her temporal world, the touchdown would be the expiration date of her visa.

Ashling arrived at what appeared to be the last photo of Rose taken before her paralysis. Rose was radiant, at the height of her career, gazing out past the photographer into her future. The progression of photos and Ashling's paintings lead to this moment of apotheosis, coming before a shattering that no one could have foreseen. When Ashling extracted the photo from its frame, she found not one, but two others stacked behind it. The first was of an elderly woman—dark complexioned, curly hair, shriveled, face wrinkled. The other was of Charlie, taken several years before, holding the hand of a pretty, young woman. Ashling told herself the spike of jealousy in her chest was irrational. She knew that Charlie must have had lots of relationships.

The next time she sketched Rose, she showed her the photographs. Rose broke away from the sewing-machine and gazed at the images. "That's my mother. Poor *Mameleh*. She was grizzled with age." Tears glistened on Rose's feathery lashes.

It was time to ask. "Did she really die just a few days after your stroke?"

Rose nodded. "Mother was in dreadful health. She was a Holocaust survivor, smoked non-stop, and had emphysema. She was dying inside for years."

Ashling knew little about the Holocaust—a few lines in a history book, a shadowy idea about showers and death chambers. Now she was in the presence of a human being one remove from that horror. She would educate herself.

She looked at Rose. "I am so very sorry. And then she died right after your stroke?"

"Yes. The shock was too much for her. A last straw. She died with a cigarette in her mouth."

Ashling tried to imagine it—this woman with the furrowed face, sucking on the lifeline of a cigarette while her daughter's life as she knew it evaporated in a flash of horror.

Rose glanced at the other photo. Her sigh was a groan. "I was very fond of Serena."

Ashling waited. Breath held, hoping for more information, unable to ask.

"All of us were heartbroken when Charlie called off the engagement."

Ashling's heart started up a drumbeat. "Why did he break it off?"

Rose stared at the photos. "I don't know. They were away when I had my stroke. Couldn't be contacted."

Probably felt guilty for being out of reach, Ashling thought.

"Since then, he dates girls half his age. No fear of them working out."

Rose's words were acid shooting through Ashling's veins. This was why Charlie was keeping their relationship secret. She was another girl half his age. And maybe it was also why Rose, and Lionel acted as if they were not aware of the relationship—it was just part of a pattern.

"My men devoted themselves to me," Rose continued, in a ghostly whisper. "Maybe they thought they could cure me if they lavished enough attention on me."

The convoluted nature of this tapestry was becoming dimly visible to Ashling. Rose's stroke had ripped apart the family fabric, and they had all knotted themselves back together in a twisted weave. The words spurted out of her mouth before she could stop them. "I thought Jews talked openly and freely. Aren't you supposed to be great debaters, Talmudic, or something?"

Rose stared at her. "We are. We were in our family. That's one of the things that changed." A choked laugh escaped. "And aren't the Irish great talkers too?"

"God, no! Sure, we talk about everything under the sun except the things that are most intimate. And we're taught not to question, to accept everything on faith."

"I think we have guilt in common, isn't that the going belief?" The shadows were lifting from Rose's eyes, her brow unfurrowing.

"I suppose. I think Catholics have the added value of shame."

"Catholicism is pretty deep seated in Ireland, I understand."

"It's engrained. We're all completely immersed. I believed every word I was told until I was fourteen. Then I started questioning."

"Why then?"

Ashling stared at Rose. Remembered her fractured innocence. The whiskey breath of the priest in the confession box.

"I started to be aware of hypocrisy more. Girls, who everyone knew were pregnant by fathers or brothers or uncles, were whisked away for months. No one knew what happened to the babies."

"Things like that happen here too, of course."

"Right. But it's such a huge country maybe it can absorb it all? Ireland is so small it's like a pressure cooker. And so Catholic, it's stifling. And so remote it gets away with murder."

Ashling thought of the painting Charlie said reminded him of Diebenkorn. Of the girl with the dark cloud behind her head. The cloud of accumulated poison Ashling intuited all around her even before she was fully aware of it. The dark that had compelled her to leave.

"If it was that intense, was there a vacuum when you stopped believing? Our family was never religious, so I can only imagine. Needing to replace it with something."

Rose's words delivered a blow to her belly. "Like another religion?"

Rose shrugged. "Or anything."

"My little brother was born around then. I think I threw myself even more fiercely into family."

Ashling's skin grew chill. She had tried to drown out her shame of betraying her mother by becoming a mother to the whole family. Even though it was her father's fault. Then she tried to be a good nun for them. She did what Rose's men had done to her—made a fetish of family.

Rose ran her fingers along the sleek fabric she was cutting. "The funny thing is that you are the one who has come farthest toward helping me, Ashling. Because, in addition to caring, you're bold. You challenge me." Rose reached over and grasped her hand. "I know of course that I'll never walk again, but you've given me hope." She squeezed.

Ashling returned Rose's squeeze, then gently extricated her hand from her vise and massaged the grooves where the blood flow had been staunched.

GALLERY

August 14-15

Ashling curled up on the couch in the living room, comforted by Charlie's sounds from the kitchen—a cork popping, crystal clinking. Lionel and Rose had retired to bed, and Wilfred had disappeared after dinner. Ashling noticed he had started to go out on Saturday nights after Charlie arrived.

She opened her mother's latest letter.

Colm looks for work every day, poor chap, but the economy is still hopeless here...

We opened up your exam results as you asked. You got top marks. You're a great girl. You'd have your pick of schools now, pet. I'm sure we'd be able to give Sister Ignatius the push if you threw your hat in the ring for that posting. Wouldn't it be grand if you were the one to be teaching our Dermot? The poor little chap is already getting more asthma attacks with the prospect of going back to school.

Ashling laid down the letter. The skin on her back was clammy. Now, if she didn't come home, she'd not only be turning her back on a good sensible job that could keep her family afloat, but also leaving her innocent brother at the mercy of the sadistic Sister Ignatius.

Charlie arrived with a tray and glasses, and a dish with hummus and olives.

"You look like you've seen a ghost, is everything okay?"

She had never told Charlie about the pressure to teach. And now her family would like her to narrow it down to just her village of Timaleen and she'd never be free.

"Same news. I'm looking forward to that wine."

Charlie sat down. "Sure you're okay?"

She nodded. He poured her a glass and she sniffed and took a sip.

"It has a hint of…berries?" It was much easier to talk about wine. She liked the sudden rush to her head and the pleasant prickly dryness on the back of her tongue.

Charlie nodded. "Syrah was a favorite of Thomas Jefferson. He was an oenophile."

Ashling giggled. "I wonder if that question will come up on my citizenship exam." She munched on a Greek olive. "Any news?"

"They want further clarification—more information on the history of previous helpers and more details as to why you are unique."

"And no response from my application for the lottery visa, looks like."

Charlie shook his head. "No. But Bill said we should definitely re-submit. We won't give up."

Ashling sipped. She glanced sideways at her letter from home. She drank more wine.

Charlie's gaze wandered over to the sewing machine. "I can't believe Rose is sewing. And I'm still astounded that she let you paint her."

Charlie stroked her hair, but his eyes meandered back to the busy sewing station.

"I'll finish the series on Rose tomorrow. I'll be ready for you to see it," she told him. She knew the work was good.

Charlie turned back to her and raised his glass in a toast. "*Eccellente*! Here's to your painting. And to a successful visa application."

Ashling raised her glass but her arm was heavy. "You know, two weeks from Tuesday my visa expires, and my return ticket to Ireland is for that day."

Charlie nestled her hand in his and squeezed. "We're going to make this work whatever it takes."

Charlie was holding her hand in a vise grip, like Rose had. Maybe this was a feature of twins—identical gestures. She flashed on Rose telling the doctor that Ashling was her companion, and not answering when asked if it was short or long term. She wished Charlie was as vehement about getting her an art related job. Everything felt fragile now, but tomorrow, after he saw her painting, surely, he would switch his focus to helping her work in that direction.

Charlie poured more wine. Ashling drank deeply. As Charlie's kisses heightened in intensity, she imagined she was in a private lounge with her lover and let her worries slide away.

Morning sun rays crept through her curtains. Ashling hopped out of bed. She had slipped out of Charlie's room at an early hour and had hardly slept with the double excitement of her trembling body and the heady anticipation of showing him her work. It overshadowed her fear of being sucked back to Ireland and to a life she didn't want. A life that wasn't her own. And of whether she would ever be able to make love without black thoughts interfering.

She wrapped herself in Rose's robe and went straight to her easel to apply the finishing touches. The robe had become inseparable from her painting now. It inspired her. It carried a vestige of Rose's successful dancing days.

Ashling arranged the series as if she were showing it in a gallery. She used every available surface—the bookcase, the bed, the chair, the bedside table, the floor. The earliest paintings were near the door—they were the most naturalistic. As they progressed, the style changed, the figures were more apt to float and soar. Then, in the final few, the lines were less defined, the gestures expressing the internal dynamics of the subject. The painting of Rose's stroke appeared at first glance to be a blank canvas, but on close examination the dust particles that floated in the aftermath of Rose's big bang were clearly there. Then the last painting materialized as a faintly discernible figure emerging from what might have been a snowstorm, a force working its way towards the viewer, gaining definition, pushing out from the canvas. The whole series moved from the innocence and completeness of the child to a maturity, fragmentation, then a return.

She was ready.

Charlie tap-tapped just after 11a.m. and came in with a tray bearing steaming mugs of coffee and plates with *pain au chocolat*. He engulfed Ashling in a hug and kissed her softly—a morning kiss. His arms slid along the silky fabric, then he jerked back as if his fingers had been singed. His eyes widened. Ashling realized he hadn't seen her in the robe before.

"Rose gave it to me as a gift."

He continued to stare as if the robe were blinding him. He blinked. "Of course. Why not?" He gulped his coffee. "The last time I saw her in this she was skipping around her apartment, drinking coffee as we are now." His voice was high. He trained it down.

Ashling nodded. He was seeing a ghost. She wasn't sure if she should take it off.

"It looks great on you." There was a catch in his voice. "Okay, show time?"

She inhaled deeply, then led him to the first painting and explained the progression. She left him there. She eased herself onto the bed between two upright paintings, tucked her feet under her, and gathered the folds of the robe around her body. She felt like a geisha, offering up her artistic favors.

Charlie began his tour. He cast his eyes over the paintings, looking closely, examining, mumbling what sounded like affirmative noises, nodding. Ashling watched the back of his head and pushed down her anxiety. She sipped her coffee but was too nervous to do more than nibble at the pastry.

Having examined the first few paintings, Charlie came and planted a chocolaty kiss on Ashling's lips. So far, so good. Charlie continued his circumlocution of her room/gallery, and Ashling followed along, remembering the creation of each piece, the progression of the series.

The ones he was looking at now were where the secret photos began to push into the open and exert their influence, where the layers of subtext piled up, and her painting process had become more dancelike. She noticed that Charlie was lingering longer over these. His back was straighter, his chin jutted out, his sounds grew softer. As he rounded the corner towards where she was poised on the bed, he was so focused that he jumped when he saw her—he appeared to have forgotten she existed. She thought that was a good sign.

Charlie refocused back on the painting to her right, seemed to breathe it in, then continued at the pace of a 500-year-old turtle to move to the next, and the next again, as he turned the corner towards the final few. Ashling glanced again at Charlie, but this time all of her attention was riveted on him. His back was a taut sheet stretched to breaking, his neck an iron rod. He seemed to barely be breathing.

Charlie stepped in front of the painting of Rose's stroke. His upper body snapped back as if he had been pushed on the chest. Ashling sprung to her knees. Charlie readjusted his spine and continued to peer at the painting. He moved in closer, he stepped away, then he settled center, still as an obelisk. If she hadn't been afraid to send a word into the forbidding silence, she would have asked if he was all right. He seemed to stand there for an eternity. She raised her coffee to her lips, was unable to drink, and eased her mug back onto the nightstand. The faint sound stirred Charlie, and he turned slowly around.

Ashling was shocked when she saw Charlie's face. His features had gathered into a set posture. His amber eyes were dull, his jaw hard, his skin pale. A light had gone off inside.

"There's some good work here, Ashling…" The voice was cold and formal, a stab to her chest.

She stared. She swallowed the lump in her throat, gathered up the folds of her robe, jumped off the bed, and faced him. "You don't like it." The words spilled out. She had seen his reaction with her own eyes, and he was clearly moved.

Charlie stood still and continued as if speaking from memorized notes. "I do like your work—in general."

"What do you mean—in general?" Ashling inhaled deeply. Of course, this was about Rose, but… "How can you like my work 'in general' and...what?..not 'in specific?'"

"I don't have to like everything you do."

"Of course, you don't. But I thought you said I was improving."

"It takes years and—"

"Maybe I'm losing perspective." Ashling was striding around the room now, building up momentum. "I know it will take years for me to grow and develop, but I really thought this work was good."

"It's hard to judge your own—"

"Charlie. You're speaking in platitudes."

"I believe I was the one who encouraged you."

Ashling stopped. "Of course, you...I...." Her pulse was racing. She remembered her family back home, her mother's grateful letters. "You've been so good to me, and my family...I didn't mean..." She calmed her breathing. Charlie was a powerful man—he held sway in art circles. Her whole future was at stake. She couldn't say something stupid that might jeopardize it.

Charlie crossed over to her and drew her head to his shoulder. He led her to the bed, eased her down, and sat beside her. A wave of exhaustion swept over Ashling. She knew in her gut what had just happened, but she couldn't call Charlie on it. It would be defying him. Nothing he had said was a plausible criticism because he didn't have a professional response. How could she fight the ghost of Rose?

Heavy as concrete, her head drooped, found the pillow and she sank into its softness.

"Ashling, you know I'm heading back to the city early today, but I'll be back up Friday." He continued to speak, but the words sifted through a thick filter. She didn't move. She heard soft footsteps padding across the floor and was on the threshold of nothingness when the door clicked shut.

Ashling slept through the afternoon and into the evening. Her sleep was restless. Her stomach rumbled and as she regained some semblance of consciousness, she remembered she hadn't eaten anything since the pastry Charlie had brought. Still, she didn't have the energy to get up. A bell rang in her head, and she squeezed the pillow against her ears to drown it out. She saw a flash of blue pants by her bedside and screamed. Then she heard Lionel's voice and saw him standing beside her.

"I knocked, several times," he said.

The bell really was ringing—the actual contraption above the bed.

"Sorry, Rose has had a relapse," Lionel said. Ashling could hear the raspy cough from the next room.

When Lionel left, Ashling roused herself. The room came into focus—her own private gallery showing, which had been a total failure. The scattered work looked forlorn—it had absorbed the sting of Charlie's rejection. Her insides were a blighted van Gogh sun.

The letter from her mother on the bedside table caught her eye, the familiar pink notepaper.

...Breda and Brona give out to me for comparing them to you. They say I'm holding them to too high a standard. Everyone is so proud of you, Ashling, for doing so well in so short a time.

If they could see me now. Eyes blurry, hair askew, hopes in shreds.

You're saving our lives here, love, and we'll never be able to thank you enough.

She tried to block out her mother's voice. A huge anger rose inside her towards her family, a red-hot flush, fanning outwards from her heart. She threw on her robe and dragged herself to Rose's room.

CORRESPONDANCES

August 17

Ashling stood over the kitchen stove and stared at the butter spitting in the frying pan. She slid in the slices of bacon. She thought of all the work that had gone into her paintings of Rose. She wondered if Charlie would ever be able to see beyond the tragedy of his sister's paralysis.

Ashling was in a daze, picturing her own face in the bottom of the pan burning around the edges when Lionel raced in, and grabbed the pan from her. The flames rose up and slashed the sides. The bacon was a charred mess.

Rose's whistle sounded from the bedroom, and Lionel dumped the pan in the sink. The whistle shrieked again and mashed in Ashling's head with her internal bells—soon she'd have a full orchestra in there.

Later that day, exhausted from Rose's constant calling, Ashling returned to the kitchen and took a scrubber to the burnt pan.

She had a sudden need for a cup of tea.

She veered over to a cabinet, stood, forgot why she was there. She walked back to the sink and resumed scraping the pan. She remembered the tea and put the kettle on the stove. Then she dedicated her entire heft to scouring.

The smell of burning curled around her nostrils. She heard the sizzle and swung around to see the tongues of fire flicking against the sides of the tea kettle. The water had burned dry. She snatched up a towel, grabbed the blackened kettle from the stove and shoved it under the tap. The pulsing heat seared her fingers through the nubby fabric. She was going out of her mind.

Ashling's breath rapped to the rhythm of the speeded-up thrum in her head. The pressure from a summer spent mostly indoors pushed against the inside of her skull. She jammed her palms into her temples to stop the bursting—the charm of Charlie's seduction, her painting frenzy, the fear of mauling mountain lions and dive-bombing crows, the locked windows and doors.

In her bedroom she opened the curtains and glanced out. No lurking shapes out there. She hadn't heard much about the Peeping Tom lately and had forgotten about him in the melee. She gathered up her easel and Alcatraz sketches and stepped outside her room. Gentle snores wafted from Rose and Lionel's room as she tiptoed down the hallway, found the key, and opened the front door.

Ashling suctioned in a breath when her foot touched the earth. Nothing blew up in her face. No guard squad materialized from the bushes to force her back inside. She closed the door behind her and paced to find a good spot for her easel. She remembered the day she visited Alcatraz, and her fantasy of prisoners lined up on the prison island facing San Francisco, painting. She might as well be on a prison island herself now, she had no idea how to physically leave this house and get somewhere, anywhere. To San Francisco. She remembered she was somewhere in Mendocino County. She peered into the bushes to find the start of the driveway but couldn't see an opening. She settled in to painting. *En plein air,* like her Irish predecessors.

When Ashling heard Lionel's footsteps in the hall she opened the door and walked inside. She glimpsed him disappearing into the kitchen—like the White Rabbit again.

"How is she?" she asked.

Lionel looked at her through bloodshot eyes. "Weaker. If she doesn't improve by tonight, we'll call the doctor. She said she'd like your hot lemon drink."

Ashling put the water on to boil. She inhaled down to the tips of her toes. "I'm painting outside today." She waited.

Lionel sliced a lemon wedge. He didn't speak. Maybe he was too exhausted to care. Or maybe he just didn't.

Ashling was completely immersed in her painting and lost track of the passing hours. Wilfred emerged from the camouflage of bushes and stopped, staring at her. She gasped.

"I didn't hear a car. Don't you get dropped off?"

"My buddies won't drive up; I have to walk it."

"Is it that scary?"

"It's not actually a driveway. More like a dirt road. You've been on it."

"Only the night I came here but I was asleep." She cleared her throat. "I was thinking of taking a walk there now, I didn't get to my judo workout today."

"It's a bit tricky. Would you like me to come with you after I check on mom?"

Ashling got goose bumps. She was in some kind of skewed universe—maybe everyone in the house really was friendly and would be fine if she just left, and all of her fears were phantoms.

She walked with Wilfred and looked for the place he had emerged from. The path came through the trees, and then turned at a sharp forty-five-degree angle, so that from the house it looked like a continuous row of foliage. As they stepped into the lane Ashling saw what Wilfred meant—the driveway was mostly gravel and dirt, and the trees formed a canopy above. It also zigzagged in such a way that every few feet it looked like it came to a dead end. "I'm getting dizzy just walking," she said.

"Yep. It's a maze."

"Do you have a long walk to the end?" she asked.

"About 17 minutes. It's fine in the light, but I've gotten lost sometimes after dark. And I've done it a million times."

The thought of being on this lane in the black night sent Ashling's skin crawling. What if she had to escape? Would she have the guts? Not one person in the world outside of this household had a notion where she was. She didn't even know where she was herself.

Beeps and bells aroused Ashling over and over again throughout the night. Rose's chest heaved; her cough scraped her ribs. Ashling heard choruses of male voices as she finally drifted off to sleep. She thought of Charlie, how he had betrayed her trust with his response to her painting. It was a kind of lie—a lie of the spirit. Had he lied about other things—about the work he was doing on her visa, having a pal in Immigration, keeping her in mind for the gallery job? About his feelings for her?

The following morning, wrapped in her robe, her eyelids drooping from exhaustion, Ashling sat in a chair by Rose's bed. The doctor had come, diagnosed bronchitis, and started Rose on a course of antibiotics. The fringed lamp cast shadows on the floor and walls. Rose, propped up on pillows, held on to Ashling's hand. Wilfred sat in the dim corner, leafed through a magazine, and cast worried glances at his mother. Lionel stood beside Ashling's chair and withdrew a thermometer from under Rose's tongue.

"99.7—getting back to normal." He shook the slim rod.

Rose looked at him with feverish eyes. "Why is it that I always get sick right after my annual checkup? And this time it happened twice."

"It's a coincidence, Mother," Wilfred said, and stood up. Ashling could feel his breath on her neck.

"Coincidence, my foot. I go through this every *fershtunkineh* year," Rose said.

"You can't blame Dr. Talbot, Rosie." Lionel's voice was clear and firm.

Rose jerked her head. "And why not? The same doctors were useless after my stroke. People do recover from strokes, why not me?" Her voice had an edge of hysteria. She squeezed Ashling's hand.

Wilfred moved closer to the bed and his leg touched Ashling's shoulder. She shifted but had nowhere to go—her chair was pinned against the bed frame. Wilfred formed a boundary on one side, Lionel on the other, and Rose held her hand like she would never let go.

"You know they did their best, Momma. It was too late by the time they arrived," Wilfred said. And his voice, too, sounded stronger. The men were starting to stand up for themselves.

Rose's shoulders quivered with a mounting rage. "Speaking of too late, if it weren't for you," she glared at her son, "my little girl might be alive."

Wilfred dropped. He listed to the side against Ashling, and she didn't dare stir.

"Rose, you're exhausted, you need to rest." Lionel's voice was concerned but strong. The pitiful tone was gone. "And that's the fever talking, Rosie. You know he was just a boy."

Rose squinted at Lionel as if trying to bring him into focus or figure out who he was. "You're the one who's hardly spoken to him since she died."

Ashling expected Lionel to cower under the assault, but instead he straightened up. "I couldn't bring myself to talk about it—to anyone," he said.

A prickly silence settled in the room. Both Wilfred and Lionel placed their hands on the back of Ashling's chair and she had a sensation of being surrounded—an intertwining of lattice arms at her back and Rose in front. Rose was fuming. Air whooshed through her lips. Her nails dug in and out of Ashling's palm.

No one spoke.

Gradually Rose's breathing calmed, and her fingers switched to a stroking motion. She glanced up at Ashling, at her husband and son. Her eyes softened, lost their slant, and a smile escaped from her lips as she found the tone she was searching for. A silent one.

Lionel and Wilfred both looked at Ashling and lifted their hands to rest them on her shoulders. She exhaled relief, knowing that some iota of progress had been made. Rose's husband and son were starting to break away from their dogged allegiance to her. Maybe Charlie, her twin brother would follow suit.

Ashling's bones suddenly felt heavy with the burden of daughterhood. Wilfred and Lionel's hands were leaden on her shoulders. She maintained a stillness for a few moments, then touched both men's hands briefly, lifted them from her and stood up. Wilfred faltered and re-adjusted himself. Ashling leaned in, kissed Rose on the forehead. Rose gave her a soft pat on the cheek. Ashling's brain cleared—a veil had been lifted. Her posture was straight and her movement effortless as she turned and walked from the room.

Ashling entered her bedroom. Her paintings of Rose pulsed with life and reached out like old acquaintances. She circumnavigated the room, moving back and forth, in and out of sequence, looking at each painting. She fell into slow motion judo, raising her legs in dancelike kicks, circling her arms in twists and sinuous curls. She viewed the paintings from stillness and from motion, drawing in an impression of them all, singular and combined.

She saw that the works were as much about herself as they were about Rose. She had stretched and deepened as a painter while she traced Rose's own progression as a ballerina. Rose's dance work had increased in complexity as she matured and trained and performed, and Ashling's, in her own way, had gone through a growth spurt that summer as she encountered new experiences and crossed new thresholds. She thought it ironic that a turning point for Rose was the sorrow and despair over the loss of her daughter, a personal tragedy that had eventually deepened her artistry, and that Ashling herself had been painting this profound pain as she herself struggled to face up to the loss of her own innocence and girlhood.

Rose's stroke had been literally a death blow to her mother, but metaphorically it was one to Charlie, and to Lionel and Wilfred. Ashling knew how dedicated Charlie was to Rose, and she admired that. One thing she understood was family loyalty.

She had been too stricken in the moment of Charlie's rejection of her paintings to be objective. It still hurt that he had discounted her work, but how could he be neutral?

She executed a sharp judo kick into the air and emitted a cry. "Ha!" She had more artillery in her artistic arsenal. She marched over to the first Rose painting and turned its face to the wall. Then she moved on to the next, and with deft strokes, like reversing a pack of cards, she swiveled each painting around, so their backs faced the room. From the closet she retrieved and set up her series on Alcatraz. She still found it hard to believe they were hers—they were so far removed from anything she could have conceived when she arrived in this house. She had experimented with neutral shades of brown and black and grey, and with linear, geometric shapes, austere compositions, and intense tones.

In her Alcatraz work, Ashling had attempted to look at the world she was painting straight on and not allow her senses to interfere, but beneath the surface all was chaotically shifting. She had painted in a frenzy, as her senses—gustatory, visual, tactile—were deliciously crammed. Her world was also filled with the corollary—Rose's demands, Lionel's hazing, Wilfred's wanting, all of their projections, her own haunting—and this must have embedded in her work as well. She flashed on Baudelaire's *Correspondances*, where he wrote of the confusion of and interrelationship between the senses—*Ayant l'expansion des choses infinies...qui chantent les transportes de l'esprit et des sens.* The mysterious relationship between everything in the universe, the transport of the spirit.

As she arranged her paintings around the room, her second gallery showing, Ashling allowed all of these thoughts to flit through her consciousness, to land, to linger, to take off again, to return. Her Alcatraz series was an expression of what her insides were like as she wandered through this strange house posing as a normal human being.

EN PLEIN AIR

August 20

Ashling straightened her spine and let her whole body fully own Rose's robe as she approached the kitchen. Charlie was bent over the coffee grinder, shoulders sloped, cowed. She inhaled the rich aroma and vowed not to be tempted by that coffee.

Charlie glanced up from under his eyelids. "Rose's antibiotics have kicked in, but I'm going to hang out for a few days just to be sure." Ashling detected an undertone of apology.

"Coffee?" he asked.

She shook her head and filled the tea kettle with water.

"Ashling." His voice was pained. "I was…terrified when I saw your paintings of Rose. You managed to capture…the interior." His voice cracked. "And it hit me, how much we gave up afterwards."

He turned to face her, his eyes glinting. "I'm sorry."

She nodded.

She turned away from his handsome face and opened the tea caddy. "I'm nearly finished with my Alcatraz series."

Charlie gaped. "You have another series? You must have been painting non-stop."

She looked boldly into his eyes. "You did promise me a painting retreat, Charlie. Unless I'm needed today, I'd like to carry on. I'm finishing the last one."

He blinked. "That's fine."

The water spit and squealed as she splashed it into the teapot. The tea leaves released their earthy aroma, battling it out with the flashy North Beach beans.

Ashling carried her easel and canvas outside and set them up a short distance from the house. She returned to her room and loaded up her arms with supplies. Rose caught a glimpse of her as she passed the living room.

"You're painting outside?" Rose's eyes were wide. Her color was high and her voice excited.

"Lionel. Maybe I could venture out for a spell while Ashling is there. The fresh air would be good for my lungs. I could get… acclimatized."

Ashling realized she wasn't the only one who had hardly set foot outside of the house all summer. Who knows how long Rose had kept herself cooped up?

"If you're really sure Rosie…" Lionel's first words were halting, like the old Lionel, and then he continued in his more assured voice. "You're right. You could start with ten minutes."

Ashling remembered her half joking thought about them being vampires.

Wilfred emerged from his room carrying a large object wrapped in a white sheet of paper.

"Aren't you going to work?" Ashling asked.

"I'm taking a few days off to help out with Mom." He handed her the packet, and Wilfred offered to hold her supplies. "It's a gift for you," he said.

Ashling couldn't stop the warm flush to her cheeks. She peeled back the wrapping and revealed a handcrafted wooden easel. "Oh, it's beautiful."

He smiled, lowering his eyes. "Will I set it up for you?"

"Yes, thank you."

Stranger and stranger, Ashling thought.

Lionel took hold of the handles of the wheelchair and Rose dangled her wrist in the air. "Ashling, hold my hand please."

Charlie stepped into the hall and Wilfred returned and stood in the living room archway. Rose closed her eyes, took in a huge breath, Lionel pushed her chair, and they processed in tiny increments over the threshold as if they were the royal family making an exit.

As she encountered the light, Rose gradually raised her lids and exhaled in a steady stream, "hhhmmmmm." She patted Lionel's hand. "Go, dear. I'll be fine with Ashling here."

Lionel kissed Rose on top of her head and Ashling unglued her eyes as quickly as she could—she had never seen Lionel show any physical affection in the entire time she had been in the house. He went in, and Ashling had the feeling that the three men were all standing just inside the hallway, looking out. Then she heard their footsteps as they went about their business.

Ashling set up her canvas and arranged her brushes in preparation for painting. She shuffled her sketches, studied each one, mixed paints, studied the sketches some more. She applied a brush stroke. And another. Wilfred's easel was sturdy—much easier to paint on than the flimsy fold-up one she had been using. She realized that she had forgotten a couple of drawings and turned to go inside. Rose looked at her, startled.

"I'm just popping in—"

"No!" Rose's pupils expanded into little black moons.

"I'll be back in a jiffy."

"Don't leave me." Her voice had an edge of panic.

A timer dinged inside the house and Lionel sprinted out. He looked from Rose to Ashling. "Ten minutes, Rosie. Have you had enough?" Ashling still found his new, or old, confident voice a bit of a shock.

Rose exhaled. She grew calmer. "For my first time, yes." Lionel wheeled her back in.

Maybe she has an allergy to light, Ashling thought. That would explain the drawn curtains all over the house. She dashed in, retrieved the drawings, and focused back on her canvas. She stole a glance at where she thought the concealed entrance to the driveway was, then turned all her attention to her painting.

Ashling could hear the whirr of Rose's sewing-machine from time to time, and the chatter of the men in the kitchen. Like Magritte's painting, *Les valeurs personelles,* in the San Francisco museum, where the blue sky and white clouds formed the interior walls of the room, inside and outside were reversed. It was strange to be the one on the outside. If she wanted to leave she could walk down that driveway—if she could find her way.

Ashling's painting was a rendition of the image she'd had of Alcatraz prisoners lined up in front of easels, facing San Francisco. The figures that emerged were viewed from behind, and the line extended off the canvas into infinity. Some of them gazed directly ahead, others were absorbed in their art. She noticed her own body was leaning towards the secret driveway.

Rose came out again in the afternoon and read. From time to time, she took a deep gulp of air.

She glanced over at Ashling's canvas. "It just dawned on me that I haven't seen any of your paintings—too wrapped up in my own misery. That's not my series, is it?"

Ashling explained it was the last painting in a second series—that the dance one was complete.

"I want to see them. Is that all right?"

A current of trepidation zipped through Ashling. She nodded. "Yes. I might even finish this series tomorrow afternoon if I can keep going."

"I have all my men here for a few days, so you keep on painting, my dear. I'll have a little family party tomorrow night—sort of a reception and show your paintings. We'll make the men do all the work."

That evening, Rose and Charlie planned the reception. Ashling had painted nonstop all day, pushing away thoughts of Charlie, and felt like a pressure cooker when the steam was building. She was bursting with the effort of avoiding him.

"Want to take a short walk, Wilfred?" She hoped it sounded casual.

Wilfred shot up, and Ashling caught the ghost of a smile on Rose's lips as they walked together down the hall.

As soon as they opened the door, they both shivered with cold.

"Let's see what's in the hall closet." Wilfred opened the door and shuffled through the clothes. He found a sweater belonging to Rose and handed it to Ashling. He grabbed a jacket for himself and it hung loosely on his frame.

"It's way too big on you," Ashling said.

Wilfred nodded. He pulled a huge waterproof cape off a hanger. "Look at that. I haven't used it since we moved from New York."

"It would fit two of you, now." Ashling laughed. Wilfred stashed it away in the back of the closet.

Ashling stepped outside. Her eyes acclimatized, and she saw the pinpricks of stars and the barely perceptible arc of the moon. A smidgeon of light escaped from the tightly drawn living room curtains.

"Do you wanna walk around the house?" Wilfred asked.

Ashling looked at the looming tree shapes. "It's a bit boring going around in circles, I'd like to walk the driveway path."

They headed for the entrance, Ashling trying to steer herself as much as being steered. They made the sharp forty-five-degree turn and were immediately plunged into darkness. She had the sudden rush of cold fear, the head spinning and sensation of falling that she always felt in the pitch dark. She gasped.

"Are you okay?" Wilfred reached out and touched her arm.

She managed some sound and eased away from him. "Whoever designed this?"

"My mother spruced up the existing design. She wanted to put off anyone from finding us, and I guess we did everything she wanted." There was a note of criticism in his voice she had never heard before.

Ashling's heart went out to Wilfred, for what he had given up. Then she checked her own heart. She had to curb this feeling—that she had a responsibility to make everything all right for everyone else. What Rose said was true—it wasn't Ashling's obligation to parent her parents or her siblings. And, neither was it her obligation to stay with Rose or help her men. Wilfred was perhaps on the road to figuring out what he had sacrificed. Charlie could at least see he'd been blinded by the intensity of his involvement with Rose. Lionel seemed like he might be starting to relate to Rose like a husband and lover, rather than a nursemaid and lackey. And Rose was on some forward journey.

Ashling came face to face with a tall black mass of trees, and Wilfred held her lightly by the elbow and directed her around. She dared to look to the right and left—dense forest as far as the eye could see. Black upon black. "That compass you made with the diamond jewel-bearing would come in handy now," she said with the voice of a little girl. She glanced up, searching out the moon. Wilfred's eyes followed hers to the sliver. "A waning crescent. We're a few days past the Gibbous," he said.

"Oh." Ashling breathed easier. She could be a character in an Edwardian novel, stepping out with her cousin—it seemed silly now that she'd ever thought he might be a Peeping Tom.

"The cycle is winding down," she said.

He nodded. "We're nearly at the New Moon."

"The Dark Moon." Ashling shivered.

"Are you cold?"

She shook her head.

"Ashling." His voice was so low she had to incline her head towards him. "My mother really hopes you'll stay." There was a trail of wistfulness to the words—his mother wasn't the only one who hoped that. Ashling pulled the sweater tight around her chest and walked on, her footsteps crunching the gravel. She stole a glance at Wilfred—a boy in an overgrown jacket lost in a dream. He caught her gaze and smiled shyly.

She heard a car whizz by, and stopped, arrested by the sudden sound.

"This is where I meet my buddies in the mornings," Wilfred said.

They were standing on the edge of the woods, looking at a two-lane road. Ashling's body froze. She cleared a constriction in her throat. "How far is work from here?"

"Willits. About 40 minutes."

The mention of an actual place name was a blow to Ashling's solar plexus—though she had a clue from the newspaper heading, she had become used to thinking of her location as nameless. As a prison. But there was the road out.

"Not much traffic," she said, as casually as she could.

Wilfred laughed. "Who would want to come out here? The gas station up there is an unofficial stop—if someone wants to get the Greyhound to the City."

"San Francisco?" She could see the red and yellow of the gas pumps.

"Yep. Gets in early evening to the City. I went with my buddy once and we stayed overnight at a hostel."

"I remember it was a long trip when I came up with Charlie," Ashling said. "Maybe four and a half hours."

"It's even longer on the bus because of the stops."

So, it left sometime in the early afternoon from the gas station. It felt important to Ashling that she had a map for a way to leave of her own accord.

From somewhere deep in the trees there was a distant yowl. It could have been a mountain lion, or a coyote. Ashling's fear flew back, and she instinctively moved closer to Wilfred. Their arms brushed, and she felt him quiver. She inched away as imperceptibly as she could.

"I'm ready to go back now," she whispered.

He nodded. "You lived out in the country in Ireland. Wasn't it dark there?"

"We were near the ocean so there were usually lights from the coast." And she made sure never to be out alone on the night of the Dark Moon.

Ashling decided she was going to walk the path alone that night and test herself. The thought turned her insides black with fear. She stepped into the shower to waken her senses. She couldn't let stupid nerves stop her. She thought about her Alcatraz paintings, the depths of blackness, the layers of fear. She eased off the hot water tap, increased the cold, eased off more on the warm, added more cold, tried to keep her gasps quiet as she shuddered, thinking her lungs would burst. She managed three minutes under the icy splinters.

Ashling set her alarm for 3 a.m. and laid her travel clock by the pillow. She woke up just before it was due to ring and turned it off. She slipped on her judo pants and her jacket, picked up her flip-flops, and tiptoed to the door. She pried it open and closed it behind her. She listened and heard gentle waves of breathing. She crept down the hall to the door. She found the key and let herself out.

A blast of darkness smacked her, and she sought out the moon. She tiptoed in the general direction of the driveway entrance and hit a blank wall of trees. She reoriented herself, groping with her fingers, a little to the right and to the left, until finally her hand fell through the opening. She took the deepest possible breath, and stepped in. The darkness engulfed her. She stifled the urge to scream, grabbed a tree branch to stop the sensation of falling, leveled her breath, and forced herself on. She groped through the pathway that she had tried to memorize on the walks with Wilfred. After the second turn she wanted to go back but pushed each leaden foot in front of the other. Whether she ever needed to do this or not, she wanted the satisfaction of knowing she could. Leave. And face down the dark.

She walked blind, navigating the path, right, then left, then right. She stopped herself from leaning on the moon—its light would be gone completely in a few days. She made it to the end of the path and stopped. Her stomach lurched. She breathed in the black air and turned back around.

Ashling arrived at the house breathless and trembling. She willed her fingers not to shake as she turned the key. She stole to her room. She was filled with the darkness.

She crossed to her Alcatraz paintings and placed them in order, thinking of the viewing the next evening. She had half consciously brought them into being, crafted and modulated them to a certain pitch and intensity, and now, the skewed angles, brown and grey palette, shadowy figures crouching behind bars or barely visible in corners, were screaming back at her. The bars put her in mind of the portcullis in the castle near her home in Ireland. In medieval times, the owners dropped it down to keep enemies from entering, but they also had a second portcullis which could be used to trap someone attempting to escape. The second portcullis had been lowered in this house, and she was trapped, peering through the latticed grille. But it was dawning on her that her jailer was actually herself.

She had thought the painting she just completed was the end of the series. Now she felt it wasn't. It needed one more. She lay down on the bed. She crashed into sleep and dreamed of the deep black cell in Alcatraz. She dreamed the cell was in her heart.

COUP DE FOUDRE

August 21-24

Charlie eased the cork out of the bottle, and when it popped, poured the champagne into crystal flutes. He raised his glass. "To Ashling!"

Her paintings were arranged as in a gallery. Ashling felt strangely numb as she clinked glasses with Rose and the men, all of them a study in black and white elegance. She sat and sipped, adorned in her new Gucci dress. They sampled the hors d'oeuvres.

They began with the series on Rose. Charlie was much calmer this time—he knew what to expect. Rose, Lionel, and Wilfred drank in the paintings. They made low sounds of approbation or affection at the earlier ones of Rose as a child, admiration in the middle and flowering period, then drew quieter towards the end. The hair rose on the back of Ashling's neck when Rose mentioned yin yang, light and dark, balance. She, herself was floating in an in-between space, with no clue what was going to come next.

When Rose approached the painting that depicted the moment of her stroke, she halted, and applied the brakes on her chair. The three men turned towards her. Rose leaned in to the canvas, she narrowed her eyes, she inched closer. They all watched.

She turned to Ashling. Her eyes were crystal moons. "How could you know what it was like?" Ashling returned her gaze. She had imagined a searing blast, like a bomb or a fire. And then the floating debris.

"The punishing flashes of light that set my brain on fire…" Rose's lips were a quivering bow. "Just the fact that you cared about painting me was enough—that the work is so good is a bonus."

Ashling's cheeks were aflame. "Thank you."

"Imagine all this in a gallery, Chas. I'm not the expert, but it looks fabulous to me."

Charlie nodded. "It is."

Ashling's insides roiled with confused emotion. She squeezed out a smile, and stood up, splashing her champagne. She tore off a corner of baguette and chewed to soothe her gut.

"I was really drawn to Alcatraz when I took the trip to San Francisco," Wilfred said. "You've captured the beauty of the place, but also the eeriness."

"Did you volunteer to be locked inside the solitary confinement cell?" Ashling asked.

"No. I passed." Wilfred laughed. "I remember the remains of the plumbing, and the factoid about the warm showers."

"Right. They weren't allowed cold water."

Rose peered at the painting of the prisoners at their easels. "Why not?"

"So they couldn't toughen up. The water in the bay is freezing," Wilfred said.

"Though it didn't stop them trying to escape, anyway," Ashling added.

"They're trying in this last painting." Rose narrowed her eyes. "It's fairly abstract, but that's what I get."

Charlie also looked closely at the painting. He turned to Ashling. "Is the series done?"

Her heart drummed in her ears. "I'm thinking now that it's not, though I haven't a notion what the last one should be."

Charlie's question confirmed Ashling's hunch. Like the children in fairytales, she had one final task to complete before she felt free to leave. A wave of nausea coursed through her and she swallowed hard and coughed.

"Water?" Lionel asked, and placed a hand on her shoulder.

She shook her head. "Air."

"I'll take you outside," Charlie said.

Ashling stood close to Charlie in the dark beyond the house. The light spilled through the living room curtains and she could hear the excited voices from inside. Charlie took her arm and steered her further away from the entrance. She didn't want to feel the tingle—she intuited a need to keep a separation from him. She didn't have much time. She was in a race between finishing, leaving this place, and getting on a plane, or not. And there was Charlie.

"Ashling." The way he said her name, like music, caused her heart to sway.

"When Rose had her stroke…I was on vacation with my fiancée. I left no contact information. I did that a lot, then." He lowered his eyes.

Ashling took in a deep breath. She and Charlie were even more alike than she had thought—feeling guilty for things that weren't really their fault and compensating by excessive loyalty to family. Maybe this would be a bond if it could be made healthy.

"You know I have a return ticket to Ireland for a week from Tuesday, the same day my visa expires," she said.

Charlie touched her shoulder and set off shimmerings of desire. "You can't leave us." His voice was naked and urgent, and Ashling felt he was right. She couldn't leave, not yet. She was beginning to dimly perceive all the connections between this family and her birth one, to see the patterns she had replicated, the dependency engendered, but if she got on the plane to Ireland in ten days, she would just be running full circle. No one would believe her word over that of Father Dempsey or Reverend Mother—the Church really did rule the State. Even if someone believed her, it would take a revolution to make a dent in the armor of religion. Her art would be her contribution, but she needed to resolve her own maelstrom first.

"You're so right about the Alcatraz series needing another piece," she said. It was one of the reasons she was so attracted to Charlie. His eye. His judgment—when he was honest.

"And it's good enough to exhibit," Charlie said.

Ashling thought she might elevate like a rocket—shoot away and join the stars. His lips were on her neck. He looked smolderingly handsome, and she had a mad desire to grab him by the hand, plunge headlong into the darkness, and make wild love in the deepest woods.

She suddenly remembered her black cell dream. That was it! The last painting. Blackness.

The voices from inside grew louder. "I'm not sure tonight is a good night," Charlie whispered, his voice dusky with desire. Ashling nodded. "They're all keyed up, alert," she said.

When they went back in, Rose and Lionel and Wilfred were still chattering with excitement. Ashling excused herself quickly and said her goodnights.

Inside her room, Ashling grabbed her sketch pad. Her hand zigzagged across the surface. She was sizzling with thoughts of the black cell she had to paint. She didn't know if it was the Alcatraz cell, a small box of a room with a metal door that allowed not a smidgeon of light. Or one room in an endless row of rooms. She continued to draw deep into the night and slept with sketches strewn like leaves atop her sheets.

Next morning, Ashling set up her easel outdoors. Rose sat in the wheelchair a short distance away and read.

Ashling looked at her painting in progress. It wasn't right yet. It looked enough like a cell, and the shades of grey and black were working to create shadows and menace. She made her brush move; had faith it would help her find her way.

Rose closed her book and turned her chair towards the house. "I'm going to try again in the afternoon," she said.

"Is it getting easier?"

"The fear, you mean? High noon is hardest in summer—the light can be intense."

"Does it...physically...hurt you?" Ashling wasn't sure if they were talking about light or fear.

"These days they call it post-traumatic stress. Strong light can bring back that first moment of horror." Rose glanced over at Ashling. "You painted it somehow, and I hadn't spoken to you about it. Not about that moment."

Ashling paused her brush. She was painting a sky over ocean beyond the Alcatraz cell—a white dash. She had been thinking about escape, that she had to be able to paint the possibility of escape before she could feel free in her heart.

"Rose, I really don't know exactly how I did that, in your painting."

Rose's breath jerked.

"Are you all right?" Ashling crossed to her side.

"Yes." Rose calmed her breathing. "I'm fighting it."

"The fear?"

"The fear, terror maybe, of the light."

Ashling held Rose's trembling hand. Though she had intuited Rose's horror in that moment of the stroke as a blinding blast, her imagination had never extended to anyone actually having a fear of light.

Darkness, yes. That one she knew all too well.

Ashling guessed it was late morning by the spikes of light pushing through the bedroom curtains. The whispering voices from the living room were low and intense. Lionel's and Wilfred's had the new edge of confidence, Rose sounded less imperious, Charlie more vulnerable. As she stood up her head swam, and her knees buckled. She had only had tea and toast for days—maybe a reaction to all the gourmet shenanigans. She slipped into the bathroom and took a quick, cool shower.

Ashling headed on jittery legs to the kitchen. Charlie, Lionel, and Wilfred were in the living room, gathered like a cabal around Rose, heads almost touching. She greeted them, and they pulled apart, smiled, and returned her greeting almost in unison. They looked like Cheshire cats. Rose was beaming with a look of pride and gratitude that Ashling had often seen in her own mother, Lionel's smile had a tinge of paternal appreciation, and Wilfred's a glint of the admiration she had seen when she caught him stealing glances. Charlie's smile was forthright and happy.

Charlie rushed into the kitchen after her. He glanced towards the living room and kissed her quickly on the lips. "Coffee? I brought your favorite—chocolate raspberry."

Ashling carefully adjusted the flame under the kettle. "No thanks. It's tea I need."

"Rose is still so excited about your paintings, Ashling. She even said she'd come to San Francisco for an exhibit."

Ashling blinked several times. "Jesus! That's huge. What's next? Moving there?"

Charlie bounded from grinder to coffee pot. "Who knows? I can't wait to see your final painting."

He began to massage her shoulders and Ashling felt a crumbling in her heart. His touch still sent a quiver, but the current was weaker. Maybe this was normal in the ebb and flow of a relationship.

"You're a miracle worker," he whispered.

"My family in Ireland puts me on a pedestal. You're beginning to sound like them."

"I'm glad we do. We're a motley crew, but…we're very fond of you, Ashling. Now, why don't I make something *delizioso* for breakfast?"

Ashling spooned out her tea leaves and set the tea to brew. Maybe *amore* meant lover, but "fond of" surely did not equate to love.

She collapsed onto a stool and in her half-sleep state, the smell of garlic and onions tickled her nose. Her head drooped from tiredness and she had the thought that maybe Charlie's endearments lacked magic because she was anaesthetized from sheer exhaustion. Her eyes closed. The next thing she felt was Charlie gently stroking her neck as he slid a spinach frittata under her nose. Ashling looked at it and her stomach lurched.

"Charlie, it looks delicious, but I feel a bit queasy. Could we save it for later?"

He poured her a cup of tea.

Ashling set up her easel outdoors and placed the cell painting on it. Rose sat beside her with her book open. "I'm going to finish it on my own," she said. "You don't need to read everything to me—there's nothing wrong with my eyes!"

A weight flew off Ashling, the shedding of a chainmail skin. She smiled.

She focused in on the painting. It still wasn't right. Her mind wandered to Rose and her fear of the light, and her own opposite fear of the dark. Her nighttime forays into the woods. Images of dark grilles. An Irish confessional. Black vestments. A grey portcullis.

"Rose, I need to step in for a sec. Will you be okay?"

Rose drew a long breath through her nostrils and exhaled. "Go. I'll read with your voice in my head."

Ashling dashed in, retrieved some sketches, and raced back out. "Are you alright?" she asked, out of breath.

Rose nodded. "I made it." They both laughed.

"It's like running a marathon," Rose said. "To fight the fear."

Ashling's head spun and tilted. She had the sensation of falling through blackness. She reached for her easel to steady herself, and as she did, the thought came to her. She had to paint the very dark itself. The painting had to be all black, like the cell in her heart.

Ashling painted furiously all day. She experimented with different brush strokes, shadings, and textures. She lumped on the paint, laced through it with her brush and palette knife. It began to resemble the raised maps they had studied in school where you could feel the mountains and rivers. It was a new terrain, with hills and valleys, peaks and slopes, secret spaces to hide. She kept her arm moving. She was the marathon runner, and if her instincts were right and her talent aligned, Charlie would help exhibit her. He wanted to, just as he still wanted her romantically. She continued to paint into the early evening, until she finally dragged herself to her room, and still fully dressed lay on the bed and plunged into sleep.

A few hours later, Charlie's signature soft rat-tat-tat on her bedroom door woke her—their secret code. He entered carrying a steaming mug of tea. Ashling peeked at him through her blonde eyelashes—he still reminded her of Brando. She propped up on her elbow and sipped her tea.

"Better?" Charlie sat on the side of the bed.

"A bit. I still feel dazed, though. I think I need about a week's sleep."

"How's it coming?"

"It's coming. It's really close."

Charlie skimmed her cheek with his finger. She felt like a china doll that was already part broken and any sudden jolt would jiggle the fault lines and cause her to crumble. Charlie leaned over and kissed her. Gently. He slowly undressed her, and though she felt something held back in herself, she let him.

Ashling and Charlie dozed, their bodies curled together like two quarter moons. She wanted them to stay this way forever, paused in their love shape, released from responsibility for future moments. A huge sadness weighed on her heart, but she didn't know why.

Ashling slipped out of bed in the early morning, bundled herself into her judo pants and a t-shirt, and tiptoed to the kitchen to make tea. To her surprise, the front door was flung wide open, and Rose was already up and sewing in the living room.

Ashling cradled the hot mug in her hands and eased herself into a chair near Rose.

"Ashling. Charlie and I talked about your Immigration status."

Ashling nodded. She inhaled the steam from the tea.

"Your visa expires in a week," Rose said. She paused her sewing and picked up her coffee mug.

Ashling remembered the Polish cleaning lady coughing up blood. The young British woman watching her lover disappear on a bus to Mexico. Jorge worried that he and his parents would be deported. She imagined herself becoming anonymous, head down, constantly dipping below the surface in a sea of illegal aliens. Or returning to a prison-like existence at home.

"I know," she said.

"We had an idea, a plan. It's delicate...It involves. . .marriage."

Ashling's heart stopped. Then it raced. Then it seemed to stop again. Everything flew through her mind like a fast-rolling film—the weeks of wanting Charlie to say he loved her, the dream of a combined love and career, the promise of San Francisco together.

"Marriage?" she asked, testing out the word, the concept.

"Yes," Rose said, with a smile in her voice.

"But Rose. I. . ." She was afraid she was getting what she had thought she wanted too quickly. And why was Rose bringing this up and not Charlie unless it was only meant as a legal ploy?

"Charlie has submitted the papers, they know you want to stay in the country, but he's doubtful the Third Preference option will work."

Ashling's mind kept racing along with her heart. Back to her fantasies of herself and Charlie. Her art piling up. Marriage hadn't been in that picture yet because she was still only twenty-one. But later. So, did it matter if it was earlier?

"I don't know what to say..."

"You know I think of you as a family member already, a daughter. So, if you were to marry Wilfred, you'd really be my daughter."

Ashling stared hard at Rose's lips. She shot upright and spilled her tea.

"What? Whose idea was this?"

"All of us are in agreement." She sounded calm—like she was speaking perfectly normal words.

"You mean that you've all been discussing me behind my back, planning this whole thing."

"It would be just for the green card, to make you legal. You could paint as much as you liked—we could get another girl to do the light housekeeping so that you would only have to be here as company for me when I needed you."

Ashling turned her back on Rose. She paced back and forth. She inhabited some liminal realm part way between sanity and insanity. The ever-present bell inside her head jangled. She picked up speed.

"We all love you so much, Ashling."

"What does that even mean? My family in Ireland love me too, as long as I'm taking care of them."

Ashling kept her back to Rose. It would be painful to have to look at her.

"But we're looking out for your welfare. This would be a really smart move for you and for your family."

Ashling stopped, spun around, and faced her. "You and my bloody family!"

Rose recoiled. "What?"

"I said, you and my bloody family. Is this all part of some grand plan? An arranged marriage!"

"It's just a marriage on paper."

"Is Wilfred clear on that point?" She crossed over to the window and tried to calm her heart.

"Wilfred is shy about it. But he wants you to stay."

Ashling heard the door to her bedroom open and close, and then Charlie was in the room.

"Is everything all right? I heard voices."

"Chas, I thought it was a good time to bring up about marriage. But..."

Ashling turned her back on him. Couldn't bear to look in his eyes. He came up behind her, moving towards her, his bare feet padding on the carpet, getting closer. He reached out to her. As her father had done all those years ago.

"Don't...touch me."

He did not stop. He moved with the hubris of Father Dempsey, of men steeped in their own power.

Ashling swiveled around. "I said—no." She planted her feet, raised her arms to waist height in a judo stance, readied herself.

Charlie choked out a laugh. "Come on. Don't play with that. I'm trying to..." His arm stretched out, still reaching.

"I said, don't touch me." Her voice was ice. A definite no.

Charlie ignored her and kept on. His fingers landed on her shoulder. She snapped. She dove in, grabbed him by the sleeve, dragged him off balance, and landed him on the floor. She heard Rose gasp.

She walked away from him. Her breathing came faster. Her throat stung. Her eyelids hardened.

Charlie sprung up, eyes glaring. "What the...?" He walked rapidly towards Ashling. She stared him down though her sight was blurring. Her power filled her up. She braced herself, yanked him forward by the shirt, slipped his foot from under him and sent him flying towards the floor.

She could see Charlie's shape; she could feel his anger. She gulped for air. She was suffocating. She had to get out.

She bolted down the hallway and out the front door. She plunged into the early morning fighting a collapse into nothingness. She lunged towards the driveway entrance and edged through the skewed opening.

She could hear her own breathing, fierce and wild as she sliced through the darkness. Her skin was glacial. Her eyelids calcified.

Somewhere behind her, Charlie's voice called her name. The family was trying to keep her prisoner, but not in any way that would be recognized by the law. Maybe they didn't even know it themselves.

Her heart convulsed. She was wheezing now, hauling breath from her body. She heard it in her ears, her skull, her chest, her lungs, her stomach. She crashed face down on the ground.

Now she was in the tunnel. She was weightless, insubstantial. Images flew by at high speed like flip books. Her parents and siblings, their arms reaching for her, grasping. Her father reaching for her, grasping. Charlie and his family, arms reaching for her, grasping. Reaching into her heart.

Her breath was a separate thing. Her body was losing form, her spirit losing will. She could easily give in, let herself be drawn down that tunnel towards the silver light.

An eternity passed.

Her lips parted, and she tasted dirt. The shock of earthy soil snagged on a brain switch and shifted her into judo-mind.

She gathered in her scattered energy. She lit a fire under the old dragging memories, the endlessly repeating cycles, and let it all go up in flames. A breath filtered through the smoke. A spark rose from the ashes and cleared her thoughts: She would live. She would fight. She would paint.

She instructed her lungs to draw in air. To expel it.
To breathe in again. To breathe out.
In. Out.
She heard voices.
She slipped into black.

IN THE DARKNESS OF TIME

August 25-28

A sharp point jabbed her thigh, exploded into her rib cage, and cannon-balled her heart straight up to the ceiling. Her brain caught fire with terror, and a current blasted outward from her chest like a radiating star. Her body pressed back from the impact and she felt her imprint, supine on a soft surface. Alcohol fumes stung her nostrils, and a hand swabbed her thigh. An arm pulled a cool cotton sheet up to her chin, and she faded back into rest.

Her eyelashes blinked half open, the lids like metal pushing into her eyeballs. She was on a bed surrounded by shiny steel bars. She saw blurry figures, shimmering blues and whites and greys. Whisperings swirled in her ear.

Hands raised her up and supported her back, helping to propel her forwards as her bare feet skimmed the cool tiles. She passed a mirror. She saw a face, white as plaster, lips enlarged, eyelids swollen almost to closing. Her face.

She was a mummy whose body had been in the same position for ten thousand years. Her eyelids lifted one millimeter at a time and light glinted off the metal bed frame. Through slatted lashes she saw Charlie sitting on a chair by the wall. Wilfred sat beside him. With their lowered heads, slumped shoulders, and magazines held at half-mast, they looked like misty debris from a shipwreck.

A nurse, in blue, sat on a chair close to the bed and held a chart in her lap. Sun filtered in through venetian blinds and threw bars of shadow across her uniform. Barely breathing, Ashling drew in the stillness.

The starched pillow was cool on her cheek when she finally tilted her head in slow motion towards the nurse. Charlie sprung up and rushed to her bedside. He took her hand. She had no strength and her hand just lay there in his. The nurse left and returned with a man in a blinding white coat.

"Ashling, I'm Dr. Gendel."

The whiteness stung Ashling's eyes. She opened her mouth and tried to speak but nothing came. She fixed her gaze on the doctor's copper eyes. She dragged the words up through her throat. "What's wrong with me?" Her voice was a whispered croak.

"We've sent bloods for testing, but we're pretty sure it's nothing serious," the doctor said. Ashling blinked and tried to bring the picture into focus. Wilfred crossed over and stood beside Charlie.

"Do you have anybody in your family who has had such attacks?"

"My brothers…asthma."

The doctor shook his head. "No, it's not that." He looked at Charlie, then back at Ashling. "Mr. Rosen told us they are your family here. Is it all right to speak in front of them?"

She blinked a yes.

"We're almost certain that you had a giant panic attack."

"Why did I pass out?"

"It happens sometimes with a severe attack, but we can find ways to help you alleviate the stress."

Ashling pictured a cocktail of stress swirling in her throat, stopping up her voice and breath.

"The main thing for the moment is a stress-free environment. And avoid hot showers and alcohol," the doctor said.

"Will I be able to do judo, later?"

"You'll have to use your own judgment. Find your own balance point."

Tears bubbled behind Ashling's eyes and lingered. Crying through these bladed lids would be unbearable.

Ashling didn't remember how she got back to Rose's house or how long she slept. She raised her arm and touched her fingers to her heart, the rise and fall she had always taken for granted. She eased herself out of bed and slipped on her Chinese robe.

Four sets of eyes looked at her as she stepped into the living room. Rose opened her arms and enfolded her. "*Bubalah*. My girl." Her salty tears stung Ashling's cheek and Rose's heart shuddered against her own. "I'm so sorry for my part in this. I was selfish and wrong to try and hold you. I know that now."

Ashling nodded. She had the feeling there had been a family conference, and a kind of reckoning. She kissed Rose's cheek.

"I'll make your tea," Charlie said. "And toast?"

"And a boiled egg, please."

She felt calmer than she ever had in her life. Probably shock.

The words rose up and toppled off her tongue. "I have to finish that painting before I leave."

Wilfred jumped up from his chair. "I'll set up your easel and get your supplies." He sounded like a big brother.

Outside, Wilfred placed her painting on the easel.

"This is the last one in the Alcatraz series?" he said.

She nodded. "Then I'll be done."

He stood there a moment.

"Ashling. I hope you will stay in touch with our family. We don't want to lose you."

Ashling smiled. She felt the subtle surrender of possessiveness. That he was trying to give her space

"I would like that, Wilfred."

He smiled, shyly. He turned and went back into the house.

Ashling stood in front of her easel and stared at the canvas. The sunlight filtered through the trees and dappled her face. She could hear the voices from inside the house—a discombobulated symphony. It reminded her of her family in Ireland when she told them she was leaving the country—her Renoir canvas that dissolved. This family was more like a splintering Pollak. But she knew they would all rearrange and be okay.

She had never painted anything with just one color before. She remembered the vigorous way she had painted the rest of the Alcatraz series—how she had put her whole body behind it. Her instinct told her that this needed a different approach—that she had to come from another place. A point of stillness.

Ashling's hand moved without any conscious will on her part. Her brush swirled through the thick layers of paint, and she stumbled upon subtle shadings of color through texture. She was an explorer, wading through a lush, undiscovered forest. Time slowed down. She had no fear. She was absorbed in the black.

Lionel wheeled Rose out in her wheelchair. She had asked if she could see Ashling's earlier paintings and held her old portfolio in her lap.

"Ashling," Lionel said. It was the first time he had ever spoken her name. "Would it disturb you if Rose sits with you?"

"Not at all. I'm winding down."

Lionel smiled, and went back inside. A calmness spread over Ashling. She saw that Lionel was just a slightly more controlling version of herself as she ran and organized her family back in Ireland. That was why she had been so angry at him; he was a warning to her of what she would turn into if she didn't look inward and deal with her past. She was happy too for Lionel, that he was different now, was pulling himself out of that trap.

Rose opened the portfolio. Ashling retreated back into her world. She could hear Rose's soft insect wing sounds.

Her arm slowed down. She came to a stop. She laid down her brush, took a step backwards, and looked at her painting. A shiver coursed through her body. The paint rose up from the surface of the canvas and spilled out over the edges of the frame like it had life and breath.

Rose cleared her throat. Ashling jumped. She had forgotten she was there. Rose held up the painting of the woman in a blue dress, framed by the archway of dangling hawthorn, a smile shaping her lips into a long-ago remembrance.

"Is that your mother?" she asked.

"Based on her, yes. On a moment recollected from when I was six years old."

"It's beautiful, all light and mystery, and reverence."

All of her life since, that day had remained a clasp on Ashling's heart—the feeling of owing her mother something like freedom. Even as a small child she had internalized the need to revere her elders, to accept without question what they asked. To follow the rules. In separating from Rose, Ashling knew she had the courage now to separate from her mother. And in doing so to have a healthier relationship with them both.

Rose glanced over at Ashling's new painting. "Finished?"

Ashling angled it so Rose could see. Rose moved in closer and looked. She took a deep breath. "It shimmers—with a dark mystery." She glanced back at the other painting. "Almost at the other end of the spectrum."

Ashling felt a shifting in her cells. "I'm older now." By about a thousand years.

Rose looked again at the black painting. Then her eyes sought out Ashling's eyes.

"This is about you, isn't it? The whole Alcatraz series."

Ashling nodded. "I didn't know that when I started. I was drawn to the topic and had to travel through it, then immerse myself."

"Yes." Rose's voice was a wisp of sweet sadness. She reached over and gently clasped Ashling's hand. She held it for a long moment, and then she let it go.

Ashling had an image of her first view of Rose—slumped over, untidy, haggard. Time had been reversed. Rose had journeyed backwards to her proper age and also found a new sense of purpose, while she herself had sped forwards. Ashling laughed to realize that. She heard the laugh resound in her head without the accompaniment of bell ringing or alien orchestrations.

She stretched out on her bed. The drapes were open, and the greens and browns no longer made it look like a place of death. A vase of wildflowers stood on the bedside table and breathed.

She felt as if her brain had been removed, polished up like a diamond, and then put back.

Ashling thought about her enchantment with San Francisco. She had a notion of it being a Promised Land—about as far away from her family and home as she could conceive of journeying to. She had made it a repository of all her hopes and dreams, a holy grail.

Maybe the true grail was finding out there wasn't one. That True North was knowing where your own skin ended, and others began. Only then could you reach out and help. Fight for yourself, and for others. Speak in an authentic voice.

Charlie came in with a cup of tea. He dipped his eyelids as if she were a stranger. She did feel different, that polished diamond in her brain shone all through her. The cup was warm as she cradled it in her palm and sipped in sustenance.

His eyes landed on the backpack and the small pile of clothes. "You're really leaving us." His voice was a lament.

Ashling didn't trust herself to speak yet. She returned to the closet and slipped her Renoir dress off the hanger. It smelled of anisette and amaretto, of Charlie. She remembered the magical dinner at Vanessi's, and her offering to come work with Rose. It had all been an elegant manipulation. She crossed over and laid the dress on the bed, as if she were laying down a child to rest. It wasn't her anymore. She took a step away from it. Charlie's eyes lingered on the dress.

Ashling removed the short black velvet skirt from the closet. That still felt like her. She folded and placed it in her backpack. She found the royal blue dress with the black oval pattern that Rose had bought her. It was free-flowing and elegant. She packed it.

She felt Charlie's eyes on her as she continued to remove and fold her clothes. It was a film scene playing in slow motion. His guard was down, and in the glassy gaze of his eyes she saw the layers of hurt, the clouds of confusion. Maybe he was such a master manipulator he didn't even know it.

"I'm going back to San Francisco tomorrow," she said, surprised by the calm in her voice.

Charlie stared at her. "Ashling," he said, and it was like a breeze in the forest. "Ashling, I really did…do, have feelings for you." His voice cracked, and his eyes welled up. Her heart crashed. She had fallen in love with this man, and despite his betrayals, her insides were a wash of emotion. He tilted his neck forward and teardrops slipped down his cheeks. With his lowered head, stooped posture, and slightly swaying torso, he looked like he was an old man praying.

Ashling dragged her eyes away from Charlie. She crossed to her paintings and began to stack them up. She would need to create a portfolio to apply to graduate school. She had the brochures for the California College of Arts and Crafts, and the San Francisco Art Institute. She would research other colleges. They must have counselors she could talk to about finessing her choices and direction. And advice about financial aid and legal status.

She held the business card that Sophie had given her and remembered she was interested in women's stories. Ashling's Rose series was one of female empowerment. It traced the journey of a young girl pushing past and through tremendous obstacles to achieve success and fulfillment, facing a devastating setback, and then returning to a new life with renewed possibilities. The Alcatraz series was Ashling's own journey of overcoming fears of entrapment. Her reckoning with her own past encounters which colored her outlook. Her encounters with men who held power over her—her own father, Father Dempsey, Charlie—of recognizing that her most potent jailor was herself, that she had the power to say no. In facing down the dark, letting herself paint through it, she now had the courage to go further. To go beyond herself and paint the unspeakable.

"I'll drive you back when you want to go," Charlie said in a small voice.

Ashling thought of the rich leather seats, the leisurely drive, the sweet sense of safety. The grandeur of the illusion.

"I'll take the bus."

She would call the Y and see if they had a room for a few nights while she got reoriented.

"The car would be better with all your paintings. Unless you want me to store them for you. Until you're ready?"

Ashling placed her passport and ticket to Ireland on one side of the bed, and on the other side her U.S. Social Security card. Eeny, meeny, miny, moe.

"I'll let you know when I decide, thanks."

Charlie blinked. He glanced at her with glistening eyes, opened his mouth to speak, but nothing came. He slipped from the room.

The air shifted, got lighter.

Ashling flipped on her Walkman. She leaned her back against the bedroom door and slid to the floor.

When is a dream just dreaming?

Her lava tears bubbled up and scalded her cheeks.

When should a lover go?

She cried away all the old dreams of Charlie.

Somewhere way back

In the darkness of time…

She cried away all the old family trappings—it wasn't worth the price of life. She knew in her private knowing, the pressure of keeping things locked up inside. One day Ireland would burst out too.

She stood, crossed back to the bed, picked up her Irish passport. The imaginary bars she had erected around her family home shrunk to slivers and slip-slided away. She lodged her U.S. Social Security card inside her Irish passport.

She breathed in. She breathed out.

The polished diamond in her brain—it would be the jewel in the compass for her new world.

Acknowledgements

Vinnie Kinsella for his keen editing eye. Rene Denfeld for her encouragement and support.

Ellen Kesend, Mead Hunter, Suzanne LaGrande, and Mark Montgomery for their friendship and comradery in our writing groups, and for their brilliance, invaluable advice, and insights on writing. For holding my feet to the fire! Special thanks to Ellen for above and beyond.

To Corey and Alex for keeping me on my toes! To Adam, for his never-ending belief in me, and his love.

About the Author

Gemma is an award-winning director, screenwriter, and educator. She was the founding Artistic Director of Wilde Irish Productions in the San Francisco Bay Area, and since 2012 has been the Artistic Director of Corrib Theatre in Portland, Oregon. Her short film *The Wake* was the winner of the Silver Knight Award at the Golden Knight Film Festival, Malta; her feature screenplay *Eye of the Storm* won the Robert and Ellen Little Screenwriting Award; and her screenplay *Wedding Bells* won the American Gem Short Screenplay award and was optioned by Fox Broadcasting. Her first novel was *Fiona: Stolen Child.* She lives with her family in Portland, Oregon.

Made in the USA
Middletown, DE
06 September 2022